Dear Reader-Friend,

I am so pleased to be a part of Silhouette Desire's 10th anniversary MAN OF THE MONTH promotion, and to return to the Blaylocks, the family in *Midnight Rider* (SD #726) and *The Seduction of Jake Tallman* (SD #811). Readers have often requested a return to the Blaylocks. Jake is a Blaylock cousin, and we met the Blaylock family in Dan's book, *Midnight Rider.* The bachelor brothers were just too tempting, and *Blaylock's Bride,* Roman's story, reopens the saga of the Blaylock family; Rio's story is next. The setting is unique: small-town Jasmine, Wyoming (similar to the towns I travel through every summer), filled with ranchers and farmers from the valley, stuffed with wonderful characters and surrounded by the Rocky Mountains.

Poor Roman. A darkly brooding hero, he's given up on love, hoarding himself in his work and ranch. He was just too fascinating to leave moldering. So I tossed Kallista—an exciting, furious woman out for revenge—into his lap and, as a writer, enjoyed the fireworks.

I hope you enjoy the Blaylock family, bound by love and land, and I look forward to hearing from you, my reader-friends.

*Cait London*

Dear Reader,

April brings showers, and this month Silhouette Desire wants to shower you with six new, passionate love stories!

Cait London's popular Blaylock family returns in our April MAN OF THE MONTH title, *Blaylock's Bride*. Honorable Roman Blaylock grapples with a secret that puts him in a conflict between confiding in the woman he loves and fulfilling a last wish.

The provocative series FORTUNE'S CHILDREN: THE BRIDES continues with Leanne Banks's *The Secretary and the Millionaire*, when a wealthy CEO turns to his assistant for help in caring for his little girl.

Beverly Barton's next tale in her 3 BABIES FOR 3 BROTHERS miniseries, *His Woman, His Child*, shows a rugged heartbreaker transformed by the heroine's pregnancy. Powerful sheikhs abound in *Sheikh's Ransom*, the Desire debut title of Alexandra Sellers's dramatic new series, SONS OF THE DESERT. A marine gets a second chance at love in *Colonel Daddy*, continuing Maureen Child's popular series BACHELOR BATTALION. And in Christy Lockhart's *Let's Have a Baby!*, our BACHELORS AND BABIES selection, the hero must dissuade the heroine from going to a sperm bank and convince her to let *him* father her child—the old-fashioned way!

Allow Silhouette Desire to give you the ultimate indulgence—all six of these fabulous April romance books!

Enjoy!

Joan Marlow Golan
Senior Editor, Silhouette Desire

Please address questions and book requests to:
Silhouette Reader Service
U.S.: 3010 Walden Ave., P.O. Box 1325, Buffalo, NY 14269
Canadian: P.O. Box 609, Fort Erie, Ont. L2A 5X3

# CAIT
# LONDON
## BLAYLOCK'S
## BRIDE

SILHOUETTE *Desire*®

Published by Silhouette Books

**America's Publisher of Contemporary Romance**

**SILHOUETTE BOOKS**

ISBN 0-373-76207-0

BLAYLOCK'S BRIDE

**Books by Cait London**

Silhouette Desire

*The Loving Season #502
*Angel vs. MacLean #593
The Pendragon Virus #611
*The Daddy Candidate #641
†Midnight Rider #726
The Cowboy #763
Maybe No, Maybe Yes #782
†The Seduction of Jake Tallman #811
Fusion #871
The Bride Says No #891
Mr. Easy #919
Miracles and Mistletoe #968
‡The Cowboy and the Cradle #1006
‡Tallchief's Bride #1021
‡The Groom Candidate #1093
‡The Seduction of Fiona Tallchief #1135
‡Rafe Palladin: Man of Secrets #1160
‡The Perfect Fit #1183
†Blaylock's Bride #1207

Silhouette Yours Truly

Every Girl's Guide To...
Every Groom's Guide To...

Silhouette Books

‡Tallchief for Keeps

Spring Fancy 1994
"Lightfoot and Loving"

*The MacLeans
‡The Tallchiefs
†The Blaylocks

---

## CAIT LONDON

lives in the Missouri Ozarks but loves to travel the Northwest's gold rush/cattle drive trails every summer. She loves research trips, meeting people and going to Native American dances. Ms. London is an avid reader who loves to paint, play with computers and grow herbs (particularly scented geraniums right now). She's a national bestselling and award-winning author, and she also writes historical romances under another pseudonym. Three is her lucky number; she has three daughters, and the events in her life have always been in threes. "I love writing for Silhouette," she says. "One of the best perks about all this hard work is the thrilling reader response and the warm, snug sense that I have given readers an enjoyable, entertaining gift."

Together again—To my new editor at Silhouette, Joan Marlow Golan. Thank you, Joan, for giving me my start in writing, for your patience in teaching me how to write many moons ago.

Thank you, Melissa Senate, for being you, for being supportive, for building my career and for the wonderful years we've had together.

A special thank-you to my dear readers, who have asked to see more of the Blaylock family after reading *Midnight Rider* and *The Seduction of Jake Tallman*.

Author's Note: The research for the Bisque Cafe was done at the Paint Cafe in Springfield, Missouri, where I painted my first smiling, belly-up hippopotamus.

# Prologue

"You're safe here with me, little bit…here on Llewlyn land," Boone said to the little girl holding his hand. The wind sweeping across Llewlyn land was chilly, Wyoming's early September ablaze with fiery quaking aspens amid the fir and pine trees; fur thickened on the animals now, a natural preparation for winter. On the Rocky Mountains above Llewlyn Ranch, the bears were fat with summer berries and fish and honey stolen from wild beehives.

Boone Llewlyn lifted his head, letting the wind—filled with the scent of the land, of the pines and earth and fields—flow through his shaggy gray hair and caress his leathered skin.

He was old now, bent by age and shame. Boone kept the little girl's fragile hand cradled in his large, rough palm, his scarred heart filling with love.

This was his grandchild, Kallista May. Her green eyes and sleek silky hair came from his mother, that stubborn edge along her jaw from Llewlyn blood. At six, and dressed in her favorite red jacket and boots, she was too thin, and had seen too much of life's dirty ways.

To remind Boone who had the legal claim to the little girl, her mother would come to tear her away soon, and Boone's wounded heart would weep. The cruel game used the girl as a pawn, to assure monthly payments to her mother and to Boone's son, her father.

Boone swallowed the emotion tearing through him. He treasured his inheritance, his parents, and the land that had been left to him. But in his thirty years away from this valley, he'd amassed a fortune and spawned two irresponsible sons...bigamists and careless, lazy men now—Boone couldn't bear to have them near his land.

So he paid them all—his sons and their harem of wives, married illegally under different names—and in return, they kept his secret from the good people of Jasmine, the Blaylocks and the rest. He'd bought his sons free of bigamist charges, because he couldn't have his grandchildren publicly named as illegitimate.

As a young man, he'd been in love with Garnet Marie Holmes, but she had wanted to stay in the valley. He'd turned to another woman and the world—and both had shamed him. Sara had been knowing, cultured and totally devoted to creating the picture of success that Boone had wanted then. Still in love with Garnet, he hadn't asked for love or comfort, and had chosen his glittering, cold wife to suit his needs for power and money. When the babies came, they had less of her than Boone and still hunting his fortune, he'd left them to survive in her care. Sara had burned out her life long ago, mourned by no one. In his pursuit for money, he'd forgotten that a child was a precious gift, and that it took care to make a child feel proud and strong. And so his sons were weak men. Their wives were— Boone didn't want to think of the greedy, immoral women his sons had chosen.

After a time, Garnet Holmes had turned away another

suitor, Cutter Lomax. Because Boone wouldn't lend money to Cutter and had stopped his land schemes, Cutter believed that Boone had caused the ruin of his life. After that, Cutter bitterly blamed the loss of Garnet on Boone, and a long-term feud began. Garnet soon married Luke Blaylock, a fine man, and together they'd had a beautiful family. Boone had always loved Garnet Marie, and wished her well; he couldn't bear to let that dear sweet, honest woman—or the rest of the valley—see inside his black shame.

*He had to protect the land from his sons. Llewlyn land was for his grandchildren, if they came back....*

Boone studied the Herefords grazing in the field; he barely noticed the deer moving along the fence. He'd created legalities to protect himself and Llewlyn land, but he mourned his grandchildren...The Innocents whom he wanted to claim for his own. Yet he couldn't shame his parents...or truth be told, himself. His pride and his shame had made him weak, though he loved his sons.

He held the girl's hand and kept her safe—while he could, this tiny precious part of his blood, though she didn't know it.

There were other Llewlyn children who didn't know he was their grandfather, and when they came to him, dropped off by a careless parent, he treasured every moment. The children all believed him to be a friend of the family.

"You remember to come home, here to Llewlyn land, when you want...when you're grown, and you remember how beautiful you are, how much I love you," he said to Kallista May and watched her trusting, freckled face turn up to his. He knelt beside her, enfolding her in his arms, and wished he could protect her.

Ten thousand acres of Llewlyn land would belong to his grandchildren. If they decided to live in the valley, they would each have their portion. If they did not, trust funds would be set up for them, and every one—when the time was right—would know who they were, and the proud blood that ran in their veins.

He held the little girl closer; she was a Llewlyn, already proud and strong. He'd given her that, and if she needed him through the years, he'd come for her.... "You remember, Kallie-girl, to come back home, to Llewlyn land."

# One

"If there is one thing I don't need, it is that sassy-mouthed, high-nosed female. Big Boone wanted her back. I don't. I haven't seen her for four years, and that's fine with me. But I promised I'd get her here, just like the rest on his list—back on Llewlyn land, then she can fly off on her broom when she wants." Roman Blaylock rubbed the cheek Kallista Bellamy had slapped four years ago, with enough power to send him reeling back against the shelves loaded with ceramic bisque, waiting to be painted.

High on the Rocky Mountains behind the combined ranches of Roman and Boone Llewlyn, a lone wolf opened his throat and bared his aching soul to the moon. The sound suited Roman's brooding mood; he settled into the shadows of Boone Llewlyn's sprawling front porch.

The sound of the shattering bisque echoed in the April Wyoming night as Roman scowled, recalling the scene four years ago. He remembered the shattered ceramic shop and the big dragon that had crashed down on his head. He'd caught the broken tail, uncertain what to do with the furious woman who had just shoved his chest again. As a piece of shattered bisque bumped down his cheek, he'd wanted to kiss her, wrap her so tight against him that all that heat would burn away the cold years stored inside him.

Kallista had glared up at him. "Go ahead. You beat your wife. What's one more woman?" Her green eyes had ripped down his dusty denim-clad body to his Western work boots; then her gaze had burned a slow, insulting path up to his face. "You've just destroyed my shop and terrified your wife. You've been drinking…you're a mess…and you are a bully. You are not shoving your wife around in my shop. Get out."

He had forced himself to let go of the dragon tail. As it crashed, he realized that he was clutching a smaller dragon in his fist—when he uncurled his fingers, it smiled cheerfully up at him. As his usually mild temper soared, the dragon had shattered on the floor. The remnants of white bisque around his Western work boots had been symbolic of his dreams long ago. He'd pushed his face down the good twelve inches to hers and spaced out the words. "I do not beat my wife."

Kallista had flipped back her long, sleek black hair and leaned forward to meet his glare with her own. "Debbie said you were rough and things between you were not good. I assume that meant—"

"Me? Rough?" The implication that he'd hurt his wife, perhaps sexually, was a hard slap to his pride.

"You are a violent man and now you are drunk."

The scorn in her tone had hitched Roman's temper higher, at the same time feeding his need to taste those red, moist lips. The woman was raw passion, steaming, no-holds-barred. He wanted a taste of that undiluted emotion and it bristled from her—he had wanted to reach out and take…

Boone had just served him two shots of whiskey and a

careful reference to Debbie's ongoing love affair with Thomas Johnston. Roman had not been aware other people knew of Debbie's affair and he'd tossed back another whiskey at the exposure of the lie he'd been living in his less than perfect marriage.

"I have never hurt my wife," he'd told Kallista firmly.

"She can't bear for you to touch her, and she's frightened of you—I saw it just now, when she ran away."

Debbie's lies, her deceit and his own, had covered the reality of their tortured marriage. Her withdrawal of their savings to pay the bank's mortgage could cost him Blaylock family land, his heritage. He'd mortgaged the land to build the house she'd demanded. "She's got reason to run," he'd said before he'd stepped from his leashes, snagged Kallista in his arms and kissed her hard. When he was finished feeding on her mouth, he'd stepped back and promptly received another hard slap.

"Out." The memory of Kallista's voice, icy and accusing, still stung Roman four years later.

With the April night fragrant and still around him now, Roman leaned his chair back into the night shadows covering Boone Llewlyn's massive front porch. Lights twinkling, the city of Jasmine, Wyoming, sprawled down in the valley.

Deer slid silently through the field, coming down to water at the stream, and Roman knew he'd fight to keep Blaylock family land. In another century, Boone's ancestor, a second son of an English lord, had found a lasting friendship with Micah Blaylock, a rough woodsman descended from an Apache princess and a passing Spanish conquistador. The unlikely friends, Blaylock and Llewlyn, had settled in the valley; they had wagered who would marry and produce the first child. Llewlyn had sent for his fiancée, while Micah had gone bride-shopping down the Natchez Trace. Micah had rescued a French seamstress from her first night in a brothel, and they were married. Both women produced sons, born so closely together that the friendly argument about who was the firstborn was never settled, and through the years, their friendship deepened. While the Blaylocks became a huge robust family, the Llewlyns dwindled until there was only Boone.

*Boone.* A man who treasured his inheritance, his land, haunted and fearful that he could not make amends for his tragic errors....

After Boone's illness two years ago, Roman had moved into the Llewlyn House and had joined his spread with The Llewlyn, making them easier to manage. He'd plowed through the mountain of paperwork that had accumulated in Boone's illness...and had been shocked by what he'd discovered—the children who had stayed at Boone's ranch through the years had been his grandchildren. As executor of Boone's estate, Roman had sworn to draw those children back to Llewlyn soil and their heritage. Kallista and the rest had been protected by Boone Llewlyn; he'd threatened to cut off the payments to their irresponsible parents if anything happened to the children. Boone's bigamist sons and their shallow, coarse ex-wives used the children to torture and bleed money from him. When he came too close, loving the children, the parents swooped in and reclaimed them. Big Boone couldn't stand the thought of his grandchildren knowing that he couldn't protect them, so he became their safety, their friend.

Ashamed of failing his sons, Boone would not have them desecrate the Llewlyn name—not in Jasmine, at least. His pensions kept them away and Big Boone's shame had been a terrible secret that Roman had sworn to keep.

Roman's own shame ran deep; he'd hidden his empty marriage from his family, deceiving them. In a family whose foundations were rock solid in marriage and love, Roman had discovered on his wedding night that his petite bride couldn't bear for him to touch her. In public, Debbie had cuddled him, but behind bedroom doors...

Roman again rubbed the cheek that Kallista had slapped four years ago; the stubble was as rough and the memory burned, insulting his honor—his family's honor. The Blaylocks were known as loving family men and Kallista's accusations had scored his pride.

Across a small slope Roman's dark empty house stood in the moonlight. Built years ago for his bride, a home for their daughter until she died, Roman Blaylock's ranch home had been swept clean of his dreams. In the distance, the moonlit silvery squares of the windows taunted him, the Rocky Mountains rising sharply behind it. It was now an empty monument to what he had wanted—a family as close and loving as his parents'. His marriage had been a lie from the first, and Debbie's child wasn't his. She'd been his only teenage sweetheart, but Roman had felt more like a big brother than her beau. When she became pregnant with another man's child, Roman had come to Debbie's defense, giving her the protection of his name.

Roman slammed the emotional door shut on his pain. He had enough to think about, managing his own ranch, The Llewlyn, and acting as Boone's executor.

The sprawling two-story, turn-of-the-century house was stuffed with collections and antiques and memories of the beloved children—The Innocents Boone used to call them—who had passed through its doors. Roman surveyed the vast farm, covered with goats, pigs, sheep and cattle grazing in the moonlit pastures and thought of Boone.

As a young rakehell, Boone had left Jasmine to see the world. Thirty years later, a changed and worn Boone returned permanently to his family's land and began building his secret empire. Whatever he'd done in the past, Boone was determined to make amends. A big man, he was nevertheless gentle, beloved in the town and yet alone, as if the shadows were his safety.

Roman understood loneliness; perhaps that was what

drew the two men together—lone wolves sensing pain in each other.

As executor of Boone's estate, Roman had promised Boone on his deathbed to bring Kallista back to the land. Spoiled, fiery, and strong-willed, Kallista was the last woman Roman wanted to deal with—but he would, for Boone.

Roman ran his hands through his shaggy black hair. It had taken a year to find her, and tomorrow she'd arrive.

He ripped off his shirt and boots and to unwind the tension in his body, began the slow series of strenuous Tai Chi exercises Boone had taught him.

Kallista turned her key in the Bisque Café's lock and stepped into the shadowy interior, closing the door behind her. For reassurance, she touched the dangling silver half-moon earrings Boone had given her. "Remember who you are. Remember me and this place as your home. Come back to me, Kallie-girl, and the land where you'll be safe."

Troubleshooting for Boudreaux Inc. at a French resort in Nassau, she was too late to see Boone one last time, but she'd come back. She spoke a variety of languages, skimming from one position to another as easily as shedding clothes and putting on new ones. And in her lifetime, the only home she'd known was with Big Boone Llewlyn.

*She owed Boone Llewlyn her life and her soul.* Roman Blaylock's takeover of Boone's beloved land and animals was obvious to Kallista; Roman had moved in with Boone before he died, and he'd taken over....

Moonlight skimmed through the big windows and settled upon the white ceramic bisque, shaped into tiny animals, plates, cups, statues and lamps. A row of dragons on the top shelf reminded her of Roman Blaylock's big hand wrapped around a broken dragon tail, the shattered remains on his dirty Western boots.

He'd been rawhide rough that day, a six foot three cowboy with leather gloves tucked in the back pocket of his jeans, raw with dust and sweat and leather chaps, tracking down his petite wife and calling her out.

Debbie had been managing Kallista's shop—began on impulse and on the advice of Hannah Blaylock, an interior decorator and a friend. While Kallista did not often visit Jasmine, she'd created the shop to please Boone, and he'd backed her financially. It pleased him to help her, and the Bisque Café in Jasmine was more his dream than her own. He'd once said it was like having her near—but she wasn't finished seeking a sense of belonging that had always eluded her.

Boone had kept the books on the café, pleased that it made a small profit, and through the years, various managers had taken care of the daily business. Kallista had built the shop six years ago, and Debbie, Roman's wife, had run it until four years ago, when Roman Blaylock had torn it apart in a brawl with his wife's defender.

On one of her infrequent visits to Jasmine, Kallista had come out of the back room just in time to see Debbie's wide-eyed horror and the smaller, slender man punch Roman's rock-hard stomach. Roman had easily shoved him backward, blocking the next punch. The whole shop had seemed to pop and crackle as all the shelves, laden with unpainted bisque, quivered and toppled.

The other man had reached for Debbie, huddling over her, protecting her as would a lover. Roman's burning black eyes didn't flinch as pieces tumbled down upon him, hitting his head, his broad shoulders and bouncing off as if nothing could hurt him. He'd ignored the thin trickle of blood from his forehead as he'd said one word to Debbie and the man, "Go."

The word sounded like a whip cracking and an icy shiver had shot up Kallista's spine, instantly followed by rage. His head had snapped back from her slap, more from pride than from the blow and she'd remembered the fiery hell in his black eyes. Then that quiet, solemn cloak had ripped away and he'd looked like his Mescalero Apache and Spanish conquistador ancestors—untempered by civilization—jutting, blunt bones pressing against his taut dark skin, black brows drawn into a fierce scowl, gleaming black hair dusted with bisque chips.

"You're not keeping Boone's land, Mr. Blaylock. Not while I am drawing breath," Kallista promised, tearing away her memory of Roman four years ago. She leaned against a wall, years of traveling lodged in her body, draining her. She dropped her flight bag to the floor and freed the tears burning her lids. *Boone was gone. The man who had always been her anchor.*

Through her childhood, she hadn't known her father and her mother had dropped her on Boone Llewlyn, the man she'd come to love for a lifetime. A big rangy man, with a huge heart, an ugly face and gentle hands, Boone had shadowy ties with her mother, lit by thunderous emotions that young Kallista couldn't understand. He was always there, waiting for her with a bear hug. She was safe then, in Boone's strong arms, while her mother met yet another lover, married again, and came to collect Kallista once more. Fury had raged between Boone and her mother; violence and hatred sprang from her mother, while Boone's emotions ran to frustration and pain. As a girl, Kallista understood none of it—only the safety that her mother would repeatedly rip away. As a restless adult, she'd always come to Boone, salving herself against the world until she was ready to seek again.

*She should have come back more... taken care of the only man she'd loved, who had shown her that men had hearts and loved. She should have come back sooner... now Roman Blaylock, as executor, had his big, greedy hands on Boone's ranch.*

Kallista moved through the shadowy shop, lined with ceramic bisque on the shelves. The tables and chairs were empty now, but according to Hannah Blaylock who had managed the shop with others, the people of Jasmine loved painting their own designs on the ceramic bisque. Kallista picked up a dish lettered in a childish scrawl. "For My Mom. Patty Blaylock."

Patty was Logan Blaylock's ten-year-old daughter, and Else, the Blaylock's eldest sister, had painted a big cup and saucer in an intricate design, duplicating a high priced Italian manufacturer's. Kallista replaced the plate on the shelf and began checking the names on the bottom of the fired and painted ceramics. The Blaylocks, a close family, liked coming to paint their designs, though the male Blaylocks were conspicuously absent. The huge Blaylock family wouldn't like her shaking Roman's tight-fisted grasp over Boone's estate.

An experienced troubleshooter who knew she was in for a fight, Kallista began making mental lists. First, she would check on the care and feeding of Boone's beloved pigeons, his goats and sheep and the rest. She skipped her usual cool logic and hurled herself into the passionate dislike of Boone's executor. *Somehow, she would rip the estate away from Roman; she would expose his greed and*—she glanced at Boone's house, overlooking Jasmine, the lights glowing in the April night. Kallista stooped to jerk her small bird-watching binoculars from her leather flight bag and aimed them at Roman Blaylock's house, which sat on the other hill. The house was dark, proof that Roman still lived in Boone's home. From Hannah, married to Dan Blaylock, Kallista had learned that Roman had moved into Boone's house when the old man became too ill to care for himself...and Blaylock hadn't moved out when Boone died a year ago.

"Squatter." Kallista muttered the Western term for those who would settle and claim another's property. Enraged, she hurried out of the shop into the sweet-scented night.

* * *

The flashy little sports car soared up the Llewlyn ranch road, gleaming in the moonlight. Roman appreciated the skill with which the driver changed gears, easing over the bars of the cattle crossing at the massive iron Llewlyn ranch gate. Then the sports car geared up again, hurling around the moonlit curves, that led upward to Boone's big, two-story house. Roman flinched when a cow and calf wandered onto the road and the car's tires squealed to a stop. The car slowly eased off the road, around the cow and calf and began more cautiously toward the house. Whoever was driving the car was mad enough to ignore a few fresh cowpatties. The car skidded to another stop beside Roman's big dented pickup and Kallista Bellamy hurled her body out of the door.

Roman eased into the shadows, the exercise sweat on his body cooling in the night air. He watched her free stride toward the house, waist-long hair floating out in a black wave behind her. She glanced at the pigpens, the pigeon house and the cattle. She stopped in front of the steps, braced her hands on her hips and studied the house as if looking for one missing board, one untended potted fern.

She moved gracefully, her taut body eloquent and rippling with passion, impatience and fury. She looked the same as that day she'd slapped him, all fiery hot and full of life, and an unfamiliar restless hunger moved inside Roman. He shoved it away and studied Kallista's long, curved athletic body, her pale heart-shaped face. In a classic style, straight back from her forehead and tamed by large silver combs on either side of her face, Kallista's hair swung around her restless body like a curtain of sleek heavy silk.

In the framed picture beside Boone's big carved four-poster bed her face wore a soft, tender look, her eyes luminous and green. Her smile at the photographer—probably Boone—was warm and loving.

Now, Kallista's frown was cold and furious. Beneath her black shiny jacket, she wore a body-hugging black sweater and black jeans that fitted like a second skin. Roman's body tensed as he noted the lush curve of her hips and endless legs. Her black combat boots added to the dangerous female-warrior look.

She hesitated, studying the old flower bed, heavy gold daffodils bent beneath the weight of raindrops. For just a heartbeat, her frown softened. Then, she flew up the steps in the easy movements of an athletic woman on a mission, and punched the doorbell furiously. Before Roman could move from the shadows, she had banged her fist on the door. In the next second, she had begun muttering and had extracted a small black kit from the huge leather bag slung over her shoulder.

When she crouched to pick the lock, Roman found his mouth drying at the curve of her hips. The instant desire to place his hands on her startled him, and he spoke too roughly, "The door isn't locked. You're a strong woman and I don't want the stained-glass window broken. It was Boone's mother's treasure," Roman murmured, moving out into the moonlit square on the porch.

"I know what that stained glass meant to him." Kallista took a step backward, her narrowed almond-shaped eyes ripping down his body, pausing on his bare chest and then jerking back up to his face. At six foot three, Roman stood a head higher than her and Kallista's frown said she resented looking up to him. She jammed the worn lock-picking kit into her bag. The firm edge to her jaw and the thrust of her chin reminded him of Boone. "I want you out of here. Now. You don't belong here, not in Boone's house."

Roman took his time in answering, stunned by the exotic scent curling from her—part anger, part cinnamon and silk, and all woman. Sleek, tough, sophisticated and...wounded. From Boone's file, Roman knew the shadowy corners of Kallista's life. "He wanted me here."

She glanced again at his bare chest, hesitated for a heartbeat, and then jerked her gaze back up to his face. "You took advantage of a dying man. You moved in and took over. You're probably bleeding his estate dry."

In the fraction of a heartbeat when she'd glanced at his chest, wildfire heat shot through Roman's body, stunning him. She'd tensed just enough to prove that she'd been aware of him. At thirty-nine, Roman considered his sensual years behind him—if he'd had any—and settling gently into middle age without the complications of a woman, Roman wasn't prepared for the sensual jolt slamming into his midsection. "I see your opinion of me hasn't changed. You should have called. I tried to contact you for a solid year after Boone's death."

He noted the trembling of her fingers before she gripped the porch railing, gleaming with the rain that had passed. "I didn't want contact with you. I don't know what Boone saw in you."

In the moonlight, Roman saw her resemblance to Boone, that sweep of feminine jaw clenched in rigid, righteous anger reserved for bullies and those who would hurt others. "Boone wanted me here...to take care of things."

"I'll just bet," she snapped back, locking her arms around herself. "I want to see everything. Now. I want to see what you've sold off, what you've destroyed, and oh, yes, the books. I want to see just how much you've siphoned off into your own accounts."

"No one has ever accused me of being dishonest," Roman stated tightly, and wondered why this woman could set him off so easily.

"Afraid that I'll see something I shouldn't?" she taunted in a silky purr that raised the hair on Roman's nape. "Something that might be missing? Something expensive?"

"It's ten o'clock at night. Why don't you come back in the morning, after you've had some sleep and cooled down?" Roman managed after taking a long, deep breath.

Kallista knew just how to insult his pride. She'd launched her contempt without shielding it. But then from his file on Kallista, Roman knew that she wasn't sweet—she was a fighter.

She folded her arms across her chest, slanting a suspicious look up at him. "And give you time to fix what you've done? No."

Roman locked his jaw before he said too much. "Let's try this another way. I'm the legal executor of Boone's estate. What makes you think that you have the right to examine anything?"

She shimmered in anger, as though she wanted to launch herself at him, and tear him from Boone's property. Then, for just an instant her bottom lip trembled and Roman prayed she wouldn't cry. He fought a shudder; he knew his limits. One tear and he'd go down like the proverbial ton of bricks.

"He was my friend. I loved that man," she said finally and the raw pain in her tone tore at Roman's heart, matching his own love for Boone.

"He left you something." Roman reached past Kallista and opened the door. He noted the distinctive recoil of her body from him—the "wife beater." "After you."

She arced an eyebrow and nodded curtly. "You first."

Roman smiled tightly and remembered his mother rapping him on the head when he forgot "ladies first." Kallista didn't trust him. Spitting mad, she looked like a weary, fragile kitten backed into a corner she didn't understand. The tension in her expression was for Boone, a man who had kept her safe. Roman wanted to fold her into his arms, to keep her safe, just as Boone had wanted. Instead he curled his hand around her nape, tugged slightly and she leaped back, her indrawn breath a hiss of warning, as she gave him room to pass.

"Wipe those boots." Roman Blaylock's broad, tanned back rippled in front of her, gleaming with sweat and rain,

and the primitive impulse to draw her nails slowly down
the smooth dark surface, stunned her. When he turned, a
mocking lilt to one corner of his hard mouth, Kallista
forced her eyes to stay locked with his, keeping them from
drifting lower—to that wide, fascinating expanse of his
chest, tanned and lightly flecked with damp curling hair.
The man was physically potent, enough to send women
swooning, especially with his dark warlord scowl and
shaggy, poorly cut hair. A physical man, she repeated,
catching the scent of rain on his skin, sweat and a dark
stormy presence. Roman moved like a mountain lion,
smooth, rippling—a predator aware of his surroundings, his
power. In Kallista's experience, men who looked like Roman knew how to use their looks and she wasn't interested.
She focused on her mission—to see that Boone's beloved
house hadn't been sacked.

A sweep of Roman's hand invited her to look—the house
was just as she remembered, big and cluttered, filled with
pictures of people she didn't recognize, other children
latched to Big Boone's safe body. The old upright piano,
which had been Boone's mother's, loomed in the shadows.
The furniture was old, overstuffed, and stripped of the doilies she'd remembered. Against the wall, covered by an
oversized shawl, was the huge steamer trunk that he'd always kept locked. The hulking china cabinet was packed
with old china and glassware, which Boone had said came
from his mother and grandmother—the fascinating, elegant
collection of ruby glass circled by gold had been Kallista's
favorite. Amid other framed childish drawings on the wall
was her watercolor of Boone, a huge stick man, holding a
little stick girl's hand. Boone And Me And My Boots a
young Kallista had printed in block letters, referencing her
favorite red boots.

Emotion tightened Kallista's throat and dampened her
eyes. She never cried, and couldn't afford the luxury now,

because she had a job to do for Boone. She forced herself to scan the house, because if anything was missing…

Kallista moved past the living room into another smaller, less formal room. The chair was simple, solid lines of oak big enough to accommodate Roman's tall body. She scanned the room quickly—a television set, magazines, books, and a dinner tray placed on a coffee table that matched the chair. Off to one side, the door to Boone's study was open and Kallista entered the room in which he had held her on his lap. He'd cuddled a sobbing lonely child, deserted by her mother. He'd told her that he loved her, that love was the most important thing in the world, and that she would always be his girl, that she could call The Llewlyn her home.

*Boone…* Tears burned her eyes and she slashed at them impatiently, shielding her weakness from Roman Blaylock. "You still have his pigeons and pigs and goats and sheep and cows, don't you?"

"They're fine. You can check on them in the morning. My brother Dan and his wife Hannah have the buffalo herd. Big Al, Dan's bull buffalo, wouldn't stop tearing down fences until the herd was together. The stock is marked and can be separated."

"Uh-huh, and we both know how the marking is done, right? More for Blaylock, less for Llewlyn? What about his stamp collections and all the rest? The orchid house? I suppose you let that go to ruin."

"You won't find anything wrong with how the calves are marked. Dusty and Titus do that, and I wouldn't like you questioning their honesty." For the first time Kallista caught Roman's low tone, like a wolf's warning growl, and it lifted the hair on her nape. He hadn't defended himself against her jabs, but his tone said he would not tolerate a slur on the elderly cowboys. He picked up an issue of *Orchid Facts* magazine and showed it to her, before tossing it aside. "I'm learning."

The thought of Boone's delicate orchids lying within Roman's hard scarred palm caused Kallista to shiver. "I can't imagine a man like you taking care of Boone's orchids. What about his collections? The stamps and coins and—" Then Kallista remembered that Roman had just mentioned something more important than valuable items. "Dusty and Titus? Boone's old ranch hands? You can't fire them—they are old men now, and without homes… You know they can't take hard physical work—"

"Did I work them to death? You've really got a high opinion of me, don't you? They're sleeping in the same bunkhouse where they have for fifty years. When their times come, Boone said to bury them in his cemetery up on the hill. Don't worry, they're healthy and they've got plenty to do looking after Boone's pigeons, pigs, goats, and sheep without doing hard ranch work." Roman studied her. "You can stay here, if you want. Boone wanted you back."

"With you? No, thanks." She pushed into the study, grand with books and a massive desk. The new computer sprang to life at her touch. The cursor blinked at her—Password? "Cute," she snapped, glancing at Roman who leaned against the door frame and studied her. "That's where you keep his accounts, isn't it?"

She quickly circled the room, then stood in front of Boone's massive antique desk. She ran her hand over the solid oak wood, and tugged at the brass handle of the rolltop. The lock held. She stared at Roman. "Figures. I won't ask you for the key. I wouldn't ask you for anything."

Then she circled the room again, lifting gilt-framed antique pictures away from the wall until she found the safe. It was new, high tech and the instant she touched it, a deafening alarm sounded and outside, Boone's registered beagles began howling. Roman sighed wearily and reached for the ringing telephone. "Mike? I know the alarm activated. Kallista Bellamy is here and prowling through the house. Right. I know a sheriff has better things to do patch-ing things up with his ex-wife than to answer useless midnight calls. Mike...stop ranting. It's only past ten.''

Roman answered the second call from a wall intercom and his expression softened momentarily. "Kallista is back, Dusty...go back to sleep. She'll be here for a few days.... Yes, I'll tell her you'd like to see her.... I'll tell her that we redid the plumbing and there's plenty of hot water now for her baths.''

He smiled briefly. "I know. Females like to take long baths. Yes, I'll tell her that we have a dishwasher and a new washer and dryer. Yes, I'll tell her that you and Titus missed her.''

Kallista turned on him when he replaced the telephone to the cradle. "I'll see them tomorrow when I check out the ranch. I want a good look at what you've done to Boone's land. I should have known. I'd forgotten how convenient it would be for you to come in here and take over. Mike is your cousin and you're related to almost everyone in town. The Blaylocks had seven children and your family would come to your defense, wouldn't they?''

"They'll do what's right,'' he said slowly with the confidence of a man who had grown up loved and cherished.

She hadn't been loved; she'd been a piece of luggage her mother hauled from marriage to marriage. She didn't want him to see her pain, how much she loved Boone, and Roman's black eyes were seeing too much. Spanish eyes, the locals had called the Blaylock eyes, a mark of their heritage on their father's side—a sturdy mix of Scots and English and French on their mother's.

Kallista hurried into the kitchen, away from him, from the memories of how wonderful life with Boone had been, how safe. Nothing had changed in the kitchen, not the big scarred farm table with its plain glass salt and pepper shakers, nor the mug stuffed with spoons. The old pottery bowls were stacked on the counter and every dish was still in the glass cupboards. The big gas cookstove had several ovens and burners and a shelf spanning the top. Boone had said it was his mother's…that he'd dreamed of his wife using it, but she never had. Boone had little to say about his wife, or his children, but sometimes the faraway look in his eyes told of his pain.

The old blackened camp coffeepot that Boone said brewed the best, sat on the back of the stove.

She sucked in air. Or was it pain? Boone had sat her on his lap, poured himself a large, hefty mug of coffee and her small china cup half full, adding fresh cow's milk to complete the measure. From the past, his voice curled around her. "This is how my mother did, little girl. Sat me on her lap, and told me how it should be for me, holding my own child on my lap and passing the time of day. But it didn't come to be until now, and now I've got you. That's her cup and now it's yours. That's real gold on the rim, and those are real English roses painted on real china— see? It's so thin, you can see your fingers through it. We're going to chat about things every day, sitting just like this, big stuff, like why flowers grow, and how people should keep each other in their hearts."

The cup seemed huge, or was it because she was small and only five? Kallista slashed the hot tears from her eyes and knew nothing could take away the pain in her heart. She glanced at a woman's handwritten note, posted to the old refrigerator by a magnet. "Come over tonight. Your favorite for dinner. There's garlic bread in the foil, just place in the oven with the rest to heat. We need salad dressing and olive oil. I changed the sheets."

A fresh wave of anger slammed into Kallista, and she jerked open the refrigerator door to find a large pan of lasagna. She slammed the door, rocking the huge pottery tureen on top. Roman Blaylock had not only taken over Boone's house, he had installed a woman in his bed. "I'll look upstairs," she managed, brushing past him.

When she'd first seen the house, hiding behind her

mother and peering out at this frightening savage land, she'd thought it was a castle and Boone was a fearsome giant who might eat her. Then she'd grown to treasure and to love him and now he was gone.

The hallway was just as wide, a table placed beneath a mirror and fresh herbs stuffed into a vase scented the air. Nothing had changed. Boone's bedroom looked just the same: gleaming wood floor covered by a braided rug, her picture with those of other children by his oversized bed— a man's Western boots placed neatly in a corner, gloves and a denim jacket discarded into an overstuffed chair. Roman Blaylock slept here; his masculine scent filled the room and a picture of the extensive Blaylock family sat on Boone's mahogany chest of drawers.

She hurried to Mrs. Llewlyn's room, soft with ruffles and floral patterns, the scent of lavender and roses hovering in the still air. Boone had said that she lived long enough for his return, then she had passed away. "Mrs. Llewlyn's walnut wardrobe is missing. It's huge and has drawers—like an armoire."

"It needed repair and refinishing. It's in the barn."

"You just put it back."

Her room was just the same, a single Jenny Lind bed, ruffles and flower prints and a brass vanity table and chair. Other girls had used this same room, layered with unfamiliar dolls and tea sets, and the other bedroom reserved for boys with model airplanes and trucks. The attic was stuffed with doll carriages and framed tintype pictures and memories. Kallista leaned against the door as layers of memories pressed painfully upon her. He'd tucked her in, placed a brand-new Raggedy Ann doll in her arms and told her that she was his. She'd never felt so safe—a horrible empty chill swept through her. "Oh, Boone..."

Downstairs, Roman waited for her, a well-loved, worn rag doll in his hand. "He wanted you to have this. When you calm down, there were other things he wanted you to have.''

''You're not fit to sleep in Boone's bed.'' Kallista snatched the doll from Roman, holding it against her racing heart. One glance at the fringed Spanish shawl covering the huge steamer trunk and she knew where the doll had been stored. There would be other things in that trunk and she knew how to pick locks. She looked up at Roman's impassive expression, and knew that she was going to destroy him. If Boone had stored her doll in the trunk, there had to be other things, perhaps something belonging to a relative who deserved Llewlyn House and the ranch. ''You know, I think I'll take you up on staying here—for the night.''

When Roman nodded solemnly, she added, ''Don't try anything. I can protect myself.''

An icy chill whipped through Kallista. She'd already proven that with one of her mother's lovers—

Beneath his glossy black lashes, Roman's eyes turned warm and amused, drifting slowly over her taut body and his deep drawl curled around her. ''Now that's quite an assumption, princess—that I'd want you. What would give you that idea?''

# Two

After hours of denying that his body tensed every time Kallista's very soft and athletic one tossed on the bed in the other room, Roman gave up on sleep. When he heard her creep from her room he reached beneath his bedside table to disconnect the alarms. With Mike's romantic reconciliation underway, he wouldn't want a second awakening at three o'clock in the morning. Roman stared up at the shadowy leaf patterns on the ceiling and listened to Kallista's boots prowl through the house, built by Boone's parents before the turn of the century. The rippling electronic sound downstairs said she'd turned on his computer, and after a solid fifteen minutes, another sound said she'd turned it off. A small beam of light lasered through the shadows beneath his door, and Kallista's footsteps moved past Roman's bedroom and up into the attic. He listened to the rhythmic creak of a rocker, too small for Boone's size.

Roman placed his arms behind his head and waited, stretched out on the top of the bed, dressed only in his jeans, the waist snap unbuttoned. Kallista was the first of Boone's "Innocents" on the list and if she was any measure of the rest... Roman shook his head; all he needed with his ranch chores and keeping up Boone's silent business was a prying, nosy, bitter and sexy woman. He tossed in passionate, colorful and vibrant.

He backtracked to the "sexy," and that long-ago kiss stung his lips. She'd been surprised, her sassy, full lips parted and the collision of their mouths wasn't sweet, but rather all fire and storms and unleashed hunger, and for a moment she'd matched him. Kallista's footsteps eased down the attic stairs and pushed into his room, stalking to his bedside.

Roman's body leaped into heat, shaken by the passion in her slightly slanted eyes. Hands on her hips, she glared down at him. The rag doll peered at Roman from Kallista's big leather shoulder bag. "Good. You're awake. I want you to see me coming and know that I'm going to take Big Boone's estate away from you, piece by piece."

Kallista jerked a fat file from under her arm and slapped it on his chest. "Yes. I did pick the desk lock. You've been tracking me. Everything's in there from my immunization shots that Boone started to every address where I've lived. It's always wise to keep up with someone who might be a threat, isn't it? You bet I'm a threat, Mr. Blaylock. You're not the kind of man who should be taking care of Boone's property."

"Boone wanted to keep up with you. That's his file. He'd want you to have it. It's yours." He was just getting worked up to tell her that he didn't appreciate the invasion into his bedroom when the tears glittering on her lashes distracted him; inside Roman, a part of him slid into helpless mush. Then she reached out her hand and Roman reacted, grabbing her wrist and jerking her toward him. With a soft cry, she fell heavily upon him, and in that instant, in the soft whoosh of her curved body against his, Roman knew that he wanted Kallista. He whipped away the crushed file between them, urgent for her soft body against his. The next instant, he realized he was easy prey for her and the thought nettled; the old bed creaked as Roman flipped over, pinning her beneath him, his hands circling her wrists.

They stared at each other, breathing hard. Roman's heart leaped into overdrive, his body instantly aware of the soft, feminine thighs cradling his own. Heat plowed through him like a steamroller, stunning him, upending his control. Her body taut, Kallista did not move, but looked up at him, the moonlight slanting on her smooth cheek and brushing her lips. She purred an insinuation. "Typical. Roman wants. Roman takes. But it won't be easy and you'll lose in the end. I'll have an arrest warrant tacked to your skin so fast you'll—"

A silky skein of hair slid slowly from his shoulder, a warm caress that startled and enticed him. He stared at her hair, spread across the pillow—black, long, fragrant and wild enough to make a man want to wrap his hands in it and tame. He sucked in his breath, aware of the soft curves beneath him. He hadn't touched a woman in years—unwillingly, his gaze jerked down to her body, those soft thighs along his. Roman smothered a groan and pasted a growl over it. "That's a lot of threats for a lady cat burglar who's been prowling through my home."

"Boone's home," she corrected, her black eyebrows fierce and drawn, her fingers curled as though if released, she'd dig into his flesh. "And you weigh a ton. Get off me."

Pain shot through Roman, the memory of Debbie's fearful glance at him. *"You're so…big…I can't."*

He'd been ashamed then, of his size and power. Ashamed that the sight of him without his shirt made his delicate wife turn away, shivering in terror. But Kallista wasn't frightened of him. Her narrowed eyes threatened;

her fingers curled as though wanting to strike out at him. Fear wasn't an element that Kallista experienced now... A steady hum of tension grew between them, and Roman slowly stroked the fine skin of her inner wrists with his thumbs, unwilling just yet to let her go. Her pulse rocketed to match his own, surprising him, but then, the woman was furious. He could feel the anger driving her. "I won't take lightly to another slap, lady," he said quietly, watching her eyes and wondering how they would look, meadow green and soft upon him.

"I was reaching for my picture. Boone took the snapshot. I don't want you to have it."

She shifted beneath him and Roman felt the deep shudder, searching her pale face, despite her furious expression. "I won't hurt you. Why are you afraid of me?"

"Get off me," she repeated unevenly and licked her lips, fascinating Roman.

Her lips were full and soft and silky moist—another shudder ran through her as their eyes locked in the shadows. Taking care not to frighten her, Roman eased slowly away from her, locking his hands behind his head. He didn't shield his arousal and Kallista's eyes swept down his body, widening at the obvious thrust against his jeans.

He met her darkening gaze evenly and eased a sweep of silky hair back from her hot cheek. "Blushing, Kallista? I'd think you'd be long past that."

"Neanderthal. Leave it to you to lower the terms of this war."

"Equal terms, lady. You push. I push back. You'd better get out of my bed now." Roman fought the need to brush his lips across hers and knew it wouldn't stop there.

She shook her head and a strand of hair slid onto his chest. Roman slowly looked down at the ebony stripe, sleek against his tanned skin with its light coating of crisp hair. For a moment, he went dizzy, the image of Kallista's hair webbing across his body, enveloping him in her scents, her flushed face soft after lovemaking...

She glared at him. "I'll flatten you. You have no idea what you have just started."

"Don't I?" Roman couldn't resist running his fingertip across her hot cheek once more. He hadn't flirted since his early twenties, before his marriage, when the Blaylock sons were prowling the country, stirring up females. Lying beneath him now, Kallista had stirred him on a more urgent, fiery, elemental level that hadn't been scraped in his experimental years.

Kallista dashed his hand away, rolled to her feet, grabbed the picture and the file and stormed out of the house. She closed the front door gently, mindful of Boone's treasured stained-glass window. Her car revved in the ranch yard and Roman stood to watch her through the darkened window.

"Damn." Instead of driving back to Jasmine, Kallista's headlights soared in the opposite direction. She left the main highway to drive toward his deserted house.

If only she didn't remember his hard mouth on hers, that long-ago kiss as if he'd give his soul to her—wrapped in her unsteady emotions, Kallista had wanted to devour Roman. His body over hers had sent her senses leaping.

Fine. Roman Blaylock's rugged face and build, his soulful dark eyes, would make any woman take a second look. His skin had a tanned healthy and weathered sheen that made a woman want to stroke those hard cheeks, that unrelenting jaw, and soften that grim mouth with her own— Then there was that arrogance that just made her want to take him down and make him pay. But the nice packaging wasn't the man, and Debbie had clearly been frightened of her husband.

Kallista picked the door lock and stepped into the shadows of Roman's deserted, dark house. A modern ranch home, built of rock and logs and surrounded by pines, the

house settled into the slope of the Rocky Mountains as if
it had always been there. After testing the dead light switch,
Kallista panned her flashlight across the living room's
rough timber paneling, noting the lighter squares where
once pictures had hung. The house was cold, shadowy and
empty. The huge rock fireplace spanned one side of the
room and a rumpled sleeping bag lay in front of it. An
antique walnut church pew stood in the center of the living
room, like a huge dark monument, marking the absence of
a woman's touch. Three of the bedrooms were empty; a
fourth, a small one, was decorated in frills and flowers with
Alice in Wonderland figures hanging from the ceiling. The
tiny room was packed with antique furniture, piled haphaz-
ardly. A box of framed pictures sat on a tiny tea table, and
a collection of arrowheads, Native American beads and
hunting knives were stuffed into another box. Only the
child and the man were noted in this room; Debbie had not
taken remembrances of either with her into her new marriage.

*Debbie.* Petite, blond, blue-eyed—a dreamer, an intellec-
tual and an innocent. Debbie would always need protection,
unable to fight her own battles. Four years ago, pitted
against Roman's dark predator intensity, Debbie had paled.

Kallista had a lifetime of fighting to survive behind her;
no one had protected her—except Boone. She ran her hand
over a large scarred rocking chair, and cobwebs clung to
her hands like shredded memories. She shut the door, remembering the daughter that Roman had lost; from Hannah, Kallista knew that he grieved—or did he? Was his
grief a call for sympathy so as to shield his takeover of
The Llewlyn?

She entered a large office, lined with filled bookshelves,
and could sense Roman's dark presence. Layered with dust,
the rifle case was empty, the modern desk aclutter. The
pantry was empty, the laundry room stripped. The kitchen
was bare except for a half-full bottle of whiskey, a scattered

array of photographs, some of them rumpled as though crushed in a furious fist. Kallista smoothed a photograph of Roman holding a baby in his arms, a tender smile on his tanned, rugged face. The other pictures were portraits of Roman as a loving father and Debbie the "little woman," standing on tiptoe to kiss his cheek. A clutter of unopened mail lay on a card table. The house had been stripped, the windows without drapes. Kallista shivered; the house was a cold tomb.

She stooped to collect a crumpled ball of paper, smoothing it open on the counter and scanning it with her flashlight. Debbie's faded big loopy writing spread across the page.

"I'm marrying Thomas and taking everything. We'll need the start. I paid for it by living with you for thirteen years and by putting up with the Blaylock family. Though I appreciated you marrying me when I was pregnant with John's baby, I want a man I can share my dreams with and my mind, and my bed. With Thomas, I won't want separate bedrooms."

Kallista remembered how four years ago, in the dreadful scene at the shop, Debbie had called out Thomas's name. Later, she'd introduced him as a "friend" and a professor of literature, though their gazes had shared emotions more than "friendly." Frowning, Kallista read on.

"He would have never come after me like you did at the Bisque Café. He lets me make my own choices and I like taking care of him. I am expecting his child. I won't be back. Do not fight the divorce, or I'll tell your family that the marriage was all a sham. That you married me to protect me from gossip and that I couldn't bear to have you touch me all these years. Debbie."

In contrast to the shattering note, but in keeping with her light-brain personality, Debbie had drawn a smiley face. She also dotted her name's *i* with a circle. The P.S. was hurriedly scrawled, an afterthought.

"Thank you for being a good father to John's daughter. Michaela's birth hurt too much for me to really love her. I took the mortgage payment."

From Hannah, Kallista had learned that Roman's three-year-old daughter had drowned in a shallow plastic swimming pool, a freak accident. Roman had been in the fields, working on the tractor, and had returned to find his daughter drowned. Debbie had said she'd just run into the house for a moment to answer the telephone. He'd been grief-stricken for years, and Debbie, a fragile woman, had proclaimed to everyone that she was a good mother. Soon after the child's death, Debbie had set about making a new life to please herself.

Kallista folded the note and let it flutter into a trash basket. A fat envelope caught her attention, and she scooped it from the trash. Four years ago, the day that Roman had swept angrily into the shop, the checking and savings accounts in the name of Roman and Debbie Blaylock had been emptied. Debbie's handwriting was on both withdrawals, which left a balance of ten dollars. When pieced together, a torn overdue payment on Roman Blaylock's mortgage revealed the bank's foreclosure notice.

Though it was not the present, four years ago, Debbie's shrill voice cut into the shadows around Kallista. "I told you I didn't make the last payment because I needed the money for something else. No, I will not replace our savings, not even enough for the payments due. Sell a tractor or a cow, or something—"

Roman had suffered, but he had probably taken other women to his bed for comfort. He was certainly knowledgeable about how to touch lightly, gently, just a stroke of his fingertip to arouse… He'd showered and the scent of soap and man clung to him, his hands rough with work, strong, capable. The heat in his eyes could cause a righteous woman to melt and tremble.

Kallista wasn't righteous; she was a survivor who knew that with soft looks usually came conditions and payments. She wrapped her arms around herself and stared out into the gray predawn light to the knoll where Boone lay. Roman couldn't be trusted and he had his big fists locked on Boone's beloved estate. Cattle were milling in the pastures, sheep spread across the small knoll like a soft, creamy cloud, a dog barked, and Boone—the only man Kallista had trusted other than Channing Boudreaux—was dead.

She shivered, the empty house adding to the vacuum of her life. The impression of Roman's hard tall body on top of hers sent a hot flush through her cheeks and another shiver through her body. He'd been aroused—and so warm, his shoulders sleek and wide, rippling with power. His chest had pressed against her breasts and his heart had raced, a pulse throbbing in his throat. That pulse had become an earthquake from his stomach down to his hips, his thighs heavy, taut, upon hers. Her heart had ricocheted the pounding beat of his and for just an instant as time stood still, a flood of desire wiped away her dislike of Roman. The denim of their jeans had not insulated the heat pouring from him—or was it her?

He knew how to look at a woman, to make her respond. More than likely, Roman hadn't missed Debbie's wifely affection. He was probably used to women coming to his bed on a regular basis. Boone's bed. Kallista scrubbed her face with shaking hands. She'd come back for Boone, to make certain that his beloved treasures and his land were not sacked.

A key rattled in the door and Roman stepped into the shadows, followed by two leggy, thin dogs that moved

quickly into the shadows. He lifted his black brows and
tipped his Western hat on the back of his head. In the shadows, he looked like his Apache and Spanish ancestors—
terrifyingly masculine, dominating, arrogant, an angular
blend of sheer power. "Ma'am. You've had a busy night."

Her head went back, ready to fight; she'd seen through
those famous Blaylock ladykiller manners. The Blaylock
men were known to be courteous and respectful of
women—if they weren't, their mother had applied a
wooden spoon. "I can see why you wanted to move into
Boone's house."

"It's...convenient." He nodded slowly, watching her,
and tossed his hat to the kitchen counter. Dressed in jeans,
a work shirt and a battered flannel jacket, Roman's shaggy
black hair was rumpled, as though he'd been dragging his
hands through it. He glanced at the shadowy rooms and
inhaled unevenly.

Kallista leaned against the kitchen counter and studied
him. If he had weaknesses, this man of stone, she'd find
them. She reached into her bag, pulled out a small apple
and bottled water. She wiped the apple on her jeans and
took a bite, studying him. After a sip of water, she asked,
"You're uncomfortable here. Why? It was your home,
wasn't it?"

"I built it for my wife. I thought it would make her
happy." The words were solemn, the promise of a man
who took his marriage vows seriously. According to Jasmine gossip, Blaylock men held their marriages and their
wives sacred. Boone had said that Blaylock men got moldy
when they weren't stirred up, and she intended to do a little
stirring.

"Rumor has it that Debbie remarried quickly," she
pushed. She wondered just how much control Roman Blaylock possessed when tested.

"She did that. I wish her well." Roman spoke too quietly.

Finished with her apple, Kallista pulled out a chocolate bar and peeled away the paper. Habit caused her to lick the chocolate tip before biting; she sensed Roman tensing and she cut right to his wound, sparing him nothing. "Come on, don't hand me that. You were married for thirteen years. She was your childhood sweetheart. A professor of literature took her away from you. That had to hurt your pride."

"You want it all, don't you? To place all the pieces in a neat little picture? Well, lady, maybe the pieces don't fit, no matter how hard you dig." There was that dangerous edge, the lifted hackles, a warning of a private man as Roman ripped off his gloves and jammed them into his jeans' back pocket. He crossed his arms, looking down at her, waiting.

Too bad. She wanted to know about Roman, to prove him unfit to be Boone's executor. She munched on the chocolate bar, taking her time to nettle him. She retrieved a chip of chocolate with her tongue. "This house has been stripped."

There was that quick intake of breath as though pain had sliced through Roman Blaylock's big, lean, muscled body. "Debbie took what she wanted."

The dogs moved restlessly; perhaps they sensed the prick of taut nerves, the clash of emotional steel...

"She left your daughter's things and yours, the antique furniture." By reading Debbie's note, Kallista had insight into Roman's life, one that the extensive Blaylock family had not known. She tossed her chocolate wrapper into the trash, covering Debbie's note.

"Do you live out of that bag? What else do you have in there?"

"I travel light. I have what I need."

Roman ran his hand through his hair and looked out into the predawn light. "Debbie had her own taste. My sister, Else, brought my share of my parents' things here after

Debbie left." He scanned the house. "There was plenty of room. When Debbie...left, the bank came calling, I almost lost everything. Boone saw that I didn't. I'm paying him back."

"I'll just bet. Several of his collections are gone. The miniature animals, his scrimshaw collection. How much did they bring when you sold them? Don't tell me they're in storage. I wouldn't believe you."

"I don't care what you believe. Marsha Gerald took care of his nursing needs and he wanted her to have the miniature animals. And Boone wanted Slim Woodard to have the scrimshaw things to remember him." The words were said without anger or frustration, just a simple statement of fact.

"I'll just check with them to see if you're telling the truth."

Her threat met a mild smile. "You just do that, ma'am."

Kallista thought of the lovely old rocking chair, handed down from years ago, the massive plain walnut bed meant to last for centuries. The rocker was meant to hold mothers and babies, the creaking blending with lullabies. With a few cushions, the walnut church pew could be... She braced herself against thinking about Roman's home and found herself studying the loneliness in his expression. "I'm going to take you down, you know."

He turned slowly to her. "You're going to try. I made promises to Boone, and I intend to keep them. If you decide to stay, you can stay here."

Kallista smiled coolly. "Why, thank you, Roman. That is very nice of you. But I'd much rather stay at Boone's."

Roman's black eyebrows lifted and he reached for his hat. "Fine with me."

"I'll be staying and I can watch Boone's house. I have a little inventory I'd like to complete." She tilted her head and fed him the challenge as she took a small notebook from her bag and checked the items she had noted remaining at Boone's. "You could move back here and let me have the house."

She handed him the notebook, which he scanned. Roman smiled slowly, white teeth gleaming in the darkness above her as he stuffed it back into her bag. His finger traced the strand of hair that crossed her shoulder and he tugged lightly. The lines around his eyes deepened with amusement, his black eyes warm upon her. "Now living apart wouldn't be any fun, would it? That's what you're into, isn't it? Fun? A thirty-four-year-old woman leading a footloose, carefree life. Working as a dancer, a hotel manager, a conference planner, and now a troubleshooter for Boudreaux, Inc.? No ties, no family, just plenty of road and sky and water."

He made her roving life seem shallow, without love or roots to anyone, and Kallista tilted her head warningly. "I've been around. I make my own way and don't owe anyone. Except Boone. There hasn't been reason to stop."

"Uh-huh." Roman gently slapped his thigh and from the shadows two streamlined greyhounds came to his side. He rubbed their smooth heads. The dogs were old, missing teeth, their pelts scarred by beatings. "Boone took in racing dogs who weren't wanted. Meet Igor and Luka."

Boone had been legendary for his quiet moods and his kind heart. "I remember them. They're shivering."

Roman crouched to rub the dogs briskly, warming them. "They should be wearing their coats—little knitted sweaters that Else made for them. I'll take them back to the bunkhouse."

She reached to pet their heads and Roman's big hand caught hers as he stood. "They sense your anger. Dusty and Titus will, too. Keep them out of this. I made a promise to Boone, and I'm going to keep it. This is between you and me and Boone. Understand?"

"What was that promise?" Kallista shot at him, looking for angles to destroy his grasp on Boone's land.

Roman released her hand and jammed his big hands into his gloves. "That is between Boone and me and my wife—if I marry again. That's not likely."

"No. You wouldn't like the confines of marriage, now that you have what you want."

"I don't want a whole lot of what comes with marriage," he said flatly.

"If there is a woman sharing Boone's house with you—and his bed—get her out…or I will."

Roman's hair gleamed as he tilted his head. "You've got a suspicious mind and a fast mouth. When I live with a woman, she'll wear a wedding band."

"Yours?" Kallista asked, pressing him, looking for weaknesses.

"Keep it up," he said mildly, with a tone that said his hackles were lifting, "and you're headed for trouble."

"I've always liked a good dollop of trouble."

At eight o'clock on a mid-May morning, Kallista sat at the small desk in the Bisque's cubbyhole of an office. She'd had two weeks of investigating Roman and organizing the shop as she wanted it. Hannah, and the rest of the Blaylock women had done an excellent job keeping records and maintaining supplies. The paint shelves were well stocked, the brushes cleaned and waiting in individual pots. The shop had a small but adequate income. The residents of Jasmine liked making gifts for loved ones and decorating their homes. After checking the latest bank statement, Kallista had ordered new supplies of greenware—the molded clay shapes that were then smoothed. After baking in the kiln, they were called "bisque," which was painted and fired again to produce the final product. Both kilns were in working order. The shop was neat and airy, wire soda shop chairs and tables empty now, its shelves filled with standard bowls, cups, lighted Christmas trees and chess sets. Dragons matching the one that had battered Roman Blaylock peered down at her. Bisque ladybugs and turtles waited for painting.

Morganna, married to Jake Tallman and a cousin of the Blaylocks, breezed into the shop with Hannah. Morganna, Jake and their daughters were visiting with the Blaylocks before returning to their Colorado ranch; Jake, a cousin of the Blaylocks, had been orphaned and the Blaylocks had claimed him as one of their own.

Hannah carried a big box, and Morganna, oblivious to the darkening damp spots on her blouse, a sign that she was a nursing mother, clutched a grocery sack. After warm hugs, Morganna, a city executive turned ranch housewife and mother, dug into the box. "A shop warming gift," she exclaimed, retrieving a high-tech cappuccino maker from the box.

"Yummy. Thanks. I'd say this gift is too much, but I'm dying for a cup," Kallista murmured. Morganna read directions while Hannah and Kallista completed the start-up effort. The aromatic scent filled the shop, and soon three mugs of cappuccino, topped by whipped cream, sat on a table.

"Bagels, too." Hannah placed bagels on napkins and plopped a carton of strawberry cream cheese onto the table. She stuck a spoon in it and grinned. "Dig in. What do you think about the shop?"

"You did a good job. Everything is in order."

Hannah surveyed the shelves and the neat shop. "We tried. We couldn't take time to develop new ideas, so everything is running as you left it. Boone liked to come in here and watch, just watch, as if he were happy that others were happy. He liked to hold Delilah, our baby. He was such a—"

Kallista couldn't sit still; the mention of Boone caused the tear in her heart to widen painfully. She stood slowly, cradling the mug that had been made in the shop. "Roman Blaylock is living in Boone's house."

Hannah spoke softly. "He took care of Boone in that last year. I think it gave him purpose. But Boone gave Roman something, too. A sense of belonging. He lost some of that with Debbie and kept to himself. It was as if he felt shamed that his marriage didn't work, the only Blaylock to be divorced. We've tried to—"

"I don't want to know about Roman's pride," Kallista stated flatly and ran her finger over the top of a bisque chess knight.

"I'd heard you'd already tangled with him two weeks ago. You took right up where you left off—Jasmine is still talking about the time you slapped him and that kiss," Morganna purred silkily. "It appears that you two had a busy night, and disturbed Dusty's and Titus's sleep. The next morning, Roman slammed into the barn looking like a thundercloud. And at just the mention of his name, you look as though you'd like to tear something apart other than that bagel you're shredding—"

Morganna's gaze snagged on the long, tall cowboy leaning against the pickup outside. Her eyes widened and her lips parted as she licked them. She took a deep breath and sighed dreamily.

Hannah laughed outright. "Love. She can't wait to get her hands on her husband. Two months after Feather's birth, he's looking more worn-out than she is."

"I'll be back. Glad you like the cappuccino maker," Morganna said, hurrying out of the shop. At the doorway, she slowed, straightened her blouse and smoothed her jeans, and reached to smooth her hair. She sauntered to Jake and ran a finger down his chest. Tension sizzled between them, before Jake bent, scooped her up in his arms, and placed her in the pickup. She snuggled close to him and Hannah grinned. "He's head over heels and so is she. She still makes tacos hard enough to break teeth, but she knows how to power-ramrod a business deal and has the much needed youth center up and running. They're more in love than ever. Just like Dan and me."

The Blaylocks were a loving family and Roman, a dark maverick who had separated himself from them, concerned Kallista. "Tell me what you know about Roman."

Hannah looked evenly at Kallista and sighed. "You've been asking everyone about him.... Okay, then. It tore the heart out of him when his little girl drowned. His marriage to Debbie changed him slowly, and we see little of him. He's been taking good care of Boone's ranch and his own. He has to hire men to check fences and watch those ten thousand Llewlyn acres. It's a big operation, and he hasn't had much time to take care of his own. He won't sell, though, because it is Blaylock family land."

She glanced at her watch. "I've got to go. I'm behind on my decorating business, but if you need help, let me know. I didn't place new greenware orders because I thought you'd want to make your own selection."

Kallista wanted more answers. "Roman isn't a friendly sort then—with women?"

"You mean, does he party in Boone's house? The man is a recluse, driving Else frantic to have him back in the family. Every woman in the countryside has given up on him...he doesn't seem to notice."

After Hannah left, Kallista sipped her cappuccino. She looked around the shop and began to see the possibilities, just as she'd done all her life, settling in to make a temporary home—just long enough to see that Boone's life-work was wrenched out of Roman's big powerful fists. If she had to take it away, piece by piece, she would.

Kallista locked her hand to the counter. Two weeks had passed and she hadn't heard one dark remark about Roman Blaylock's character.

Else, the oldest Blaylock sister, and now the matron of the family, arrived, wearing her mother's pearl doing-business earrings and a warm smile. She handed a huge vining plant to Kallista and gave her a kiss. "I hear you're picking on my little brother. He's been in a bad mood and even told my husband, Joe, to back off. That's a first for Roman. Joe says Roman reeks of woman-trouble. That wouldn't be you, would it, Kallista?"

Kallista coolly met Else's amused stare. "I'm going to give him hell."

Else's eyebrows shot up. "Mind if I ask why?"

"He's moved some woman into the house. I saw a note she'd left. She's changing sheets and Boone would have never put up with that—"

Else laughed aloud and went to collect her ceramic crouching black leopard from the finished shelf. "That's me, honey. That old house is stuffed to the brim and needs a full-time cleaning woman. Margaret Berry does most of it, but she doesn't starch doilies—and neither do I. Farm living leaves little time for such niceties. So Boone's mother's doilies had to be stored. But other than that, Roman has kept the house as it was."

Else watched Kallista pack the leopard into soft wrap and place it in a sack. "I've got three unmarried brothers at the moment—Roman, Rio and Tyrell. Tyrell is in New York now, a number cruncher, a high-flying finance chief, but he flies in occasionally. Rio is girlfriend shopping and you've met him. Then there's Roman."

"Yes, then there's Roman," Kallista repeated slowly, darkly.

"When you get tired of sleeping up in the shop's loft, you might think about renting Roman's house," Else murmured lightly.

# Three

The scents of June blooming and sweet alfalfa and clover didn't help Roman's dark mood. He eased his pickup to a stop near Boone's barn and prowled through his thoughts. Other than the burning strip of flesh that barbed wire had ripped, lack of sleep, a humming sensual tension riding his body—*and* a whole lot of gossip burning his ears about Kallista Bellamy's month-long stay in Jasmine—he was just fine.

Boone's Hereford bull had decided to walk through a fence as if it were a lace ribbon. The amorous bull, seeking a friendly cow, had dragged the fence along, tearing out fence posts, until he'd become too entangled to be free...and from there things weren't pleasant. That had suited Roman just fine; he'd needed a battle royal to relieve his frustration, and First Prince gave it to him.

Roman looked at the corral and frowned. Neil Morris, the veterinarian, hadn't left the ranch, but was sitting on the top board of the corral giving instructions to the horse-

woman within it. Neil's blond wavy hair had been neatly
combed and he'd changed into the extra clean shirt he kept
in his pickup. His face was smooth, the morning stubble
gone, a warning that Neil was woman-hunting. Roman ran
his palm across his stubble-rough cheek, then damned fancy
razors that used batteries or plugged into vehicles and
Neil's bachelor-drooling look. "An honest man wouldn't
use a battery or a pickup motor to beautify himself," Roman muttered darkly, before the vision in the corral stunned
him.

Framed by the golden setting sun, Kallista's black hair
was loose, long rippling blue-black silk, as Loves Dancing
the sleek graceful mare, trotted around the corral. The flow
of woman beneath Kallista's tight black sweater and black
jeans didn't help Roman's dark mood. Neither did the sight
of his brother's angular backside perched near Neil's. Rio's
Western hat was tipped back and he had that curl to his
mouth as if he'd just identified a succulent female morsel.
Roman sucked in his breath; an infamous bachelor rogue,
Rio had been making noises about settling down; Neil had
that same female-hunting look. Dusty and Titus looked as
if their worn Western boots were an inch off the ground,
their weathered, lined faces shoved into grins. In honor of
Kallista's return, both men wore their store-bought teeth.

Roman whipped off his hat and slapped his dusty torn
jeans. He was sweaty, bloody, and his good shirt had been
ripped to hell. He blinked and looked down at the brand-
new chambray shirt that had been hanging in the closet for
a year. With a sharp note that someone had to take care of
him, Else had purchased new jeans and shirts. Now the new
jeans were ruined and his blood soiled the price tag; he had
no idea why he was wearing stiff new clothes; and damn
it, Kallista was holding court to two wife-hunters.

After a level look at his brother, Rio dropped to the corral floor and sauntered to Kallista, tipping back his hat and
grinning up at her. She returned the favor with a flirty look

that hitched Roman's bad mood higher. If she was out to make trouble, she knew just how....

He found himself placing a hand on the low gate and vaulting both legs over it. Rio slanted a look at the intruder, and his grin slid down a notch, his black eyes leveling with Roman's.

"Hello, Roman. You look like hell," Rio said pleasantly.

Drawn to staring at Kallista, Roman braced his legs apart and his boots on the corral dirt. He locked his hands to his hips to keep from reaching for her, and everyone else fell away in the June sunshine as his heart kicked up and flip-flopped over into uncertainty.

"Yeah, we'll be there for Men Only Night, Kallie-girl," Titus called. "Anything to help business get up and going. A week from Tuesday night? About seven?"

"Men Only," Rio said quietly to his brother. "I'll be there. There's a dog food bowl I want to paint for Mix, Else's dog."

"I guess I'll just have to cut you out of the herd, then, won't I, boy?" Roman heard himself say in a low, soft growl to his younger brother.

"You can try, old man. I'm really primed for that dog bowl."

Roman skipped the growling side talk and shot right to business. "Your pointy ears better settle down, boy, because this filly is mine."

A younger brother who'd had to fight to hold his own, Rio didn't back down easily. He hooked his thumbs in his belt. "She's not wearing your brand."

"She will."

"I'm sweet. You're not. You're a rangy, old lonesome wolf," Rio murmured and slid Kallista a big grin.

Kallista's furious expression burned down at Roman, but he didn't take time to examine why—Rio wasn't getting Kallista. "I can grow fangs if I have to, lover boy," Roman muttered darkly. "But you leave this one alone."

Rio's blank stare shoved into dawning awareness and a slow grin; he hooted at his brother's first interest in a woman in years. Roman damned the heat rising up the back of his neck and braced himself to take his little brother down. "Else's wooden spoon won't save your backside this time, Rio. She's not here to protect you."

"Could be you who needs her protection this time," Rio purred back and glanced at Kallista. "You're all fired up."

Kallista's mare pranced as if sensing the tension running between the humans. An experienced horsewoman, Kallista held the reins taut. "Exactly what does that mean, Mr. Blaylock? Why should your brother leave me alone?"

The brothers turned to her, and she defined which Mr. Blaylock: "You, Mr. Blaylock, the one with the sweet temperament and the price tag on your shirt."

Roman ripped the tag away and started toward her. He was uncertain how to handle this woman, but advancing into the war seemed a sensible move. "Get down from there."

With the rugged mountains as a backdrop, she was an exciting sight, a strong woman who would take the weather and stick. Kallista wasn't sweet or dainty—but ripe, all wild and passionate and furious with him. Shoulders squared, body taut with tension—she was a powerful woman, vibrant, alive and Roman admired the high-handsome look of her.

He traced the gentle rise on her upper arm as she reined the mare, and wanted to smooth the delicate feminine muscle, unlike his own. He wanted to skim his fingertips and his palms and his lips over that elegant strength and... Her legs controlled the mare and Roman's body shot to steel. His gaze jerked higher as Kallista breathed hard and her breasts rose and fell quickly beneath the sweater. Her hands tightened on the reins as if nothing could tear them away, and that was just how Roman wanted her holding him— hard and strong. Her legs flexed, locking to the mare's sides and Roman barely kept his hand from reaching out to stroke her.

Like the honed blades of raised swords, every humming emotion between them flashed in the sunshine, neon-bright, shielding nothing of the heat, everything real and honest. He ached to make those flashing emerald eyes turn to a softer, drowsy shade, to hold her in his arms and take that ripe, sassy mouth as if it were his right— He stopped in midstride, caught by the boyish excitement rushing through him, his emotions stunning him. He felt as if he'd just stepped out of a gloomy cave and in front of him was the woman he wanted. Betraying him, his body hardened, and Roman damned his lack of expertise in controlling himself. He glared at her, the woman who had turned the comfortable rhythms of his life into a hurricane of uncertainty and need.

The protective layers were peeled away from his keeping now, and he knew that he'd never needed, not like he needed Kallista. He stood and stared at her, locked in the need to swing up on the horse behind her and...

Kallista's generous mouth tightened, her face pale with fury, her eyes narrowed and burning him. Holding his look, she backed the mare to the farthest part of the corral; she nudged the mare's belly and leaned forward. Loves Dancing shot into the short distance of the corral and hurled gracefully over the gate. The mare hurled over the next gate, and sailed into the open pasture, woman and horse a beautiful symphony.

One whistle would stop the mare, Boone's favorite, and Kallista could be hurt. Roman sucked air into his lungs, and realized that he'd been frozen by the beauty of the jump, terrified for the woman he desperately wanted.

Standing at his side, Rio nudged Roman's ribs and flipped a quarter into the hair, slapping it to the back of his hand. "Toss you for who rides her down."

Without taking time to think, Roman hooked his boot

behind Rio's and jerked. Rio's butt hit the corral dirt. Sprawled in the dust, he grinned up at Roman. "You're slow and you're old and she's a fast mover."

"I can keep up," Roman tossed back and wondered if he could. On a run, he bent through the corral boards and eyed Massachusetts, a fast black gelding that didn't like the saddle. Roman reached for a fist of black mane and swung up on the gelding's back and they stretched out in the pasture, following Loves Dancing and Kallista.

Roman realized suddenly that he was chuckling and had a silly grin pasted on his face, like a boy playing chase with his girl. He noted the soft flow of her bottom on the saddle and swallowed hard; she was all woman, free and wild, and Roman's instincts told him to capture her, to claim her. She looked over her shoulder to him and scowled, then slowed the mare quickly and turned to face Roman. He slowed Massachusetts and eased the gelding beside the mare. Kallista, cheeks flushed, was glorious, the most exciting woman he'd ever seen. She eased the mare away from him and in the sunlit pasture, they moved in a slow circle. Roman wanted to stroke her hot cheek, but instead he asked, "What's got you revved up?"

"You. I don't like you." She spoke tightly, maneuvering the mare away from his gelding in that taut, challenging circle.

"Did I ask you to?" She was one hundred percent real, Roman thought, fire and flash and ready to go for him, nothing hidden. "Are you staying?"

"Just long enough to do the job on you. Boone should have relatives and they should be taking care of his property. Not you."

"That sounds interesting. Run when the going gets tough, why don't you?" he challenged and knew her for a woman who wouldn't back away.

For a blinding moment, he saw her as his wife with children and dreams between them. The image stunned him.

Kallista's silky black mane whipped around her head as a cool breeze swept down the mountains into the pasture. The breeze riffled the soft blue-black tips, stirring Roman's need to reach out and run his hand down that sleek swath. He wasn't a touching man, but now the need to touch Kallista leaped upon him, digging in.

An expert horsewoman, she turned the mare to face him. "Debbie said you hurt her, and that day at the shop, I saw her cower from you as if she was afraid you'd strike her. I detest bullies."

He admired her cutting dive to the bald truth, no softness cluttering the spring air between them. "I never hurt Debbie. She got what she wanted. What do you want?"

"From you? Nothing. I've known men like you, who hurt and take and—"

The pain in her eyes, quickly shielded, caused Roman to ache. The bitterness in her tone startled him, nicked his pride. "I won't hurt you," he said slowly, meaning it.

"You won't get the chance—"

Roman followed his instincts; he reached out a hand, claimed the front of her sweater and drew her to him for a long, slow kiss that tasted like warm honey and sunlight spread on heaven. It seemed just right, out there in the pasture, with fingers of evening shade, brushing his lips lightly against hers. She didn't move away, and Roman held his breath as he leaned closer. While slanting his lips lightly over hers, he eased his arm around her waist and gently, slowly so as not to frighten her, lifted her to Massachusetts's back.

The sweep of Roman's big trembling hand down Kallista's side to her thigh and back up again, resting under her arm, fingertips just touching her outer breast, should have frightened her. His dark heated look that slowly ran down her body, brushing her breasts and came to settle on her face, should have terrified her. Large men could send

a familiar terror through her, but Kallista wanted to pit herself against him, and take… Roman's solemn eyes were
soft upon her and shuttered, waiting for her reaction.

She'd been too stunned by his kiss to react, too surprised
that he could handle her easily, gently, as if she were one
of Boone's orchids to collect and cradle against in his rough
palm.

Suddenly she was too close to retreat, Roman's broad
shoulders solid and warm beneath her hands, his face too
close, his uneven breath warm upon her skin. His advance
was too raw, too urgent, and there wasn't time to back
away. He was testing her, seeing if she'd run. She wouldn't,
she could take what he gave and give it back hotter. He
tasted like home and excitement and whatever she'd sought
all her life, beyond the edge of now, here, this time. She
wrapped her arms around his neck and tugged him closer,
fusing her mouth to his tempting hard one.

The delight in his taste took her spiraling into the desire
to take everything from him, to push straight through to
find that exciting male mystique. She wrapped her fists in
his hair, claiming that shaggy black mass and pulling him
closer to feed upon him. Roman tasted dark, powerful, and
edgy, wary of her. Too bad. He was letting her set the
tempo and within her, unfamiliar needs stirred and smol-
dered like embers churned to life by a stormy wind. On
impulse, testing his gentleness and her own curiosity, she
moved into the kiss and let him gather her closer.

"All I want to know," Roman said unevenly as she
leaned back watching him, waiting to see what he'd do
next, this unexplored man she'd found. Ridden with mys-
tery, untouchable, cool Roman Blaylock had definitely
heated beneath her lips, a flush on his dark cheeks, his
mouth slightly swollen from hers. The rapid pulse beating
at the base of his neck proved that she'd gotten the impact
she wanted—raw and honest.

Kallista shivered; she'd unlocked enough passion in Roman Blaylock to tether her, and she couldn't afford the leash, nor the man whose fist gripped Boone's estate. "All I want to know," he repeated huskily, "is where you're going to sleep tonight."

"At your place." She watched as his black eyes heated and his fingertips pressed slightly harder into the outer perimeter of her breast.

Why wasn't she terrified? Roman had the size and strength to— Yet she didn't fear him; she wanted to challenge him and push him to the ends of whatever dark reins held him.

"That won't do, and you know it," Roman rasped, his eyes locked to her lips. "I'd want you in my bed. And I'm not good at the games you're playing."

"You are blunt, Roman Blaylock." Still…she studied his raw, hungry look, shielding nothing. She appreciated his honesty, that reluctant declaration that proved he wanted her, his fingertips caressing her lightly.

His gaze into her eyes both promised and asked, and Kallista fought the temptation to place her hand along his rough cheek, to absorb that heat into her palm. "I'd like to rent your empty house. That way I can watch you without coming close. I'll find your weakness and you'll lose. I'm very good at getting what I want."

His expression tightened grimly, the lines etching deeper between his black brows and bracketing his mouth. A hard pulse beat in his throat and in his temple, his jaw taut. "Games, hmm? I told you, I'm not a player."

"I think you are. This was a pretty dramatic statement, something right out of a cowboy movie—running down a woman and taking her upon your lap. You know your moves. You've practiced."

"Not once before have I brought a woman to ride on my horse with me," he said formally, as if vowing his life to her. The sincerity corded in his deep, uneven voice stunned her.

In a protective effort to stop the mood from going deeper, and learning too much about Roman Blaylock's experience with women, she patted his shoulder. The muscles there tensed and shifted into steel. "You're a big boy. You can take games. And I don't like men bantering about who I belong to, Mr. Blaylock. Not a bit. I've belonged to myself since the last time my mother jerked me away from Boone. You've read all about it in that file. How does it feel, knowing everything about me?"

"There are a few things I don't know." His gaze caressed her mouth.

Her face burned; Roman had referred to her sexuality, her experience with men. From the way she'd ignited in his arms, Roman would think she...

She braced herself against the flush rising up her cheeks. Then she tossed her head, letting the wind sweep her hair across her face; she didn't care what Roman thought. She didn't want to feel for him, for the years his wife wouldn't let him touch her. From the way Roman held her now, he'd had women to serve his needs.... His needs. Now he wanted her, his gaze caressing her breasts as if he wanted to...

She shifted, preparing to drop to the ground, and Roman hitched her tight against his chest, his arms wrapped firmly around her, a big hand spread on her bottom. "I could flatten you," she warned.

"I asked you, what has you so worked up?" Then Roman placed his cheek against hers, nuzzled her hair on his way to her ear, and a terrifyingly tender and sweet emotion swept through Kallista. "Are you frightened of me?" he asked in a low vulnerable tone that reached into the scarred corners of her heart.

"No, not of you," she answered truthfully against the rough stubble on his cheek, enveloped in the scents of a man who worked with cattle and green grass. She closed her eyes, and there in the sunlit pasture, scented of alfalfa and pines, she had the unlikely feeling that Roman Blaylock was holding her in his bed, cherishing her as if he'd never touched a woman before, sharing himself with her—and that he'd always be hers. The thought terrified her; she couldn't. "You put Boone's mother's doilies away. He wouldn't have liked that," she said, a light attempt to derail the deeper emotions running through her.

How could the man holding her so carefully hurt a woman? Yet Debbie had said that Roman was too raw, too rough—he'd been that way at the shop, confronting her.

When seeking sex, men changed, Kallista noted from her shadowy experience.

"You just shivered," he asked. "Why?"

She met his eyes and closed the terror of her past from her, as she'd had to do so many times before. "It's not you. You don't affect me one way or another."

"That's good…you're not afraid of me," he whispered heavily, slowly against her skin, as though he were relieved of a burden. His face nuzzled hers, an odd gesture, smoothing the contours of her face with his rugged ones, cheek against cheek, nose to the flesh at her temple, forehead against forehead, jaw against jaw, as if matching them for life. He breathed unevenly against her ear. "I don't want you to be afraid of me."

Kallista opened her eyes to the blinding sunlight, the shadows creeping from the rugged Rocky Mountains. This wasn't a man she wanted in her life, yet her fingertips dug into his back, binding him closer. She shivered and instantly, Roman's black head jerked up to study her too intently.

"Were you faithful to your wife?" Her question stunned her, shot into the sunlight before she realized she'd spoken.

He lifted his head and met her eyes, before nodding curtly. "I was. I did not hurt her…ever. And I'm doing the best I can for Boone," he said in a simple tone that rang of sadness.

"Let me go," she whispered shakily, terrified of her urge

to hold her enemy closer, to comfort him. She reminded herself that the man was ravaging Boone's estate.

Roman's fingertips stroked her cheek just once and then slid down the swath of hair crossing her shoulders. "Not before I tell you that you are a fine-looking woman, a strong woman. I like that."

At ten o'clock that night, Roman lay across Boone's bed, his arms behind his head, and tried to quiet his body's restless urge to seek Kallista Bellamy. The shape of her lips haunted him—the two little peaks on her upper lip, and that little dip between them. Her almond-shaped eyes had flashed at him, not soft and meadow green, but as brilliant as emeralds, shooting sparks at him. Then there was that sweet, fascinating curl to her lashes, like little soft blue-black brushes catching the sunlight. Her nose, what there was of it, was perfect.

Out there in the sunlight, Roman had almost rubbed her nose with his, a caress he'd reserved for the Blaylock children and Michaela.

He groaned shakily, and placed his hands on his bare stomach. The aching pressure of his lower body against his jeans had surprised him. He couldn't get the feel of Kallista, the exotic cinnamony scent of her, to leave him. That soft, firm, curved, strong body had fitted to his like—

The bed creaked when Roman turned to his side, and in the distance he saw lights twinkle in his house. Kallista had had a busy day with telephone installers and electricians, plumbers and every one of them had called Roman to let him know what a fine-looking woman was doing to his house. Ned Redmond had helped the delivery people haul in furniture. Ned was impressed by the size of the futon-folding-cushion-chair-thing. George Wyatt said she was turning the place into a jungle with all those potted plants. Else's pickup had pulled up, then Morganna's and Hannah's and the rest of the Blaylock women.

Using binoculars, Dusty and Titus had seen the women carry in mops and brooms. The two elderly cowboys couldn't wait to help and had returned to The Llewlyn for evening chores with big grins and homemade cherry pie. They bore lipstick marks on their leathery, but freshly shaven cheeks.

Kallista knew exactly how to stir up the country-side...and men. She knew how to appeal to women, eager to help. She could wreck what meager peace he'd found.

Roman forced his eyes to close and breathed deeply, the old house silent and empty. She could kiss like sweet, tempting sin, and he'd forgotten——hell, maybe he never knew the heat driving him now——that need to hold her against him, as if she were a part of him forever.

Forever didn't last, not when it came to women, not for him. His last tangle should have taught him something. He shouldn't have said that bit about getting her into his bed; he should have waited until she'd cooled down, and tried a flower bouquet. He should have... When he looked at her, all fired up, that lonesome hole in his heart warmed.

Roman shook his head; he hadn't realized he'd had a lonesome ache until he'd seen Kallista again. He rubbed his bare chest slowly, the nudge of her breasts still pressing upon his flesh. He hadn't thought about courting a woman, but now——

The phone rang and he jerked it from the cradle. Rio's voice purred softly from it, "Need any lessons in handling women, bro? From the way you took after Kallista, you do. That's a fine piece of woman, and she needs a light rein. She makes her own call, and what you've got to do is make yourself appealing. For you, that might be impossible. The little girls around might think you're something, but Kallista is a real woman——"

Roman slammed the phone down, cutting off Rio's chuckle, and stood. It was going to be a long night: he padded down to his office to work on files, and to keep his vow to Boone.

One week later it was the second week of June with bumblebees humming on the clover blooms, and the ranchers' new fields spread like green patchwork blankets across the valley. Newborn calves frolicked beside cows, and Homer Mason's tame elk had made his first sashay down main street. Flower gardens were beginning to thrive. The first lettuce greens had already been served for dinner, green beans were canned, and school was out, filling the streets with children on bicycles. In the Bisque Café's tiny office, behind the sinks where the greenware's seams were cleaned and smoothed, Kallista fed the Bisque Shop's mailing list information into her small computer, her traveling companion.

Advertising took time, but Kallista intended to get the shop into better financial shape; its income was small and steady and could grow with promotion. The Blaylock women were glad to be relieved of the shop's care, and Kallista had hired two teenage girls to come in afternoons and on Saturdays. Melissa and Jackie's cleaning of greenware and caring for the shop had helped. Both kilns were running now with Morganna's all-white table settings, which would be shipped to her. Once into the project, Morganna had run full speed ahead, until her husband Jake Tallman appeared with Lomasi, their two-year-old daughter, and their infant daughter, Feather. Jake's face had reddened as he had handed Feather to Morganna and explained in a hushed whisper that the "ah...prepared...ah...mother's...ah...formula is gone. You'll have to feed her."

While Jim Croce sang about "Bad, Bad Leroy Brown," Kallista thought about the people surrounding Roman, people she didn't want to hurt on her way to destroy him.

Jake and Morganna had found each other, Hannah's husband Dan Blaylock adored her, and always had, Logan and his wife had a happy growing brood, Rio was a carefree bachelor with a ladykiller reputation, and Tyrell was busy crunching numbers in New York. Roman was the dearly beloved of the Blaylock family; he could do no wrong, even when he had slid into his shell, remaining apart from their extensive family. He accepted all casseroles, attended all funerals, and helped his neighbors in need. But when all that was required of him was done, Roman retired to his lonely haunt—in Boone's house…and the Blaylocks had ached for him.

She didn't; she intended to tear Roman away from Boone's estate. After a month and a half, she still couldn't dig out anything bad about Roman Blaylock; at least Channing Boudreaux had given her a full leave of absence from her job, telling her to take her time with "her problem." Her problem was one Roman Blaylock, lodged like a granite mountain on Boone's land. Kallista tapped her fingers on the pink ceramic belly-up hippo lying on her desk. Did he really care for Boone, or was ill and kindhearted Boone misled by Roman, who eventually got what he wanted?

Had Roman loved his wife?

Had he been capable of love, or was his devastation merely the outward appearance of a man whose possession, and pride, had been ripped away?

How could he seem so honest—too honest and too real in his need for her?

Kallista inhaled abruptly. Roman Blaylock knew how to hold a woman against him, gently, firmly. His look down at her had been almost tender. Was it a well-practiced look designed to send a woman's heart skittering and her bones melting?

Melissa and Jackie had sighed and drooled when Roman's pickup prowled by on Jasmine's main street, the aging greyhounds sitting up in the truck's front seat like old friends. Lottie Morales had dipped her paintbrush into her coffee. Sue Corliss had painted Emma Jones's hand, and Margie Crowfoot's jaw had dropped the same time as her tiger print plate.

From the banker's cheerful wife, intent upon painting her new candlestick holders, Kallista learned an interesting tidbit—after that dramatic day at her shop four years ago, Boone had walked into the bank one day and asked to take over Roman Blaylock's loan on his ranch. It was a small bank and Boone was a member of the board of directors. The bank's decor was courtesy of Hannah Blaylock, and the Blaylock pioneer family names had been used on a wall mural. The family and town were formidable, strong, united, but Kallista would tear Roman apart—

Used to making her life comfortable wherever she stayed, Kallista glanced out into the shop, empty now, but arranged in a mass of finished ceramics, ranging from dishes, soup tureens and candle holders to picture frames and tiny animals. Hannah, Else, and Bernice had helped build a hurried display of designer dishes that young married women might want to create, but couldn't afford to buy.

Kallista propped her boots up on the tiny, scarred desk, and leaned back to sip her cappuccino from a new cup. The design was classic, and Morganna had painted it white. With the shop rearranged and repainted and her home comfortable, Kallista focused on the man she intended to tear away from Boone's estate.

She smoothed the smooth green leaf of the vine nestled beneath the window's sunlight; the plant was potted in an elegant, tassel decked elephant. Unlike Roman's rough cheek, the warm and smooth texture of the leaf was predictable, repeated on the next leaf and the one near it. Something leaped inside her every time she thought of him, of the softness in his eyes, that hard mouth easing gently against her own, as if not to frighten her away. He was much too careful of how he handled her.

Kallista distrusted careful men; they usually had reasons, or something to hide. Perhaps Roman Blaylock had perfected his spider and fly technique; his sad, vulnerable look had haunted her.

It wouldn't do to feel sorry for Roman, not when she was out to dissect him. Kallista settled back in her chair and studied the blinking light on her computer screen. With just a little more time, she could "hack"—break into Roman's computer with her own—and see exactly what he was doing with all of Boone's estate.

She glanced at the clock, set in the tummy of a black ceramic cat with a swinging pendulum tail. At six o'clock, the Tuesday night dinner crowd presented a moderate flow on Jasmine's streets. Ranchers and businessmen squired their wives with an old courtly air. In early June, the Community Garden Club had begun its good deeds and new redbud trees and prepared flower beds, stuffed with impatiens, waited to awake on Jasmine's streets. The old Western community with roots back to mountain men and drovers gently settled into the cool June sunset.

The Tuesday night Men's Only first session would begin at seven o'clock and end at ten. Hannah had said that Dan had been dragged into the shop once, mumbling and groaning. But when she had finished her project and was ready to go, Dan was meticulously involved with a chunky softball paperweight. He wouldn't leave until the ball was perfect.

Kallista tapped the pink hippo again, and with her television remote control she prepared an action-destruct movie, to make the men more comfortable. The popcorn popper and the cans of cold soda added to the aura she wanted for Men's Only Night.

Jasmine's menfolk were delicate creatures, she'd discovered. Since she'd started promoting the Bisque Café, she'd gotten guarded calls from men, asking cautiously, "Would there be other men there?" When answered affirmatively, they wanted names. Jasmine's men traveled in packs, uncertain if their manly status would be diminished by a "female activity" like painting dishes. A modern example of Western scouts for the army, several men had come during the week, cautiously looking around and explaining roughly that they were checking on something obscure for their wives. Tuesday was Men's Only Night, Thursday was Ladies Night, and Friday was Couples Night. She'd scheduled a few birthday parties, the bank had given gift certificates to its clerks for an hour after work on Wednesday and Kallista had a small, tight grip on the community, methodically circling for one bit of suspicious information about Roman Blaylock.

She sipped her cappuccino, and dragged a small box of cheese crackers out of her bag just as the bell over her shop door jingled. Roman stepped into the shop, big, solid and dressed in a crisp new denim jacket, a white shirt and new jeans. His Western boots were highly polished. He carried a sack in one hand and his Western hat in the other; his black gaze locked on her instantly with the impact of a bulldozer.

# Four

When Kallista's heart started pounding again, she eased to her feet. She gripped her cappuccino mug to keep her fingers from shaking. A tall, angular man, and trained as a Blaylock to be courteous to women, Roman nodded as she approached; he slowly closed the door and reached to hang his hat on the row of hooks provided for hats and coats. The finality of the gesture startled her, as if he'd come to stay. He looked slowly around the shop, as though scouting new and dangerous territory. He shifted the sack in one hand to the other, studying the plants and television, the weathered ladder from which ceramic cats hung by their tails. He studied the café tables and chairs and the tiles hung on the wall to demonstrate available colors. One swift glance took in the array of individual containers for brushes and the framed Paris in springtime and Venice gondola paintings. Another glance shot to the animal ceramic pots in the window, filled with growing herbs.

Then he looked slowly at her, as if he'd found what he

wanted. His scents curled around her—all those dark mysterious scents topped by soap…and the scent of new clothing, fresh from the package. One glance at his lips took her back a week, when she had pitted herself against him. She fought her shiver and the heat moving in her cheeks.

Roman Blaylock definitely knew how to pierce her protective shields, something no other man had managed to do. Her awareness of him had to do with the unexpected lurch of her body. At the sight of him—the vulnerable, wary look like a lone wolf who had come to call—a traitorous softening began inside her.

She slammed her mental door on that treacherous ache. "I suppose you came for the rent. How much rent do you pay Boone's estate?" she asked bluntly. She could forgo any niceties to a man pilfering Boone's estate.

The overhead light slanted across Roman's black brows to gleam on his cheek. A muscle crossing his jaw tensed and his eyes darkened. "I pay my way. You can stay at the place rent-free."

She tore at him; for looking so good, he deserved her anger. "Doesn't your home mean anything to you? Don't the memories make you want to live in it? How can you rent it?"

"It's a solid house. It should have someone in it."

"But not you. Why?"

His expression closed as he held out the bulging paper sack, avoiding her question. "You can't live on snacks and cappuccino."

Ignoring the sack, she warned him, "I'll find out, you know. I'll find out everything."

His next words ripped the floor from under her. "You'll have to marry me to find out."

"That's not a likely event," she managed after a struggle to reply flippantly.

"No, not likely. I've been married. A wedding ring doesn't make things right between a man and a woman, neither does trying until your heart bleeds and your pride is gone...." He made a gesture with the fragrant sack, again inviting her to take it. "It's good food...Italian night at the café. I didn't sprinkle it with poison."

Continuing to ignore the sack, Kallista searched Roman's tanned hard face, taut skin covering his high cheekbones, the lines bracketing his mouth. Pride and pain ran beneath the surface, and she sensed that he had given her an insight that no one else had seen. She couldn't afford the emotions running through her, the need to understand his secrets and that odd vulnerability. She had to destroy his grip on Boone's estate. "I don't appreciate your views on marriage, Roman."

He shifted on his long legs just once and held her eyes steadily, as if he had something important to say and he wasn't letting her barbs take him off track. "Didn't mean to say that much about it, but you're looking pretty sweet tonight and something just went soft inside me. You should be happy...have someone taking care of you, so you'll eat right and not stay up trying to hack into my computer all night. You've got a restless soul, Kallista Bellamy, and I hope you find what you're seeking."

That statement rocked her. Roman had skipped flirting and he'd said every word slowly, solemnly, as if it were wrapped in truth, straight from his heart and soul. He nodded and lifted the sack slightly. Because she was hungry, and the aromas coming from it were enticing, Kallista finally took the bag. Roman's expression changed mildly, softening as if he were pleased that she would take anything from him. "You just ran your hand through your hair again, as if you're feeling shy and uncertain.... You've got whipped cream on your lip."

Then he bent down slowly and kissed the spot where her tongue had just flicked. When Kallista inhaled with surprise and stepped back, Roman's dark eyes ripped down her body and heated. "Afraid? Of me?"

"Not a bit. And no one has ever called me shy." Trying to be careless of his attention and keep her fingers from shaking, Kallista placed the sack on the table and took out a shallow pie pan covered with foil. "Fried chicken? Mashed Potatoes? Gravy?" she asked, experienced in the usual country café fare.

"You're shy now, like your skin is dancing over your bones, and you can't look at me. You're skittish, keeping your distance from me. Are you sorry you kissed me like that? Like your walls were ripped away and you'd dived for what you wanted? Curled against me and sank into me?" he asked too softly. "Are you regretting that?"

One startled glance at Roman revealed the deep lines on his forehead, his hands hanging loosely at his side as though bracing for a blow. Why did she feel that rocketing need to comfort him? "I'm not in the habit of doing things I'll regret, Blaylock. I wanted you to know that I can hold my own."

"Uh-huh," he murmured, disbelieving her.

With shaking fingers, she eased away the foil. A mound of fettuccine *alfredo* topped by an artistic slash of chives, basil and shrimp caused her mouth to water. Another foil-covered package revealed warm crusty Italian bread. "How much do I owe you?"

"Nothing."

"'Nothing' doesn't come without strings." She turned to him slowly, facing him squarely. She wanted him to understand her rules. "I won't be obliged to you in any way, Roman. You can't come calling at my doorstep when you're in the mood."

"You'll see me coming," he answered slowly with a tilt to his black head that said she'd nettled him. "What time does Men's Night start?" he asked, scanning the shelves of bisque and the waiting brushes and paints.

Ignoring Roman, Kallista sat down and began eating. She hadn't realized how hungry she was until she savored her first mouthful of fettuccine. While Roman prowled the shop, she quickly finished the meal. She glanced up to see Roman studying the cappuccino machine. "You'll have to leave. My customers will be arriving soon. Don't come back."

Roman turned slowly, reached out to latch his big hand on a bisque dog food bowl as if he'd never let go, and said quietly, "As Boone's executor and partner, I'm responsible for fifty-one percent of this shop. I'm staying."

Stunned, Kallista stared at him. "You're not my partner!"

"Check the document you signed with Boone. It's part of the estate. I'm obliged to check on it." Roman lifted the dog bowl from the shelf and studied it. "I'll take two of these. Where do I sit? And how fat is that file you've got on me? Learn anything interesting?"

"You've got a nasty habit of tossing out too many things with one breath, Blaylock. I feel like I'm running on two tracks with you and I don't like it. What makes you think I've got a file on you?" She had notes, little things people had said about Roman, how he was as a child, when his parents died, when he grieved for his child, how well he cared for Boone— She kept shoving them around, hoping to push the puzzle into something she could destroy.

He settled into a chair, a rangy sprawl of broad shoulders and hard muscles sheathed in cotton and denim, shaggy hair blue-black under the light. The ragged cut of his hair suited the man; smooth and neat wouldn't do for his untamed look. The angles of his cheekbones jutted against the taut skin, his jaw clenching as he turned the unpainted bowl in his big work hands. Then his black eyes narrowed, burning her. "When a woman like you starts asking questions, a man feels proud."

Kallista's indrawn breath hissed by her set teeth and Roman's slow grin knocked her back another heartbeat. After

years of a cosmopolitan life-style, she'd forgotten how
small towns shared and thrived on gossip.

Two hours of the Mens Only Night passed and Kallista
hoped her smile concealed her throbbing headache. Toby
Young, an eighty-year-old friend of Titus and Dusty's, had
asked Lem Steward to join them. Toby talked overloud,
adjusting to his hearing problem. Both the new extralong,
extraviolent action movie got on her nerves, and all the men
there—including Dan, Logan, Rio, James and Roman—
were driving her quietly out of her mind with their exacting,
painful, precise painting techniques. Each man had chosen
a solid, big object—dog bowls were favored—and required
help…all with the action movie erupting in full sound.

To soothe her taut nerves, Kallista went to work on her
cappuccino machine. All the men except Roman approached to tower at her back, asking questions. Eventually
they took over the cappuccino machine, gaily steaming
drinks and whipping froth. The "gizmo" produced drinks
for the men, and after discussions of cinnamon and
whipped cream, they settled down to paint piggy banks,
softballs, chunky candlesticks and fish teapots.

Roman continued to paint dog bowls in his steady, me-
ticulous fashion. Rio seemed intent on flirting with her, and
she entered easily into a kind of dialogue she understood.
She was comfortable with Rio's light, charming banter and
his compliments. She was not comfortable with the dark
way Roman's gaze followed her as she helped the other
men. For just a fleeting second, she almost reached out to
touch his sleek black hair, that small spike of hair that
jarred as he tilted his head; she'd jerked her hand away. As
if sensing her near, Roman had turned slowly to her, his
black eyes pinning her briefly before she looked away.

When the evening was coming to a close, Roman stood
slowly as she passed. "You're working too hard. Come out
to the ranch tomorrow. You can count the pigeons and the
pigs."

That dark intense look caused her to shiver again and Roman's expression tightened as if she'd slapped him. Then he looked over her head to the woman standing in the doorway, draped in a long fur coat. The woman looked hardened by life, her face layered with cosmetics, and her bleached hair badly in need of care. She puffed nervously on her cigarette, her eyes darting around the room, then said, "Roman, I need you."

Roman glanced at Kallista, then quickly brushed by her. He took the woman's arm and hurried her outside. Through the window, the shops' neon lights revealed Roman and the woman who was obviously upset with him. She stalked to her expensive luxury car and got into the driver's seat, while Roman got into his pickup. The woman followed him in the direction of the ranch.

Kallista fought the pain tearing through her, as though a piece of her heart had just been ripped away. She told herself firmly that it didn't matter to her if Roman's women came for him, or if he hurried to be with them, when only a moment ago he'd asked Kallista—

"Women," Dusty said while swirling his brush artistically over a fish platter. "Never know why they come to see Roman, but they used to do Boone like that. Just tromp right in and start up with him. Odd women wanting something. Sometimes real young ones and those a bit older. Odd mix for Roman to be seeing, but never know what he does when he's away from the ranch."

"Women came like that for Boone?" Kallista asked. Her guardian had seemed so perfect, immune to cheap affairs, while Roman hurried toward them.

Titus placed his brush in the water cup and stretched. "This artwork saps a man. Sometimes men like to keep their romancing away from where they live, quietlike. But neither Boone nor Roman are the sneaky sort. After his wild young buck days, Boone was gone that thirty-year spell and came back different, purely lost interest. Something went out of him, out there in the world.''

Dusty shook his head. ''Roman never did play around. He palled around with Debbie for a good long while, then all of a sudden they turn up married with a baby on the way. He was working two jobs then, trying to pay for that house. He sure loved that little girl. I never understood Debbie, but she came from a good family. Her folks died years ago, just a bit before Roman and she got married. He's never courted a woman since, and those Blaylock men make pretty certain that the other bucks know who's their lady love.''

The old cowboy scrunched up his face as though running layers of memories through his mind. ''Don't really remember him really courting Debbie, either. Not the flower, hand-holding sort of cuddling sweetheart courting.''

''All those Blaylock boys act up when one of them kisses his bride. I always thought that Roman was slow and careful to kiss Debbie, when the rest were grabbing and grinning. Not that their women minded.''

Dusty lowered his voice so the other men couldn't hear. ''That Rio sure enjoys women. He's not likely to settle down quick, but when he does, he'll be like all the Blaylocks, good family men.''

Dusty looked at Titus. ''We need to make something homey for the bunkhouse. Maybe some bowls and cups. You think Roman will ever try a wedding ring again? Or he's too much of a lone wolf type?''

Kallista closed her eyes and fought the headache pounding her skull. If she had Roman's thick neck in her hands, she'd... One minute he's bringing her food and telling her about the soft feeling in his heart, and the next a woman turns up to claim him. She'd had enough of Roman Blaylock.

''Out,'' she said quietly, and then, as the men continued to debate their next projects and play with her cappuccino maker, she pasted a smile on her face. "Session is over. Your things will be ready next week."

Rio grinned and plopped his Western hat on the back of his head. "You'll miss me. Think you can go a whole week without seeing me?"

Used to friendly flirtations, Kallista shot him a practiced, sizzling look beneath her lashes. "I'll probably waste away without the sight of you. Spend more money next time."

Rio chuckled. "My big bad brother took all the dog bowls."

"Good. Profit is up. I'll order more," Kallista returned lightly, then glanced at the row of dog bowls that Roman had lined up on the shelf with the other men's work. "Luka," "Igor," and other names were on the bowls. Each name was aligned perfectly with the next, the printing bold, leaving nothing unclear—except Roman's secret life....

Later that night Roman was leaning against the building as Kallista stepped out onto the sidewalk, locking the door behind her. For just an instant, his heart stopped as she leaned her head back, inhaling the June night. With her hair drawn back into a band at her nape, she looked sleek, continental, restless, her big bag slung over her shoulder, as though she were ready to step onto a plane and soar from him. The thought slammed into Roman's midsection and left him cold. The roses in his fist trembled, startling him. They suited her—smooth, beautiful, sophisticated and they'd had thorns, before he'd stripped them away.

Boone's granddaughter paused, inhaled again and stiffened, her silver half-moon earrings catching the light. The streetlight pooled around her, a restless woman, impatient to be off, to tear him from Boone's land. Roman's fist curled tighter around the bouquet of roses he'd purchased earlier as she turned to find him in the shadows. "What are you doing here?"

"Saying good-night to you." He lowered the roses; he

wanted to hold her in his arms, bury his face in the scent of her hair, and forget the furious screaming woman he'd had to face. Margaret had exceeded the allowance Boone had pensioned her off with, and she wanted more for a trip to France. To be quickly rid of her, allowing him to return to Kallista, Roman had advanced her payment, damning himself for doing it.

Kallista's head went up, her body taut. "Are you finished with your lover?"

The bold thrust didn't shock him. His promise to keep Boone's secret wasn't an easy road. "She isn't my lover. We have business—"

"I'll just bet," Kallista stated flatly.

Roman studied her. She was clearly furious with him, this granddaughter of Boone Llewlyn's and the woman Roman wanted to hold in his arms. "You'll have to trust me."

"'Trust' and 'you' in the same sentence? No, thanks. If it's any pleasure to you, I've had to extend my leave of absence from work. This is taking longer than I had planned.... No, I don't trust you."

Roman didn't blame her; with her scent stirring him, he barely trusted himself. "The roses are for you. From me."

"You smell like a perfume counter, and it isn't the roses," she said tightly, furiously, and walked to her car. She tossed her bag into the car and after taking a second look at him, she stalked back and grabbed the roses. "Thanks."

An hour later, Roman sat in Boone's study, watching his computer screen. His Tai Chi exercises hadn't taken the ache from his body, the need for Kallista, and to settle his stormy mood, he'd pitted himself against Boone's extensive worldwide accounts. He smiled grimly; Kallista had begun prowling, trying to reach into files by testing passwords. Boone's granddaughter was thorough, talented, and persistent.

Roman reached out to type, "Hello, honey. I took a shower. No perfume smell."

After a pause, the computer began pushing words on the screen. "Who are you?"

"Roman," he typed. "I never kissed her."

The words quickly coursed across the screen, "What did she want?"

"We had business. Boone's business," he added. "You're wasting time trying to hack into this system. It's secure."

The letters ripped across the screen again. "She wasn't a woman Boone would want."

No, but his sons would, Roman thought as the screen became blank, and Kallista finished prowling for the night. Boone's sons had repeatedly married women like their mother, and Boone had blamed himself for their weakness. That was Boone's private, black hell—that he'd been a poor father, building an empire in oil fields and the stock market, and that his two irresponsible sons had destroyed others' lives.

Roman sat back in his chair. One of Boone's sons was dead—Kallista's father—the other on a hefty retainer to stay away from Jasmine. Struggling to finish his life with dignity, and denying drugs that would dull his pain, Boone's voice had been weak. "We lived all over the world, Sara and I. I left them to their mother while I went off and made my fortune. She didn't do a good job and I couldn't change them, but I tried. My sons married women like her—harsh, cruel women—and it's my sweet grandchildren who are paying the price. You make certain that you do what you can for them, Roman. Try to get them back here, in Jasmine, where my family was once strong and good and the land holds true. You'll do that for me, won't you, Roman?"

"I will," Roman had pledged, and watched the old man slip away, eased by the promise. When Boone was ill for that year, Roman had taken care of the visits from the Llewlyn sons' wives, protecting the old man and aching for him. Boone's extensive business interests away from Jasmine provided money to sustain monthly allotments to Boone's living son and a string of ex-wives, none of them sweet.

"She's on the move—" The small trail of light leading away from Kallista's house said she was on the path to the Llewlyn family cemetery. Roman reached for his moccasins, tying them quickly. He found himself smiling. If Kallista wanted to prowl at midnight, so did he. She suited his Apache hunting blood—the restless need to seek out his woman.

Half an hour later the moonlight filtered behind a cloud and Roman watched Kallista tear the rose petals from their stalks. Inside the old elegant wrought-iron fence, Kallista knelt beside Boone's grave. The bouquet of roses lay across the grave, and one hand reached out to grip his marble stone, as if to jerk him back from death. Her head was bent in mourning; her long hair shielded Kallista's face, but the gentle stir of air carried her muffled sobs to Roman.

Roman settled back into the shadows, giving her time, and slowly Kallista tore away a rose and, lifting her hand, let the petals drift upon Boone's grave. With ceremony, she covered the entire grave in petals, and stood slowly. "I know you're out there, Roman Blaylock. You're too big not to notice in the moonlight."

"I'm here."

Her voice was soft, uneven and drenched with tears. "I loved him desperately. Boone was everything to me."

"I know. He was proud of what you were, of what you became."

When she turned to him, the silver sheen of tears and grief washed her pale face. She wrapped her arms around herself. "He talked to you. What did he say?"

He nodded, remembering the old man's pain and his

shame as he passed away. Roman walked toward her. "It's chilly up here...a draft comes down from the mountains."

She looked up at the mountains and didn't seem to notice when Roman smoothed her hair back from her damp face. "He loved the mountains, that old gold mine, the hunting shack. Is it still there?"

"I'll take you up there, if you want." He'd take her anywhere, aching for her grief now.

"Boone Llewlyn was the only man I ever trusted. He was always there. I never knew exactly the arrangements that my mother had with Boone, but he always knew when to come get me. My mother would sometimes drop me off with him for months, then she'd be back, tearing me away. I was always glad to see her, but Boone—Boone wasn't. They weren't friends. Or lovers. My mother always chose men who— I look like her in a way."

He wanted to tell her that she had Boone's fierce look when she was angry, the angle of her jaw, the piercing emerald green of her eyes. Boone had said that Kallista had his mother's hair, though his was crisp and wavy. But Roman had promised to keep silent—until the time was right. Boone didn't want his grandchildren to know who he was until they came to love Llewlyn land; he'd been too ashamed of failing them.

Roman knew that the men her mother chose weren't like Boone—stable, loving, kind, generous. "He'd be glad you're back."

"Yes, well. We both know I'm not staying. But I don't want to fight over his grave."

"He wanted you to have this...it was his mother's." Roman took the small box from his pocket, extracted the opal-and-ruby ring. He took Kallista's hand, pressed his palm against hers, unable to resist the need to fit her against him, then slowly slid the heirloom onto Kallista's right hand.

She lifted her hand to study the ring, and a silvery tear

fell from her lashes to her cheek. "His family should have this."

Roman smoothed the half-moon earring with his finger-tip. "He considered you his family."

"I know. He was a loving man."

When she turned her face up to him, pale and grief-stricken, Roman could no more have stopped his hands from reaching for her than he could have stopped his blood from coursing through his body. He cradled her face between his hands and slowly brushed away her tears with his thumbs. Her hands flew to his wrists to push him away, and then her fingers stayed, digging in. Her eyes were haunted, shimmering with silvery tears, and Roman slowly lowered his mouth, wanting to ease her, to give her a tender part of himself.

The wind curled around them, taking her hair up and around his shoulders as the kiss trembled and brushed and lingered in gentle play. Kallista sighed unevenly, moving closer, and Roman wrapped his arms around her, holding her carefully. When the kiss—no more than a tasting—was finished, Kallista eased back, wary of him, her expression puzzled. "Who are you, Roman Blaylock?" she asked un-evenly, her open hand over his chest.

His answer came from his heart, as true as an arrow. "A man who wants you in his life."

"That can't be," she whispered before she eased away. She turned and began walking slowly to what used to be his home, leaving his arms empty and his heart aching.

The second week of July came hot and dry to the valley, and after another sleepless night, Roman padded down to the kitchen. He had the early hours to the call of the mead-owlarks and himself. Then dressed in their Sunday best, Titus and Dusty would stop to pester him about going to church, and then Else would call, worrying about him, and wanting him to come to a family dinner.

He couldn't bear to place his family pictures around him—Logan with his wife and five children, Else and Joe and their grown brood with grandchildren, James and Bernadette, Jake and Morganna's two daughters. Roman had deceived them, tried to portray a happy husband, and for the brief times when she had to, Debbie had pretended to be responsive to him.

Roman scrubbed his hands over his face. He'd deceived his family, presenting a married life that was a lie.

Like a fool, he'd gone to Ben Jones's auction and purchased all that old furniture, the wood running smooth beneath his hand, aching for the layers of varnish to be removed. He'd looked like a hermit, packing his pickup high with that heavy furniture, hoarding it like his dreams. He'd packed it into the barn behind the house he built for his wife. She hadn't loved him, and all the new houses in the world wouldn't have made a difference.

Rio flirted with Kallista and she flirted back, and the town had begun to wonder why Roman painted all the dog bowls available at the Bisque Café. Accustomed to making herself comfortable and settling with temporary friends, Kallista could play pool, baby-sit and throw horseshoes. Clearly cosmopolitan, she fascinated both the men and women of Jasmine. Rio had called Roman last night from Mamie's Café and Tavern. "You'd better learn how to play soon, son," he'd said in a taunt loaded with laughter.

According to Rio, Kallista knew her "moves" and she was "one fine dancer." Roman had had one boot on before he decided that if he went to Mamie's—

Roman closed his eyes as Moby the rooster crowed from the top of a corral post. He didn't know how to dance—nothing but an old-fashioned waltz and two-step, and he was rusty on that. He'd seen line dancing on television—it was intricate and sometimes a man didn't hold a woman against him. He wanted to hold Kallista in the old-fashioned way, to feel her body mold and move against his, and to know that she wasn't afraid of him.

He repeated the phrase—*she wasn't afraid of him.* Those green eyes shot sparks at him, ripped him apart, and took his heart leaping with excitement he understood too well...but she wasn't afraid. He wanted all that fine strong supple woman naked in his arms. His feelings ran deeper, down to the real appreciation of her as a truthful, all-out, go for broke woman, who knew how to handle the truth between them. He knew her scarred life, and he appreciated her strength, that quick mind. But the lurch of his body was immediate, hard, and hot when he caught her scent. Whatever ran between them could leap into wildfire with one look.

What would he do at Mamie's? Sit and brood in a corner while Rio danced with his woman?

Roman heard himself groan. There was a big distance between wanting a woman and getting her...especially one who didn't trust him at her back. Roman groaned again, remembering the feel of her body against his. He glowered at the magazine Titus had slapped on the table that contained ads for country-western dancing lessons at home. With a scowl, the leathery old cowboy had asked, "You're going to that dance at Mamie's Café, aren't you? You'd better hitch up your garters, boy, and make a move. Rio sure ain't wasting time. He ain't holed up working on records and papers with a fine-looking unbranded woman prowling the countryside. No siree-Bob."

Roman held out his big work-rough scarred hands, the palms callused. His ex-wife couldn't bear for him to touch her and yet just that once, Kallista had sunk into him and turned fiery-hot. "I'm dreaming and I don't have time for that," he muttered darkly to himself and began to make coffee.

As he ran water from the faucet, he studied the ranch

yard. Dawn was lightening the sky, and on Sunday morning Llewlyn and Blaylock ranches were quiet.

His land, a part of the original Blaylock spread, needed work, but there always seemed more to do on Boone's.

Then a meadowlark trilled and a rider slowly, quietly moved Loves Dancing into the woods bordering the base of the mountains.

# Five

"**I**'m not a believer in the sanctity of one Roman Blaylock. He's covering something up," Kallista muttered as she easily guided Loves Dancing on the mountain trail. She wanted to see the old cabin where Boone had taken her as a child just as much as she wanted Roman Blaylock to ask her to dance.

Last night, only her pride had kept her from going to Boone's house and calling him out....

There by Boone's grave, Roman had held her so gently, as if she'd break, his big hands open, yet firm on her body and— Kallista glanced up at a raven soaring through the new pale Sunday sky, the rugged mountain path ahead of her. She glanced at a movement in the shadowy pines and said, "I can take care of myself. You don't need to come."

Looking as much a part of the untamed West as his ancestors, Roman eased Massachusetts behind Loves Dancing on the narrow winding trail up the mountain.

Kallista looked over her shoulder to him, her single braid

sliding along her black jacket. Dressed in his Western hat and denim jacket and mocassins, Roman looked bred to the West, a reflection of his Apache and Spanish ancestors, and good solid pioneer stock. "You're prowling early this morning."

"I want to see if the cabin is still there by Boone's old gold mine."

"It's still there. Just like he left it."

She shot him a meaningful look, this man who held Boone's beloved land and home in his fist. "We panned for gold. I know there is some value to the mine."

"The value was that Boone gave you himself."

"He gave me magic. I knew then that men had souls and hearts." Kallista turned swiftly back to the trail and watched a chipmunk scamper up a red-bark tree. She turned back to the man she intended to destroy. "Do you believe in magic, Roman Blaylock?"

"I do now," he said firmly, locking his gaze with hers. "You're a woman who causes men to dream."

"Don't dream about me, Blaylock," she managed tightly when she could speak. Images of heat and storms and Roman's dark, strong body locked to hers, in hers, took her pulse leaping. She knew all about the mechanics of sex, but Roman was a man who would want more, take more.

A rippling snow-fed creek tumbled down the mountain and without speaking, Kallista and Roman watered the horses. She crouched and scooped the icy water into her cupped hands, drinking as Boone had taught her and waiting for her blood to cool—Roman's words had set a fever simmering in her that terrified her. When she licked her lips, savoring the past and the memories with Boone, Roman's dark eyes locked to her lips. Nettled by her immediate reaction to him, as if her skin skittered with the jolt of that one dark simmering look, Kallista frowned. "Stop flirting. I'm not in the mood."

He blinked as if startled, then his scowl shot down at

her, his voice indignant. That spear of jet-black hair
crossing his forehead quivered. "Me? Flirt?"

"It's your eyes," she muttered, wanting to calm that
spear of blue-black hair. To others, Roman might appear to
be a quiet man, but his storms could lash and prick and
ignite. "They say things that aren't decent."

"I try to be decent," Roman said, the low tone of his
voice reminding her of a wolf baring his teeth. "But you've
got an all-woman look that a man appreciates now and then.
It isn't sweet and cuddly, more like wildfire, the thunder
and lightning of a high mountain storm."

She'd thought the same about him—raw, tough, restless
and filled with leashed emotions. He could rip her emotions
from her hold and she had to defend herself against him.

"You'd know about women, wouldn't you?" she flung
at him, reminding him of Margaret's visit. Kallista stood
and whipped the long braid over her shoulder.

Roman stretched out a hand, claiming the thick braid in
his fist and slowly drew her closer. The look beneath his
narrowed lashes wasn't sweet, matching the raw temper
smoldering inside her. "You've got a nasty cutting side to
you, Miss Kallista."

"And you don't?" She'd had to learn to defend herself
at an early age—cut, cut, jab—and now she took nothing
at face value, especially Roman's troubling sweet words.
Beneath her palms, his heart was racing, pounding, as if
leaping into her care. Why? "Terrifying you, am I? Why
weren't you at the dance? Afraid?"

"Would you have danced with me?" he pushed, his dark
eyes caressing her warm, flushed cheeks, her lips, her throat
and lower to her breasts.

In that instant his other hand moved slightly, rested on
her waist for a moment and began to rise in a slow, steady
path to her breast.

Her emotions leaped into life, the need to lock her arms
around Roman and fuse her lips to his. The thought terrified

her. She'd never needed anyone but herself...and Boone. Jerking up her walls, Kallista moved away and prepared to mount. She put one foot into her stirrup and... Roman's hands circled her waist, lifting her easily. When seated, she looked down at him—furious with him, with herself for wanting more of this man, for the jolt his touch sent skittering over her skin. "I can manage by myself. You'll find out that I do what I have to, and I don't ask for help."

He nodded and swung up into his saddle and for the next two hours neither spoke, the only sound that of the birds and the rustle of the forest, the rocks turning beneath the horses' hooves. Kallista gave herself to the peaceful sense that she was coming home, and doing what Boone might have done, keeping in touch with the land—Llewlyn land. There in the valley below, Llewlyn House looked as safe as it always had, big and blazing white in the sun.

At the cabin, nestled in a clearing, Kallista pushed open the old wooden door, glanced at the cobwebs and rubble and fought tears. She placed the hand with Boone's mother's ring on her shoulder and covered it with her cheek as the memories curled around her. She realized she was speaking, her throat dry with emotion. "Boone braided my hair, his big hands clumsy for the task. He said, 'My mother had hair like this—black as coal, straight. She was a lady, Kallie-honey. You remember that it's important to have manners and act like a lady. It's called dignity and a soul has to have that.' He told me I had magic in me and it would keep me safe, and then he cried. That sweet big man simply crumpled before me and I never knew why."

The man who drew her from the doorway and into his arms was solid, warm, stroking her head as she burrowed against him. She heard the words leap from her keeping, "I was just a child, old with pain and what I'd seen...Big Boone gave me back an innocence, a shield to hold around my heart, to keep me safe."

"Hold still, little butterfly," Roman whispered against

her cheek. His lips brushed her temple. "Hold tight and cry."

Kallista fought the flood of emotions, grief washing over her once more. She wanted to fling herself from Roman's safety, but instead, her fists knotted in his flannel work shirt. "You'd like that, wouldn't you? Some sign that I was weak and that I'd leave you to Boone's estate. Well, listen, mister…I never cry."

Furious with her weakness, she slashed at him. "What good does it do? It makes your eyes red and swollen and your makeup spread everywhere—"

Disgusted that her voice trembled and tears dripped from her lashes, Kallista shuddered. He rocked her in his arms; the steady beat of his heart anchored her palm as he said, "When hearts bleed, sometimes tears clean the wound."

The shocking simplicity of his words came too sweetly, frightening her. Kallista pushed away from Roman, brushed the back of her sleeve across her damp lashes and walked to the creek where Boone had knelt beside her, exclaiming about the size of the nuggets. She crouched by the rippling stream and reached down to scoop up a handful of sand, dotted with bright gold chunks. The wet sand trickled through her fingers like fond memories of Boone. "I know the mine is worthless. This is fool's gold. There should be a sack of it somewhere at Boone's. I was only ten, but I was so happy and excited. We roasted marshmallows and talked of sailing ships—I wanted to be a pirate and roam the seas and Boone—"

"The sack is in the steamer trunk. Boone wrote your name on it. I'd say you made that pirate princess goal."

Kallista watched a rabbit scurry through the brush, just where Boone and she had planted daffodils. "I planted bleeding hearts and lily of the valley at Boone's house. I haven't planted anything since. I'm not usually around to see them grow.… I've always been restless. I suppose it comes from my mother lugging me from place to place. I know about you, Roman Blaylock. Your mother, Garnet, was a leader and as respected in the community as Else. All seven of the Blaylock children knew exactly who they were and where they were going. You knew your heritage, that you'd descended from those mountain men that settled the valley. How does that feel?''

Roman scanned the small clearing, the woodpile over-grown by brush, the red-barked pines shooting up into the blue sky like spears. "It locks a heart to the land."

"You speak about your heart as if it weren't part of you."

"It's starting to stir a bit. You're a woman who doesn't leave things the same, like a fresh spring wind." His smile was wry, charming, warm upon her, and her heart flipped and quivered within her.

Kallista stood and rubbed her trembling hands upon her thighs. She couldn't trust this man. Or could she? His words were too pure, too simple to be believed. "Was what Debbie said about you true? That you hurt her?"

Roman lifted his head to stare at the mountains, his sleek black hair riffled by the breeze, his fists clamped on the brim of his hat. "I told you before I never hurt her. I wanted...a life, what I'd seen my folks and the rest of the Blaylocks have—nothing exciting or special, just a good solid marriage. She didn't want me and it wasn't a mar-riage," he said as though the truth had been torn out of him. "After our wedding night, we had separate bed-rooms."

He'd shocked her again, giving her a private insight into his marriage. "I know. The scent of her perfume was in one—I remember it—in the bathroom leading from the bedroom. Yours was in another room, and in the tiny bath-room by the kitchen. You weren't sleeping together."

He looked down at his mocassins. "A man doesn't need much room to shave and except for my...my little girl, I wasn't at the house much. After Michaela died, we didn't see each other for days. No, we never slept together. Not even that first night.''

Kallista inhaled sharply. Roman was a physical man; his masculine aura seeming to pulsate when he was near her. In the corral, she'd seen proof of his desire. *"Never?"*

Roman frowned down at her. "You're pushy, Miss Kallista. Pushy and nosey.''

*"You did not have sex with your wife?"* she asked, disbelieving that a man who kissed like silk and fire would live for years without—

"She didn't want me." The answer came too blunt, an admission that must have hurt his pride.

"Sex stopped with marriage, so you found other women. That happens.'' She'd seen enough in her lifetime, starting at an early age. Her first images were that of her mother beneath a man, both naked. From her mother's affairs, Kallista knew everything about sex, the sounds, the mechanics, the need to move to a new partner. Had she ever been a child? Only with Boone...

She hadn't meant to taunt Roman, but his hackles were raised, his pride scored. "You know so much, do you? Well, take this in those sharp teeth and chew on it—Debbie was my high school sweetheart. I always knew we belonged together...I felt...I felt protective of her, like she needed me. It wasn't a hot storm, but I didn't expect that. I respected Debbie too much to...before marriage, and later...''

He scowled at Kallista. "That sassy mouth just dropped open. She said no. I honored that. You think I'd take a woman who didn't want me?" he demanded too quietly.

His pride had been scarred, the shocking, painful edges left open to her; she should have been afraid of him—she wasn't. She wanted to place her hand along his hard cheek and comfort him.

After studying her expression, Roman reached out and grabbed her jacket. He jerked her closer to glare down at her. "You're not sweet, lady. When I married, I took a vow to be true. You keep pushing me and——"

Kallista licked her lips, not frightened by Roman Blaylock, rather she wanted to grip his head and bring his mouth down to hers and feed upon him.

A shudder ran through Roman's tall body. "Don't look at me like that."

"How?"

"All saucy and hot, just waiting for me to make a move. Here we are, alone. You without protection——"

He sounded outraged, like a father, like Boone, and yet... She placed her palms on his flat stomach and fluttered her lashes up at him. "Protection? Birth control?"

Roman sucked in his breath. The red color started rising in his tanned cheeks and his scowl deepened. "You've got a fast, hot mouth, lady. I meant that we're up here alone and——" He cleared his throat and said roughly, "You've got no one to defend you, ah, against my basic urges."

She almost laughed; he seemed sweet and vulnerable. Roman had just admitted that he hadn't taken his wife and at the moment he was displaying signs of an outraged male who held honor high. She knew men who had kicked honor into a corner, spat on it, and took what they wanted. To the rest of Jasmine and the Blaylocks, Roman had portrayed a happily married man, he'd taken another man's child for his own, and he held Kallista when she cried—as if she were delicate. She wasn't; she'd learned to take care of herself at an early age. His honesty had shocked her and in that instant, she saw why Boone had trusted Roman Blaylock with his fortune. Roman loomed over her, staring darkly at her and she couldn't resist. She staged a quiver and fluttered her eyelashes. "Little weak me, and big strong you?"

Roman closed his lids and groaned. Then he reached down, swung her up into his arms and walked toward Loves

Dancing. He tucked her head upon his shoulder and fitted his chin along her cheek.

"You know I could make this difficult for you, don't you? When it comes to defending myself, I'm pretty good. All it would take is—"

He snorted and held her closer. "You talk too much."

"Why are you carrying me?" she asked, too curious about this man holding her.

"It feels right. When are you going to start telling me where to go?"

"Now *you* talk too much. I'm deciding how to make you pay."

"You're doing plenty of that without trying," he admitted ruefully.

"How?"

When Roman didn't answer, she settled into his arms and gave herself to the unique sense of being treasured. Temporarily. Just to test Roman, she slid her arms around his neck and turned her body to him. He trembled instantly, shuddered, and stopped walking. His voice was rough and deep as though torn from him. "You are a soft woman, Kallista Bellamy."

Surprising herself, she kissed the side of his neck, just once and lightly, and Roman shivered. His arms tightened around her and he looked at her, clearly shaken. "What was that?"

Later she might excuse her actions, laying them on her emotional return to the cabin. But for now, she gave into her instincts, that something good and true lurked within Roman Blaylock. "That was for Titus and Dusty...for you taking care of them. I checked with Doc Bennett. You see that they get their checkups and medication. You're regularly investing for them at the bank and that bunkhouse has been insulated with new heating and cooling systems. That new whirlpool probably helps those old broken rodeo bones."

"They're good men. They were Boone's friends. Don't mention the new heating and cooling systems to them. They like that old woodstove and open windows and think the vents are fans," he stated as if he was merely caring for valued family members and it was no burden.

Then he slowly lowered her feet to the ground, and Kallista forced herself to breathe as his dark look searched her face. Slowly his hands moved to her hips, opening and locking upon the softness firmly. "You're going to tear the heart out of me, Kallie," he whispered roughly.

"How do you know?" she returned and wondered how his mouth would taste upon her lips, her body. Like fever? Like silk? Like a burning wind to set her aflame? Or like freedom?

Like lightning, she decided, burning her as they touched.

"I just know." His gaze slid to her lips and lowered slowly to her chest, drawing her softness against him. He inhaled unsteadily and closed his eyes, as if everything in him had come to this one moment, this one caress. "I want to look at you. Does that frighten you?"

She shivered. She should be setting up her shields against him, and instead, she held very still in the warm strength of his arms, the gentle caress of his palms over her hips. The sense that she had come home was too terrifying to explore. Before she could catch her breath, Roman's large hands eased slowly up to her breasts and cradled them gently.

"Kallista," he whispered roughly, as if in aching awe, and eased her jacket and sweater from her.

"Roman," she murmured, wanting him close and warm against her in the sunlight.

"Look at you. You're so perfect in my hands. Beautiful," he whispered unevenly, drawing her gaze down to where his hands held her softness, his thumbs running gently across the lacy cups of her bra. He touched the dark peaks beneath the cloth and Kallista dug her fingertips into his shoulders as she sensed what he was about. Roman slowly bent his head to her breast and gently suckled her through the fragile cloth.

Riveted by surprise, by the beauty of his dark head at her breast, the sensations he created, she gripped his shoulders, digging in her fingers and tried not to cry out.

He shuddered and groaned. "You're burning, Kallie," he whispered rawly.

"Roman!" she cried out desperately, as he put her away from him with one last glance at her breasts. She shivered as Roman quickly replaced her clothing and turned away, his shoulders taut and his legs braced wide apart.

Their heat had shot to the danger zone so quickly, she hadn't time to set her defenses against Roman.

"There's too much fire in you, Kallie," he whispered roughly. "I'm sorry."

She could have hit him. He'd taken his big boot and squashed the beauty of the moment. Only the torment of his expression stopped her from ripping him apart.

Roman briskly bent and lifted her to her horse, placing the reins in her hand. The brush of his fingers stayed, just for a heartbeat, and then slid away to fist in Loves Dancing's black mane. "It won't happen again," he said in a tone that was a promise from his heart.

Loves Dancing, sensing the tension before the humans, shifted restlessly, and Roman soothed her with his hands and his voice, "Easy, girl."

*Easy.* It was all so easy for him, Kallista thought, wishing her unsteady emotions could settle as easily as the mare's. She studied Roman, the muscle clenching in his jaw. All that iron control was firmly locked in place.

"I've gotten to you, haven't I?" she asked cheerfully, just to nettle him more and to shield the emotions surging within her. She locked her hands to the saddle horn to keep them from reaching for him, for the taste of honor and gentleness and hunger.

His large hand slid to her thigh, gripping her gently. "Yes, damn it."

"You'll have to come out and play if you want me," she whispered and knew she'd have all of him, the dark secrets and what bound him to Boone and more. She wouldn't stop until every forbidden edge of Roman Blaylock had been given into her keeping. "And I don't make promises."

"The problem is that I do want you. When a man takes a woman's body, it's a promise to respect and honor, the same as if he's taking a bride. I know now that I was never really married, not my heart and soul bound to a woman." He swung up on Massachusetts and before they began the journey down the mountain, Roman's black eyes leveled at her, hot and hungry and dark with promises and she knew, when he was ready, he'd come for her.

Two weeks later August baked the paved streets of Jasmine. Kallista pared the rough clay seams of a greenware elephant; she smirked as she dampened the smoothed edges. She'd gotten to Roman on a level that had surprised her and he was holed up, wary of her. Good. He didn't know how to act with her, and for now, she had the advantage.

When she'd stopped at the ranch earlier, bringing Dusty and Titus their favorite chocolate and coconut cream pies from Mamie's Café, Roman had been at work, loosening an old fence post that had been broken. Without his shirt, his chest gleamed in the sunlight, powerful muscles shifting beneath his tanned skin. Kallista's mouth went dry, and she barely heard Dusty say, "He's trying to make up for lost time and he's got a bit on his mind lately. Worse than usual. But me and Titus had to go to the doc today and Roman remembered the appointment. He always goes with us, just to see that we tell the doc all our problems and that we get our medicine."

Roman's eyes had locked to hers and the sunlight blazed brighter between them. Then he reached for his shirt, hanging on a nearby post, pushed into it, and began shoving the old post to loosen it. Kallista had appreciated Roman's fine taut bottom beneath his jeans, his long legs braced against the ground, powerful shoulders flexing beneath the faded fabric.

Kallista had wanted to go to him and wrap her arms around that beautiful, rippling, powerful back, claiming him.

"He tries to do his best, but it's a whole heap of work out here, running these two ranches...even with part-time help, and the Blaylocks pitching in. Then he spends half the night with records and such," Titus had murmured. "I ain't havin' no woman come to the bunkhouse and clean for us like Roman said. A bunkhouse is sacred man's territory. I ain't in the mood for frilly curtains and flowers everywhere. I ain't havin' no dripping coffeemaker when a man's coffee ought to boil hard on the stove, and them grounds is good for the gullet."

While Dusty chewed on the "disabilities of having a female around," Kallista had studied Roman.

She wondered what he was in the mood for, his powerful body taut, moving impatiently. Suddenly he'd turned, strode to her, jerking off his gloves and demanded, "What do you want?"

Fascinated by the damp whorls of hair on his chest, the span of his gleaming tanned shoulders, the dark line leading down into his jeans, she managed to keep from drooling. Little kept her from saying, "You." Instead she'd said, "August is hot."

"Yes," he'd said. "Usually cools down by the end of the month."

"They're simmerin'," Dusty had noted as Roman's black hot gaze had ripped down, then up her body; in response, heat skittered over her skin, lodged deep in her belly and Kallista wanted Roman making love with her....

"Yep, and there will be kids aplenty if those two get together. Both is hot natured and soft when it counts. It'll be good to have kids on the place again, like Boone did," Titus had added sagely as Kallista forced herself not to grab Roman's black head and draw him down for another soul-searching kiss.

The sound of running water brought her back to the shop; Kallista held up the tiny dragon greenware she'd been holding, and thought of the day Roman had come to challenge Debbie. Another man was taking his wife and she had emptied their bank account; his pride had been torn and he'd had to ask Boone for help.

Kallista knew him on a level that went deeper than words. She knew she wanted Roman Blaylock to be her first lover and when she was finished feeding upon him, satisfying whatever kept her from sleeping, she'd be free to move on—and she'd untangle Roman's hold over Boone's estate.

Just then the shop bell jingled merrily, and Roman stood there, his Western hat in his hands. "I'm taking Boone's calves to sale. You can come if you want...to see how the sale and books are handled."

His gaze ran softly down her body, like gentle hands soothing and exciting her. "You're dressed just fine. Do you ever wear anything but black sweaters and jeans and those combat boots?"

Roman's blatant honesty pleased her and his wary expression caused her to want to leap upon him. She washed her trembling hands free of the greenware mud, aware that Roman had come to stand behind her in the cleaning room. She turned to him, drying her hands on a towel. "Sometimes I wear nothing at all," she said, testing him with a steamy look.

After his stunned expression and a heavy swallow, Roman scowled. "I'll just wait outside with Dusty and Titus."

Pleasure zinged merrily through Kallista. She loved teasing Roman; he responded magnificently, warily, as though unused to the play and she intended to play. She intended to tear away his shields and find the real Roman Blaylock. "Fine. Send them in, will you? I want to ask them to take care of the shop while I'm gone. We have to take care of your fifty-one percent, after all."

At the auction barn, Roman's business skills surprised Kallista, so did his large hand wrapped warmly around hers, and his fingers laced with her own. "Cattle prices are down," he explained as the calves were sold in a lot.

"Isn't there some way to keep them? Look at their eyes, Roman, all big and soft and—" she pleaded.

His hand curled around her nape. "Boone was a cattleman, honey, so am I."

"But they're just babies," she returned hotly and took his free hand onto her lap, gripping it tightly. "Do something."

Roman shook his head, then looked down to where she held his hand. His fingers laced with hers, slowly, methodically, palm against palm, as if fitting them for bed, and for life. "No. I'm following Boone's instructions."

Kallista didn't think; she went for the alternative method. She gripped his shirt with both fists and jammed her face against his. "Roman, I want those calves. I'll trade you my forty-nine percent in the Bisque Cafe. I'll work for free, *only do not sell those calves*. Please," she added a breath later.

Roman's long fingers circled her wrists and his thumb smoothed her skin as he smiled gently. "Honey, you're a softhearted woman and you don't make a good cattleman. I'll buy them back, for my ranch, and that would suit Boone's instructions. When you decide you want them, they're yours for the same price."

Later with the calves in the same cattle trailer they had come to market in, and cattlemen grinning and chiding Roman's silly purchase, Kallista glanced at Roman. "If I've embarrassed you, I'm sorry. The men at the auction were teasing you."

"You haven't. I've been teased before and they're my friends. I think Boone would have liked you to want those calves. I think he'd want you to plant flowers or a garden, too."

"I'm not staying, Roman. I like potted plants, and I give them away when I leave," she reminded him, while men with big Western hats grinned at Roman.

"You came back. The bleeding hearts you planted are blooming. Did you know those were Boone's mother's favorite?"

"Yes. He told me. She taught him how to crochet. That's a strange thing for a mother to teach a small boy, isn't it?" Boone had tried to teach her, his big rough hands moving her small ones, but she had been too impatient to learn.

"There were other things. It was a sharing." Roman's gaze lingered onto a small boy riding a bicycle and he waved. The boy grinned back, front teeth missing.

"You want children, don't you?" she asked as Roman drove away from the auction barn.

"With all my heart," he said solemnly. "But the woman to go with them is just a little problem right now. And she'd be the one to decide if she wanted my baby in her."

Because she was uncertain, Kallista taunted him, "That old-fashioned 'seed' thing, then?"

"You're in the country now, Miss Bellamy." Then his black eyes slowly traveled her body, down to her stomach. She could almost see the dreams in his eyes, the treasure of a child added to his life. "But making a baby is the best that a man can do in this lifetime. That and loving a woman. When and if it comes my time to add to the Blaylocks, I want a marriage certificate over the bed."

His sincerity, spoken in a deep soft tone, was almost a promise—one she couldn't afford. She wanted to find an evil, selfish lust in his plain words, but she couldn't.

It was dark when his pickup parked beside her red sports car. "It's been a good day," he said formally, looking across the seat to her. "I'll make certain that the calves are logged into my farm account. You saw me write the check. I have the receipt. It was a good price for them. When I have the auctioneer's payment for the calves, I'll show you the deposit to Boone's account."

She was ashamed then, of how closely she watched him pay for the calves, the questions she asked the auctioneer as to payment methods. Roman's explanation was too careful; he wanted her to know exactly how he handled Boone's money. He leaned closer, scanning her expression in the dim light of the street lamp. "You're shy of me now, your eyes all round and filled with me. Why?"

"I don't know who you are. You upset me, Roman Blaylock."

He toyed with a strand of her hair, wrapping it around his finger. "Is that good or bad?"

"I'm afraid of you," she whispered, aware that no other man except Boone had made her feel so secure—but with Roman there was that sensual edge, the need to experience him and tug away all those shields to find that man beneath. How could he be so raw, so tender and honest? Was it all an act? How real was Roman Blaylock?

"No more afraid than I am," he admitted and shifted to give her a lingering, tender kiss.

Kallista latched her fingers to his shoulders as the flick of his tongue touched her lips. She waited, entranced with the light, asking touch. "Open your lips for me, honey," he whispered roughly against her mouth.

For a moment, she fought other images of another man rudely pushing at her.... The familiar panic slid away as Roman's touch was seeking and gentle and letting her adjust to him. Testing, trusting him in this physical need, she placed her hands along Roman's cheeks; she parted her lips slightly, allowing him entrance. The gentle seduction of his mouth playing upon hers, molding, shaping, slanting, brushing, soon wasn't enough and Kallista wrapped her arms around him firmly.

"Oh, honey," Roman murmured before he eased her down into the seat. His trembling hand swept down to her hip, locked firmly to it as he moved over her. His hands swept up again, found her breasts and he groaned, his warm face moving into her shoulder and throat, gently nibbling on her skin, causing her bones to vibrate within her flesh. There in the close confines with Roman Blaylock, she was just where she wanted to be, without a notion of moving on.

Thrilled by his touch, by his hungry and tender look down at her, Kallista barely breathed as Roman drew away her sweater and lowered his head to her breasts, kissing the softness as he eased away her straps. He stared so long at her breasts, touching, exploring them that Kallista fought crying out, a heated desperation rising, a need as basic as air. Then his mouth took one breast, sucking and nibbling gently at the peak, and she did cry out, holding his head to her as he found the other.

Then just as quickly, Roman pushed up and away from her, his big hand locked flat to her stomach. He rolled down the steamy window and flashing red lights hit his face as he said, "Nice night, Mike."

Humor wrapped around the sheriff's voice as he said, "Don't let those alarms go off and spoil my love life again, Blaylock. Annie and I are coming to an understanding and if I pay, you pay. Good night, Kallista. This is going to be real interesting—"

Roman rolled up the window, his hair rumpled as he ran his fingers through it. He stared down at her. The look held and sizzled and Kallista placed her hands over his on her stomach. He lowered his touch until his palm rested upon her heat and Roman shuddered. "I'd better go."

"In the moonlight, I can see you on your horse, just sitting and looking at my house, Roman. Why?" She had to know.

His look was tender as he took her hands and tugged her upright to sit while he replaced her sweater. "I've got restless notions where you're concerned, Kallista Bellamy."

Then he wrapped his arms around her and with a long sigh, settled his cheek along hers and simply held her, rocking her gently.

He terrified her more than the bullies she had known.

# Six

After a fitful night in which she dreamed about Roman Blaylock's hungry, yet tempered good-night kiss, Kallista stopped yawning. Beyond her kitchen window, night was turning into gray. A big man jogged on the pasture bordering the pines. The predawn light slid over his graceful, tall body, sheathed only in loose shorts. He ran smoothly, a powerful athlete settling in for a steady run across the pasture. The elemental need to run Roman down, to hunt him, leaped within her. After all those sweet kisses, he could be running to another woman for satisfaction. "Typical. I should have known. So, he's got places to go, does he?" Kallista muttered as she hurried to dress in a T-shirt and jogging shorts.

She whipped the laces of her running shoes into bows, yanking them tightly. Roman had no right to walk her to her car, his arm around her waist, and to give her that sweet, dreamy kiss—to bring her hands to his mouth, smoothing the backs with his slightly parted lips, his dark eyes smoldering upon her face, promising... In that moment, she had been certain that she was all Roman Blaylock wanted.

In the cool of the August morning, Kallista stretched her muscles expertly, ready to track Roman. He was too delicious, too practiced not to have a woman waiting for him, arms open. "The man has secrets, and I'm going to get them," she said, settling into an easy run across the field.

The calves called to her, hurrying along and wanting petting. She stopped briefly, surrounded by churning calves with rough, wet, licking tongues. They nudged her bare legs, and Kallista laughed before hurrying after Roman. In her restless life, she'd had little to do with animals and found she enjoyed the welcome.

She spotted Roman's powerful body still running easily, though he had started up the mountain trail. Kallista picked up her pace. Lettie Coleman, a petite, packed and sexy single mother, a manhunter, lived just over the rise and...

Kallista ran freely, enjoying the stretching of her muscles, the hunting of Roman Blaylock in the fresh fir and pine-scented mountain air. She smiled grimly. The only man to interest her, Roman couldn't possibly know how much she loved puzzles, seeking answers and running.

She glanced at deer, watering at the stream, and felt her lungs resent the pace. She stopped, braced her hands on her knees and forced herself not to pant as she listened. A descendant of mountain men, Apache, Spanish and sturdy settler blood, Roman knew the well-used path. She didn't know the path or her heritage, other than she was restless and had black hair like her "old man." She had one love in her life, Boone Llewlyn, and Roman wasn't giving her the answers she needed.

She pushed herself into a fast run, leaped across a fallen branch, came into a low curve, sailed around it and plowed right into Roman's arms, sending him backward and off balance. He shoved her away, protecting her. He sprawled onto the brush and lay still as rabbits scurried away. When Roman's eyes didn't open, Kallista hurried to crouch by his side, and leaned down to study him.

The sweat and stubble on Roman's cheeks did little to make him seem civilized, nor the damp red bandanna tied around his forehead. His big hand swept out and latched around her upper arm, anchoring her. He opened his eyes and stared up at her. "You. Figures. I knew someone was following me."

"Sorry I'm not one of your women?" she taunted, trying to pull her arm away. Roman's grip was firm, yet not painful.

He came to his feet and braced his hands on his hips, looking down at her, ignoring her taunt and waiting.

She hadn't been forced to defend her actions to anyone, not for years, and now Roman clearly expected answers. "You're on my path," she tossed at him, and reached out the flat of her hand to shove him away, to shove away the unsteady emotions he caused within her.

Roman wrapped his hand around her wrist, tugged slightly, and when she was off balance, scooped her up until they were eye level, his arms supporting her bottom. The rough warmth of his thighs brushed against her smoother ones and Kallista inhaled sharply as Roman's gaze shot to the damp cloth covering her chest, to the hard nubs pushing at the cloth. "Why are you all revved up?" he asked curiously, peering down at her hot flush.

"Why are you out here this time of morning? Don't you have chores?" she shot back, unwilling to tell him how he fascinated her, how she ached for his mouth against hers, on her.

"Running cuts the tension I've been feeling lately. But you know about that, don't you?" The words were more of a statement than a question.

The fresh mountain air simmered like a firestorm between them and Kallista studied Roman's hard-boned face, the tension riding him…and her. Against her thighs, his body was hard, aroused. She'd been sickened by the men who had tried to force her, but Roman's arousal called to the wild, heated storm brewing within her. "Do you want me?" she asked carefully.

He'd said taking a woman's body was a promise, a bond a man should respect and honor. Could she believe him?

"You know I do. This is for you to decide."

"You're holding me off the ground. I think better on my feet."

He smiled wryly. "I'm afraid if I let you go, you'll run from me, and you're darned agile. And fast. And in shape for a soft woman. I've come to appreciate a fine, strong woman."

The curve of his lips enchanted her, his amused indulgent expression that made her feel safe…a friendly man playing with her, teasing her. She touched his cheek, ran her fingertips across the warm desire riding his skin, strolled to his eyebrows and studied the sleek black thickness. This man was incredibly gentle, and leashing what ran hot and wild within him. She'd known men who didn't restrain their passions, and this man honored women, respected the sexual bonding of bodies as a promise to be kept. She'd known few men with such honor, and one of them was Boone. "Who are you, Roman Blaylock?" she whispered.

"Who hurt you?" he returned so gently that he terrified her, opening scars that she'd hidden for years.

"Does it matter?" she asked, fearing the tears welling inside her.

"I won't hurt you, honey. But I'm sorry for the rest. I'd give it back to you, if I could." His kiss was only a nudge against her lips, and she tasted the salt of his sweat, the honesty of his heart, the promise of his body, thrusting intimately against hers.

She didn't want emotions for this man, to trust him though he grasped Boone's estate and left her with unanswered questions. Yet she did trust him on a level that frightened her. Could she trust herself?

"Let me down." Kallista pushed gently against Roman's bare shoulders, her fingertips stroking the smooth damp skin while the dawn became pink and sweet and new around them.

She stood free, braced her legs apart and considered the possibility of Roman Blaylock as her first lover. From the top of his sleek rumpled hair down his long powerful body to his worn running shoes, planted firmly on the well-used trail, Roman was a definite possibility.

"Well?" he asked, amused. A full two minutes had passed and a deer ambled by a red-bark pine and a chipmunk chattered, awakening to the day. Birds chirped overhead, leaves rustling as mountain creatures prepared to forage and live and...

Kallista inhaled, and decided to trust her instincts. She didn't have time for Roman to come courting; she'd always taken what she wanted. She ripped off her long black T-shirt to expose her sports bra. She hurled the T-shirt at him, and Roman's big fist crushed the material. His sexy, amused look vanished, replaced by shock and frustration. A tiny muscle began contracting in his jaw, and he frowned at her. "What the hell are you doing?"

She stepped out of her shorts and stood in her running shoes, dressed in her bra and her briefs. She threw her shorts at him and his other hand shot out to grasp the material. His stare down at her clothing in his hands was desperate, wary, and raw with desire. She wanted the truth Roman offered her, the raw honesty of a man and a woman tangled in desire, simmering with it, easing into sensuality.

"No," he said firmly, then dragged his hand through his hair and glanced at a hawk soaring into the morning sky.

He was perfect then—wary, uncertain, and hers.

She walked slowly to him; she studied the thrusting proof of his desire and the taut muscles of his thighs. This was her way—she trusted her instincts when they hit her, she made her decisions and explained to no one.

"No. Not like this," he said again, as her eyes raised to meet his. His gaze locked with hers and darkened. Roman tugged her into his arms and fused his mouth to hers, taking, demanding everything.

When her legs were weak, he scooped her up against him. He ran his hand along her leg, locking it around his hips, then the other, anchoring him to her, her arms around his neck.

Day and dawn hovered, spinning coolly around them. But wrapped in Roman's arms and his desire, Kallista had never been so warm and safe. As Roman poured his hunger into her, she fed upon his need. Her fists wrapped in his stark black hair, his body thrusting intimately against the shield of lace protecting her. His groan swept roughly across her cheek, the desperation of his tone pleasing her.

Still carrying her, Roman moved off the trail into a shadowy cove covered with lush, sweet grass. He tossed her clothing to the earth and eased to his knees, his mouth slanting, fusing, and hungry for her. There in the shadows of the pines, amid the clearing's lush grass and larkspur, Roman looked primitive, skin almost gold in the dappled sunlight, ridges running along his shoulders, muscles bunching. Slowly he lowered her to the clothing, tore away his own and pushed them beneath her to add to the pallet.

"I want you," he said roughly, as if the truth had been unwillingly torn from him and eased his body over hers. He smoothed away the band from her hair and gently arranged the silky length around her head, then his face rested against her throat, as if he waited to be denied. The gesture was humble and cautious and beautifully unique.

"I want you more," she returned huskily, certain that this was a moment of truth, that she would know Roman Blaylock's essence, that she would have him. She smoothed the taut muscles of his back, absorbed the rippling shock into her palms.

For those racing heartbeats, damp skin against skin, Roman simply rested lightly upon her. She slid her finger under the damp red bandanna and eased it from his head.

What caused her to smooth his hair, to want to comfort him? Was it the reverence and the tenderness with which his hand slid to hold her breast, as if it were a treasure he would hold forever?

Slowly Roman slid away her bra and her briefs, replacing them with the warm, trembling caress of his hands. When she shivered beneath him, he braced above her, tension rippling through his broad shoulders. For a time he looked down at her, frowning as if he couldn't believe she was lying in his arms, that her body lay open to his, that his arousal just touched the heated damp entrance of hers.

"Are you afraid?" he asked in an uneven whisper as his taut body shuddered. "We can stop—"

"Don't you dare stop," she returned, lifting to bite his lip. She would tear him from his leashes and devour him—find what she needed....

He jerked back, startled. Then his expression slid into tender amusement. "You want to play, do you?"

"Is that what this is?" she asked softly, smoothing her hands over his tense shoulders. Then she drew him down upon her.

Roman smoothed the side of her throat with his parted mouth, his breath rushing to warm her. "I wanted you in my bed, not here. You deserve—"

He inhaled sharply as his hand found her intimately, caressing her. Ripples of pleasure circled her and she arched to his touch, wanting more.

"Hush. Come here." Splaying her fingers through his hair, his lovely shaggy hair, Kallista drew his lips down to hers. Within her, she knew that for all the wrong men that had come at her, this was the right man—that here in this

mountain clearing with dawn shimmering on dewy grass
and daisies, this was the time for her new beginning.

Roman's big hands smoothed her gently, running from
her shoulders to her hips to her thighs. Against her mouth,
he whispered, "I don't want to hurt you, but this will—"

She cried out, a part of her yielding, tearing away, and
Roman tensed, his face against her throat. He was shaking
now, his skin damp as she dug her fingertips into his shoulders. "I can't—"

His hands ran beneath her, lifted her gently, as his lips
found her breast, suckling deeply, and the cords within her
tightened, ignited and when they were fully joined, Roman
thrust quickly. His movements were powerful, his body
gathering her closer. Stunned, but not frightened by the
intensity of his desire, shocked by her own body clenching
his, her earth-shattering emotions and pleasure, Kallista
could only grasp him closer. For the first time, she saw
passion as beautiful, the movement of their bodies a dance.
Inexperienced and uncertain how to meet him, Kallista held
him tightly as he shuddered and lay still, clearly spent. She
hadn't reached fulfillment, she knew, but the beauty of Roman's desire was enough. To hold him tight and close, gave
her pleasure; as she stroked his hair, peace she'd never
known came to Kallista. She breathed in his scent, remembered how desperate he'd been for her, the sound of her
name on his lips, treasuring her— "I'm sorry," he said
unevenly. "I..."

"Shush." Though she wasn't comfortable, stretched almost painfully, Kallista did not regret holding the man in
her arms, his humble, desperate expression shocking her.

She watched him glance down at her body, dark and light
skin tangled in the morning shadows. Hunger ignited in his
black eyes before he leashed his emotions. His fingers dug
into her hip, his palm warm and callused on her skin.
"You're cold. If you go into shock—"

Kallista watched him move through the forest shadows

to the rippling stream. He crouched, studied her briefs for moments before dampening them in the clear water and walking back to her. He was big and graceful and beautiful, and shielding her body with the drape of her T-shirt, Kallista marveled that she had held such a powerful and gentle creature in her arms, had tasted him, and that he had shared her body. He studied her expression, and sadness came upon his own. "I'm big, and rough. I'm sorry."

Kallista drew her shirt over her quickly and Roman turned away, dragging up his running shorts, as she cleansed her body. He looked so alone, so haunted as he stood with his back to her. Kallista rose to her feet, her legs unsteady, her femininity aching, burning.

Uncertain of him, she stood waiting. "Roman?"

He turned to her, anger lashing at her. She should have been frightened. She wasn't. His stare ripped down her body, then back up to her hot face. "Lady, I just tore through your body and I still want you. You should have a bed and roses and sweet talk and I didn't know how to—"

The agony of his expression caught her and Kallista took one step before her weakened legs gave way. Roman scooped her up in his arms and turned around in the small clearing as though seeking a soft place to lay her. "You're so small," he said unsteadily, concern lodged in every word. "So small and tight and damp and burning hot."

Roman sat with her across his lap, rocking her and placing her head against his bare shoulder. She kissed the damp skin there and he tensed. "We're in a fix," he stated bluntly, after kissing her forehead.

She moved against the soothing caress of his hand between her legs, a gesture meant to soothe, not to stimulate. "You evidently are. You look frazzled and worried. I'm just peachy."

"This isn't funny," he said grimly. "I don't know what to do with you."

"Oh, yes, you did," she teased and his enchanting nipple leaped to the touch of her fingertip.

"This isn't how it should be—stop that," he ordered as she bent to suckle him. He tensed and stared at her as if he'd never seen her. "Why did you do that?"

"Because you're so easy to startle. You look so stunned."

"You're still determined to have fun, huh?"

"I like to play." She could have lain in his arms all that hot August day, forgetting her past, the ugliness she'd seen, replacing it with this beautiful, new bright day. She had the strangest sense of being clean, of coming home to something that was irrevocably innocent and right and bonding.

"No more now," he whispered unsteadily.

Kallista lay back in Roman's arms and studied him. His hand ran slowly over her thighs and rested on her femininity. "Are you sorry?" he asked gently, uncertainly.

"No. It just wasn't—"

"What you expected?" he finished for her. He smoothed a strand of hair back from her forehead. His expression was a mixture of self-disgust and tenderness for her. "I haven't been with a woman since before my wife and I wanted you too much. Those incredible sounds you make— I couldn't wait. Now that says a whole lot for controlling myself, doesn't it?"

"Hey, did I ask for control?" She'd found a painfully honest man, and she'd had him for one glorious moment. Would he always be this way?

"I'm short on control with you," he admitted roughly.

She loved his blush, his boyish expression of guilt and studied the daisy she'd just placed in his hair. "Why? Why weren't you involved with other women?"

"They didn't seem right and that's the first flower any woman has put in my hair.... It's an odd thing to do, isn't it? A woman putting flowers in a man's hair?" His blush deepened beneath his dark tan and wary of her, he looked at the stream. "Nice day today. If we had our fishing gear, we could fish."

"Daisies are definitely you.... Don't change the subject. You said I seemed right?"

"Yes." His answer came as a vow, his kiss tender upon her lips. "But I'm not telling you about Boone's affairs."

The realization hit her, sickened her. "You think I did this...*because I wanted to know about Boone's business? Because I wanted to get information out of you?*"

He held her easily when she would have squirmed free. "A man likes to do the running. I haven't courted you, but I want you to know that I take what just happened as a serious matter, the gift of your body. Thank you."

His formal thank-you wasn't what she wanted—she wanted more tender kisses and hungry looks and deep unsteady groans, she wanted his body locked to hers and he'd given her a glimpse of flying and—

"Send a thank-you card. Who sets these outdated rules? You?" With that, Kallista stood free and with as much dignity as she could manage walked from Roman, a man she still wanted to feast upon, to devour. "I wasn't after information on Boone's account, Mr. Blaylock. You are a frustrating, slow-moving, thickheaded hunk of muscle and—" She realized she was muttering and despite her newly aching body, she set into a fast run to wipe the need of Roman Blaylock's tenderness away.

She stopped suddenly and found him behind her, wary and rumpled, frustrated and aching with guilt. Because she was nettled, she decided to add to his thoughtful misery, making him forget his guilt. She wouldn't have Roman feeling guilty because he made love to her. She knew exactly what she wanted, and despite the pain, she would have repeated the experience with him. She served him a tidbit that Boone had said Western men never do. "I saw you blush, Roman Blaylock."

"Damn it, Kallie. Men don't blush," he shot back,

scowling fiercely at her as though she'd scored a hit on his manhood.

She pushed her hand through her loose hair, grinned at him and said cheerfully, "I'm going to make your life unbearable."

Kallista's uncle didn't fight fair. That evidence lodged painfully in Roman's bruised side and his swollen black eye. He entered the community hall, ignored the hush that came over the extensive Blaylock family as he walked to hang his Western hat on the wall pegs with the other hats. Jasmine's Belles' Saturday Night Dinner and Dance had packed the community hall, a benefit for Doc Bennett's new clinic. Jack's Country Music band was tuning up and children who would dance with their elders milled around the floor.

He'd grown up, forced to dance with his mother when he was a boy, and he'd come to every dance since then—until his divorce. Now here he was, late and wearing a black eye, just two days after making love—after taking Kallista on that mountain trail. The sight of her body, soft and curved and fragrant, haunted his every moment. Roman took a deep breath and braced himself before he turned to his brothers and sister and their families. Dressed in a short, tight black sheath and high heels, Kallista was carrying a casserole from the large kitchen to the inside picnic tables. Her green eyes lasered into him with enough impact to make him catch his breath.

He couldn't tell her he had to meet Jeremy, Boone's only living son, to keep him from returning to Jasmine, to keep him from the land Boone prized. Jeremy wanted to sell the land, to challenge Roman's executor status, and to become Boone's rightful heir. But Boone didn't want that, and Roman had had to meet Jeremy in Cheyenne, each with lawyers. The will was ironclad, and in his revenge, Jeremy had leaped across the table at Roman. The hot cup of coffee that he'd flung at Roman, had seared his throat.

When the meeting was done, Jeremy had the choice to have his rich monthly allotment severed...or to behave and keep away from Jasmine and Kallista, or any of Boone's grandchildren.

Two days away from Kallista and Roman still felt her body open to his, that sweet tug of hunger on her lips, her light painful cry as they became one.

He frowned at Kallista, whose rigid expression told him to keep his distance.

He couldn't. His heart was in her keeping, and it wouldn't beat warm again until he held her.

Roman attempted a smile at her and the split on his lip threatened to open. She ignored him and plopped the casserole down on the table. She brushed her hand through her loose hair, flipping it impatiently over her shoulder. She looked at Rio and crooked her little finger. Rio chuckled and nodded to Jack's Country band, who struck up a fast-moving tune, perfect for country-western dancing. Rio and Kallista whirled off onto the floor, followed by other couples, while a miniature herd of Roman's nieces and nephews descended upon him.

"Uncle Roman," one of Logan's little girls was saying as Rio swung Kallista under his arm. "You never come to stuff. Aunt Else just told Uncle Joe that now she knew why you were buying up all the old furniture around Jasmine and hoarding it. She says you've got the nesting urge. What's that mean, Uncle Roman? Chickens have nests, but you're too big, and why would you want to set on a nest anyway, and why do you need more furniture, and—"

To stop the flow of her questions, Roman picked her up and placed her on his hip.

Else came to stand beside him, her hand on his shoulder. "Hello, pitiful. But at least you're wearing a nice dress shirt. Here, let me take off the price tag."

"Stop fussing after me, Else."

With years of experience in tending Blaylock males, Else ignored his protest, and pushed his arm up to rip away the tag. "You'd better explain the bruises to her, and quick, brother dear. Your sweetheart is dancing with lover boy. If she thinks you were fighting over a woman—"

"Can't explain and she doesn't know she's my sweetheart." Roman burned a warning message to Rio, who had just winked at him as he set Kallista into a series of fast turns. Else studied Roman. "Well, you'll feel better after you eat," she said finally, in a tone that reminded him of their mother. "I've been saving Mother's best cameo for you."

"I'll be over to get it," he said, and Else would understand that he'd finally found the woman to wear it.

"Wild rambling roses are hard to tame, little brother. This one has a steel backbone. But you hurt her, and I'll have Mother's best wooden spoon after you."

"Taming isn't what I've got in mind," he returned easily, used to Else's worrying about him.

"I'll bake the wedding cake," she said, swatting his backside as she winked at him.

Roman wanted the soft feel of his lady in his arms. Dan and Hannah danced by and Dan threw Roman an amused look.

"That's some shiner, Uncle Roman," one of Else's teenage boys said around the mouthful of carrot cake he'd just snatched.

"Awesome," his buddy agreed, munching on a chicken drumstick. "Why are you glaring at Rio? What'd he do? Man, that dude is a mover—hey! Why did you give me this kid? Jeez, a little girl— Ruffled panties?" he gasped indignantly as his hand supported her bottom. "Here, Mike. You hold her."

"Dance?" Roman asked Kallista after tapping Rio's shoulder with enough punch to warn him.

"No," she said, sending a brilliant smile at Rio. She wasn't going to show Roman she'd missed him. A woman had her pride....

"We can all dance together, a threesome," Rio offered cheerfully and stepped back when both Kallista and Roman scowled at him.

"People are watching." Kallista stiffly gripped Roman's shoulders and he placed his arms around her waist as the music began. "I cannot abide brawlers," she stated coldly, looking away from him.

Unused to dancing, and to sharing his thoughts with a woman he treasured, Roman stopped moving. "I'm sorry."

She avoided his eyes. "You look awful."

If he couldn't hold her just once more, his heart would tear away. He lifted her chin with the tip of his finger. "Can I hold you?"

"We're on a dance floor. What exactly do you think you're doing now?"

He needed to hold her, to know that she was safe from parents and an uncle who could harm her. "Holding you close to me, Kallista. Close to my heart."

She shivered, a blush rising on her smooth cheeks. "You're embarrassing me."

"Making love on the side of a mountain trail wasn't what I'd planned. I didn't want to be away from you."

Her look up at him steamed, lashed out at him, as though he was a man who made love to a woman and then went whistling on his way. She hadn't expected anything from him and that hurt. He'd told her he would be bound to her, if they made love.

Roman slid his hands down her arms to her hands and lifted them. He simply placed his face within her keeping and prayed that she wouldn't turn him away.

# Seven

A man can do a lot of work when he can't sleep at night, Roman thought, as he eased out of his pickup and told the aging greyhounds to "stay."

At six o'clock the morning after he'd seen Kallista safely home from the dance, Roman had already done a day's work on Boone's accounts. In the two days he was gone, Kallista had prowled through the house, and the exotic cinnamony and feminine scent kept him stirred too much to sleep. She'd tried to pick open the new lock on Boone's steamer trunk in the living room. She'd been through the desk, and his divorce decree had been moved. She'd studied the big ledgers accounting for Blaylock and Llewlyn livestock. Roman noted with a smile that Kallista had gone through his bedroom, and had rummaged through his underwear drawer. The woman wouldn't stop, and he appreciated her dedication to Boone.

Sometime during the hot August night, while every pore, every molecule, of him ached for Kallista, Roman had ordered those fancy at-home dancing lessons. Around four, he'd milked the cow that Titus loved, but couldn't curl his arthritic fingers around the teats; Roman had made his rounds of the orchid greenhouse, checked the pigeons, and fed the livestock. Then he went to see Else, who served him breakfast and his mother's cameo. With tears in her eyes, she ran her hand over his head, shook him lightly, and slid their mother's ivory tatting shuttle from her apron. "Dad gave it to her. It was his mother's and came West on the wagon train with her mother."

Rio, looking for a home-cooked breakfast, entered the kitchen and straddled a kitchen chair. "Feed me," he said simply to his eldest sister.

"Here's the butter churn. Get to work." Else playfully thumped him on the head. By the time she served him pancakes, the butter had turned to a lump, waiting for the buttermilk to be drained and pressed away, and salt to be added. Rio quickly devoured the five huge pancakes on his plate, washing them down with two cups of coffee and orange juice.

Roman waited until he had Rio's full attention. He looked at Rio steadily until his younger brother lifted an inquiring eyebrow. "The next time you dance with Kallista, it can be at our wedding," Roman said.

Rio had almost choked on his last bite of pancakes, then he began to guffaw. Else's wooden spoon, applied to his shoulder, reminded him of his manners and who ruled in her kitchen.

"Anytime," Roman offered levelly, calling Rio out, if need be. "When Men's Night Only comes around at the Bisque Café, you get lost."

"Now why would I want to paint ceramics when you're taking up all the good dog bowls?" But Rio's look at Roman was a mixture of brotherly pleasure and amusement and love.

*  *  *

Now, standing on the sidewalk in front of the Bisque Café at ten o'clock in the morning, Roman gripped the tiny white box in his fist. His mother's cameo pendant and a tatting shuttle handed down from a wagon trail bride weren't exactly courting material. Roman closed his eyes, inhaled deeply to gather his courage, and wrapped his hand around the doorknob. He thrust the door open and stepped inside. A table of women, happily painting bisque and chatting, looked at him. Faced with a horde of curious stares and wanting to make his stand as a suitor for Kallista's hand in marriage, Roman resisted the urge to run...and the flush rising up his nape.

"'Morning, ladies," Roman said. He removed his hat as he and all the Blaylock males had been taught to do.

"'Morning, Roman," they replied in chorus.

Just then Kallista came from the back room, a smile on her face, and Roman's heart flipped over at the sight of her black sweater, shorts and boots. Her legs were smooth and fine and tanned and long and... He took one look at Jasmine's ladies and summoned his courage.

"I'm out of dog bowls," Kallista whispered as Roman walked slowly to her.

She was so fresh and pretty and sweet. Roman bent to kiss her parted lips lightly. "I'm wanting more than dog bowls, honey," he said as her eyes widened.

His next words shocked her. "Do you like kissing me?"

*Only as much as she liked breathing....* "Kissing is an activity that I—"

He smiled slightly, wistfully. "Uh-huh. You kiss every man as though you want to suck his soul from him."

"I do not! How dare you come into my shop and call me a tramp!" Her mother had been a tramp and all her life Kallista had fought the mold. The hand she had just shot out, knocked over a mug, resting on a shelf. Roman caught the mug, and replaced it.

"Oh, I'd be the man to know you're not, wouldn't I?"

he said, reminding her of how well he knew her body's innocence. His hard mouth shifted as though pushing back a smile, the skin beside his eyes crinkling with humor. "It seems to me that I might be special to you."

She strained to be calm and lied, "No, not at all."

Roman took her hand, pressed a kiss into her palm, and tried not to spit out the taste of clay. Then he pressed the box with his mother's cameo and the tatting shuttle into her hand. "These were my mother's. I want you to have them."

Maizie Murdock's cheerful voice sliced through the silence. "You Blaylock men can purely make a woman's heart race."

"How's Else's husband, Joe? I heard he had a brush with pneumonia," called Wanda Hightower.

"Joe is just fine." Roman almost faltered, but he focused on Kallista and spoke quietly. "I never courted Debbie, but I'm courting you. You're the first woman in my life and you'll be the last. I'm not happy that we've got the events backward, but in my heart, you're already my bride."

She'd probably had men give her mountains of flowers, and fine jewelry, and they'd probably have taken her to some exclusive Caribbean hideaway to say the same thing, but he had to take care of Boone's land and meet his promise.

"Oh, Roman..." Tears shimmered in her eyes, and Roman tumbled into their meadow green depths.

"I'd tell you about the promise I made to Boone, if I could. But I can't. I'm sorry. Else wants to bake the wedding cake, so I'd appreciate it if you'd let her."

The single teardrop glittering on Kallista's lashes ripped through Roman's heart. "I thought it would be a good start if I took you to dinner tonight. If you like, I'll pick you up after work and—"

Kallista's fingers brushing lightly over his bruised eye

stopped him. She looked at him with clear emerald bright eyes, searching his face. "I like," she whispered softly.

Shaken with emotion, Roman gripped her wrist, pressed a quick kiss onto the fine skin, and managed to walk out of the shop without a backward glance at the woman opening the small box. If he'd stayed, he'd have dragged her into his arms for a kiss that would have shocked the good ladies of Jasmine.

He sat in his pickup, gripped the steering wheel until he heard it creak. He couldn't tell Boone's secrets to the woman he wanted, and yet he'd asked her to trust him in the most basic of ways. Would she?

Well, fine, Roman thought with disgust hours later. He gripped the steering wheel of his pickup and veered around the buck deer sashaying across the highway. Luka, pressed by Igor, leaned against Roman's shoulder and he reached to pat the greyhounds reassuringly.

The telephone call concerning the girl came just an hour before he was to pick up Kallista. Breaking their first date wouldn't help her trust him. There had been deadly silence at the end of the telephone line when he'd called. "I have to go somewhere" wasn't exactly a good excuse to a woman he wanted to claim, but it was as good as he could offer.

The girl was Boone's grandchild, the same as Kallista, and Roman had a promise to meet. He forced himself to think about the girl, and what to say to her.... To tell Kallista that Hyacinth Walker was her half sister would necessitate unraveling Boone's secret, his disgrace that his bigamist sons had taken women under other names and irresponsibly produced innocent children. Margaret Walker wanted Boone's monthly checks, but did not want Hyacinth. The girl had been abandoned at a sleazy motel with Boone's telephone number and enough money to buy a hamburger. Though terror trembled in her ten-year-old voice, she didn't cry and it would be midnight before Roman could reach the trucker's roadside motel.

"I can read, you know. I know exactly what my mother wrote on those papers. I've known how to steam envelopes open since I was five," Hyacinth stated as haughtily as she could. "Don't call me Hyacinth. That's a sweet flower name and I ain't no posy."

In the afternoon light, the man who had slept on the room's other bed was even more tough-looking than she first thought. The only good thing about Roman Blaylock was Big Boone's Luka and Igor. Hyacinth remembered the greyhounds and when they curled up on the bed beside her, she released her tight grip on terror...but she hadn't cried, not one drop, not since she read the papers her mother had sealed in the envelope...before dropping her off at the motel. All she had was her small Barbie suitcase and the pride that Big Boone had given her on her last visit. She held tight to the two greyhounds on either side of her, the only part of Big Boone she could hold. "Mister, if you didn't have Big Boone's dogs, you'd be road dust on my boots right now."

She eyed the man with the black eye and the burned throat. He wasn't no pretty-perfume smelling man, his hair black and shaggy, and his skin tanned by sun—like Boone's. There were calluses on his hands, and Boone had said calluses showed a man worked hard, and most working men were good, because they didn't have time to be anything else. "My mother signed papers that said she didn't want me. I saw Boone's name on them. So you hauled me into some judge-friend of yours and adopted me right after breakfast—I liked that bacon and egg breakfast, by the way. I purely hate dry cereal and water. I got a Blaylock name stuck on my butt now, and one wrong move on me, buddy, and I'll make you sorry...Dad," she added sarcastically, just to dig at him. "I said I'd go with you, but it's only 'cause you got Big Boone's dogs and he's dead and some-one needs to take care of them—boy, you sure don't talk much, do you?''

"It seems to me that you're doing fine all by yourself."

"Just laying down the rules, mister."

"While you're working hard at that, think about what you want me to call you."

Hyacinth stared at him, her mouth open. No one ever gave her a choice. "Man. You mean I get to pick a name?"

"You ought to have a name you like. Just make it simple and something to go with Blaylock."

Then because too many promises had been made to her and broken, she tried not to get excited. He was even tougher looking than he'd been last night, his dark stubble had thickened, and the lines cut into his face. His black hair was coarser than hers, and one spear shot over his forehead. "Are you an Indian?" she asked.

"Part. Part Spanish. Part homesteader."

"Mmm. A mongrel. I won't hold that against you. But we'd better be driving to Boone's house. Are Dusty and Titus still there?" They were kind old men with faces like aged leather, and she loved them—until her mother tore her away.

Hyacinth studied the man who had collected her, fed her, and bought her new clothes. "I'll think about that checkup with the doctor. Boone took me to him when I was little, so if Boone did it, I guess it's okay."

Roman Blaylock reminded her of Boone—kind to ani-mals, quiet, steady as a rock and a man who kept his prom-ises…like when he said he'd wait outside the bathroom when she showered. He'd gently used a brush on her tan-gled black straight hair, and fastened two new bright blue barrettes in it—he said he'd picked them and the new tooth-brush and toothpaste up on his way to get her. Boone used to come after her, now and again, and when he did, he was mad—not at her, but at her mother. And like Roman, Big

Boone had always brought a large bag of just perfect girl things.

The man knew she liked blue, and his voice was soft when he apologized for her new pink jacket; he hadn't been able to find a warm blue one. No one but Boone had ever cared about her love of blue, a reminder of clear Wyoming skies.

Hyacinth scrubbed her hands over her face and dried the suspicious dampness on her new bib overalls. She sank into her new hot pink jacket and looked out at the rugged Wyoming mountains flying by the pickup window. When a girl's mother didn't love her, it hurt awful bad. She hadn't known her father. This man didn't look like a father; he looked like a cowboy and he kept a flat, old dried-up daisy in his wallet.

"Just what do I call you?" she asked, sorry for digging at him throughout the long trip. A man who picked the meat from café hamburgers and fed them to the old greyhounds in pieces couldn't be that bad.

"You call me what you want. But I'm going to ask you to help me…and Big Boone."

"Buckoo, I'd do anything for Big Boone," she said, meaning it, as a spear of pain shot through her. Boone had been her rock, and now he was gone. Roman had that same slow way of speaking, as though he thought all his words out before opening his mouth. And when he said them, he'd abide by every word.

"You remember how Boone asked you not to say anything about how you came to stay at his house…about how he came after you, wherever you were? That's what I'm going to ask you to do…all anyone needs to know is that from now on you're my daughter…and you're a Blaylock."

"What's being a Blaylock got to do with anything? My mother had lots of last names."

Roman's hard face softened as he smiled at her. "You've

just picked up a whole lot of relatives, Hyacinth. They'll be there when you need them. I will be, too. Every day...every night...you're not going to be alone anymore."

"And Dusty and Titus?" she asked cautiously, not wanting to give them up in exchange for Blaylocks. In her experience, everything came with strings and trade-offs. "Do I have to put up with some witch called Mrs. Blaylock?"

"Not at the moment. But I'm working on it. And she's not a witch. She's got my heart."

Hyacinth stared at the man, her mouth open again. What kind of a man talked about his heart and a woman as though they were the same thing?

"I could cramp your style, buddy. I'm good at cramping styles. My mother said so." Hyacinth wasn't proud of that fact because her mother had been bitter about her "little tagalong."

That night, Hyacinth settled into the small familiar bedroom and the greyhounds slept on the floor. Fully dressed, she lay very still and gripped her Barbie suitcase. The man was working downstairs, in Boone's office, and he'd told her to come down if she couldn't sleep.

The man wasn't so bad, she thought, easing around Luka to stand. He reminded her of Big Boone and she'd have to trust him, for now. If Big Boone trusted the man enough to let him take care of all the Llewlyn's fine things, then... She descended the stairway and, holding her suitcase, stood in the office doorway, studying the man.

He turned to her, then glanced back at the computer screen where words were flying across the surface. "That's from my...someone I like."

Hyacinth came to study the screen. "She's a hacker, and a good one. She's trying to open your security systems."

"She's smart," Roman said in fond, proud tones. "And pretty, too. She looks like you in a way. Black hair, green eyes, pale skin."

"Have you put the make on her?" It seemed an honest question and one Hyacinth had heard the adults in her life ask.

Roman frowned sternly at her, and Hyacinth began to giggle. "That's what men do. Women, too. Didn't you know?"

"Are you hungry?" he asked, and she knew it was an effort to derail her. Because she felt sorry for the poor lonely, beat-up, embarrassed cuss, she said, "Sure. Feed me something. I burned a kitchen once, and I don't want to do that to Big Boone's house."

By the next evening, Hyacinth had discovered that Titus and Dusty and every animal on Boone's place adored Roman Blaylock. She was soon in love with Rio and Else and all the rest of the Blaylocks who just happened to drop in with clothes and food. Whenever she felt uncertain, she'd feel Roman's big hand on her shoulder…just like Boone's. "This is my daughter," he'd said proudly introducing her as if she were a top prize at a family show.

"You need some games on your computer and your hacker-woman is back," she said around a mouthful of peanut butter and jelly sandwich. She sat on the sofa in Boone's office, watching Roman punch in numbers to the computer. "Okay…I'll stay until things aren't sweet. But your cooking ain't much."

"Isn't much," he corrected. "But I'm glad you're staying," he said as though she pleased him. "We'll start you on chores, first thing in the morning."

"Holy hell," Hyacinth exploded, remembering all the cleaning work she'd done for her mother. "If you got me here to make a slave of me, think again…."

"I thought maybe taking care of the pigeons, to start. It's planting time, and I'd like you on the tractor with me to see if the rows are straight. Then that barn cat had kittens and we can't find them. I don't want to sink a pitchfork into hay and find—"

"Okay, okay." Hyacinth tried for a bored tone when she couldn't wait for morning.

By the end of the week, in which Roman spent every day with her, Hyacinth was in love with her new dad. She slept in his worn, soft shirt, just as she'd done when Boone kept her safe.

# Eight

**R**oman glanced in his rearview mirror. He was a pitiful specimen of a man courting his intended bride. His hair was too long, past his collar, and in Cindi's, formerly Hyacinth, enthusiasm to show him how useful she could be—and to make up for the sow and piglets she'd released into the new sweet corn—she'd scorched his only good shirt. His jeans had bleach spots on them and his emotions about facing Kallista were just as unstable as the denim cloth.

He'd ached for her, embarrassed himself by calling out her name in a morning dream—his body bearing a constant sensual ache that hard work didn't diminish. He dreamed of Kallista's warm drowsy look as she lay beneath him—all that soft sweet skin rosy from lovemaking.

He'd plundered her body and given her pain; she hadn't an idea of the full measure of pleasure. Roman rubbed his forehead; what did he know about lovemaking? A teenage experiment in the back seat of a car, and the shattering one

with Kallista beside the mountain trail, did not make him
an expert of any kind.

He didn't have time to study what women wanted during
lovemaking; he just knew how he wanted to love Kallista—
long and slow and sweet, taking care to treasure every inch,
every memory of every touch. However, keeping Cindi oc-
cupied, clean and dressed was a full-time job—and making
her feel as though she belonged. The girl's rage and guilt,
her emotions concerning her mother, led to the mortifica-
tion of bedwetting. Dusty and Titus wouldn't purchase un-
derclothes for her, and Cindi didn't want anyone in town
to know she wasn't in control.

Roman had taken her driving through several towns, and
when she was cried out and tired and curled against him,
he'd asked her if he could purchase more underwear for
her. Since they were away from Jasmine, he'd said, no one
would know. She'd agreed on the condition that he purchase some for himself, some spiffy new silk boxer shorts,
because she figured that was fair. Wearing silk, which was
not righteous on a man bred to the West, was a small price
to pay to make her feel more comfortable. Though she
changed into Roman's shirt at night now, she still slept with
her gift from Boone, a tiny suitcase close at hand.

Who was the man who had called earlier that week? The
call haunted Kallista—he'd said he was her uncle. Though
she had hunted for years, she hadn't been able to find any
record of her father or his relatives. It was as if everything
having to do with them had been erased.

Then she saw Roman through the shop's front window
and stopping thinking about anything but him. From the
shop's workroom, Kallista watched him open the door. In
the week since she'd seen him, Roman's bruised eye had
healed; dressed in a shirt with a scorch mark on his flat
stomach, jeans with white blotches and wearing a wary
look, he looked delicious. The thin, black-haired girl with

him was dressed in a T-shirt, big overalls, and running shoes. The little girl carried a big white box and she looked up at him as though she adored him. Kallista sucked in her breath. With her hair in "puppy dog tails" on either side of her head, tied with colorful bands, and the spray of freckles across her nose, the girl was the exact image of herself.

Kallista placed her hand over her stomach, the familiar sight stunning her. Boone had once stood with her, like Roman did now, bending low to whisper that she was as good as everyone else, and precious, and there was nothing to be frightened of as he introduced her as his "little friend." *There's nothing to be frightened of, Kallie-girl. Just hold your head up high. These are my friends and yours, too. You're wearing new clothes and you're prettier than that new filly.*

Roman's big hand on the girl's shoulder said she belonged to him, proving true the rumors that he'd brought his long-lost daughter to Boone's home. Mort Raznik, known as the fastest mouth in the territory, and Wilma Nigel gossiped that Roman's times away from Jasmine were spent with another family—a high-nosed society woman who'd had his child. Roman had said that making a baby was the most important thing a man could do, and when he gave his body, he gave his bond. A searing pain shot through Kallista, tore down her stomach and ripped it open—Roman had a daughter he'd never mentioned and a bond to another woman....

Kallista gripped the small greenware dolphin in her hand until it broke, falling into the cleaning sink. She'd wanted to run away from him. She'd wanted to call him out, face-to-face, to tell him that he didn't matter—but standing there in that pose, looking at her as though she was everything he wanted, Kallista's legs went weak.

Every day Titus or Dusty had arrived with a crudely crafted paper box, fashioned with tape. Inside was a perfect orchid, resting on tissue paper, and Roman's bold, blocked

initials. Just the sight of the blooms caused Kallista's heart
and soul to weep.

He'd caught her prowling in his computer, but she didn't
want to chat with him there, or on the telephone when he
called. She wanted to see his face, see how a man who said
such sweet things and gave Blaylock family keepsakes to
her, could then stay away one whole week, turning up with
a little girl and using her as an excuse.

*Orchids weren't going to help Roman Blaylock.*

Kallista inhaled unsteadily, forced a tight smile down at
the girl, and pinned Roman with one glance. He had that
wary, vulnerable look that curled around her heart. "We
brought you something. This is my daughter—"

The little girl shoved the big flat box at Kallista, then her
small hand tightly gripped Roman's tooled leather belt.
"The name is Cindi. I dot my *i*s with hearts. Cindi Blaylock
is the name. You know my dad. This is him…my dad,"
she said with pride, as though showing off a new bicycle.

She eyed Kallista; Cindi's small jaw said she'd fight to
hold her own. "I don't like sharing. He's mine."

Roman gently shook the girl's thin shoulder. "We talked
about this, remember? You're special to me in one way and
she's special in another."

"Yeah…I guess so. It's okay…until it isn't." She
grinned at him and then at Kallista, and back at Roman.
"He's in love with—"

"Hush." Roman's gaze slid slowly over Kallista's face,
taking in too much that she couldn't shield from him.
"You've got circles under your eyes, and you look thin."

Who did Roman love? The girl's mother? Kallista forced
herself to speak quietly. "I'm working to make a profit for
Boone's fifty-one percent."

"You're a pretty good hacker. Ro…er…ah…Dad thinks
you're smart. Say, I like those black combat boots. I'm
going to school here, when it starts."

Roman's gaze locked on the cameo at Kallista's throat,

tied by a black velvet ribbon. "I missed you," he said finally.

She didn't want to feel that impossible tug, that sudden lifting of her heart. Why should she want to touch him? Why should she trust him? The man offered her nothing but himself.

"Are you going to a funeral? Where did you get those neat moon earrings? Is black your favorite color? I like blue." Cindi peered up at her, then at Roman. "You guys can kiss, you know. I've seen that mushy stuff before. Yuck. Aren't you going to open this box?" she asked.

Roman reached out to smooth a long strand of Kallista's hair from her throat. His fingertip traced the velvet ribbon tied close to her throat and her pulse leaped to his touch. "I thought Cindi and I would get started painting ceramics—together. What do you recommend?"

"No more dog bowls," Cindi said, eyeing the unpainted bisque on the shelves. "The present is for you. Me and Dad did it. We ruined the first and second batch, but we did it the third time. Made a hell of a mess—"

She frowned up at Roman, who had just nudged her, and corrected carefully, "We made a big mess."

When Kallista opened the box, four starched and ruffled doilies lay neatly inside. Cindi peered at them, touching one high ruffle with her fingertip. "Can't believe that sugar water does that. We sat and starched Boone's doilies. My dad said these suckers need to be under flower vases. I'm going to plant some flowers at my dad's—at Boone's house, just like you did when you visited him. Did you know that I stayed with Boone when I was a five-year-old kid? We played poker, but now me and Dad play cards. Are those the prettiest doilies you ever saw? Boone's mother made them. Else is making me a dress with a collar that's crocheted from a long time ago. But I don't know if I like dresses."

"These are the prettiest doilies I've ever seen. You did

a good job," Kallista murmured, and wondered why she allowed Roman to take her hand, smoothing her fingers with his thumb.

"I'd like to try that date again," he murmured.

"I guess you liked the orchids. Titus said you had 'tears ashimmerin'' in your eyes. I made the box. Dad says he knows someone who would like to come take care of the orchids, and of the pigeons, too. They were kids at Boone's once, just like me. If he can get you to go on a date with him, I get to stay overnight at Else's with Patty Blaylock...'cause I didn't try to run away once this week. Ro...Dad kept me too busy, right with him every minute, and I was tuckered out, like Dusty said. But this place is okay and I might stay—" At Roman's gentle nudge, Cindi glanced up at his slight, warning frown. "Whoops."

Her eyes widened innocently. "I got a new bike. Pink. Not blue. But it's okay. Better than okay. Has streamers from the handgrips. Ah...I think I'll just go look at that big bunny on the shelf."

Alone, Kallista turned to Roman. When had she become so fragile? Where were her shields? All it took to destroy her walls were beautiful orchids. Roman walked into her shop with a little girl who was her exact youthful image, and all her determination turned to mush. "Take a note. I don't make second mistakes."

He spoke in the hushed tone she'd used. "You're mad."

"That's an understatement, Blaylock. I don't like broken dates, and I should have known better to trust you in the first place. I have to know about your daughter—did you love her mother?"

He searched her eyes, then shook his head. "No, I didn't."

"Figures. You've claimed a long-lost daughter and you didn't love her mother. You don't explain anything, do you?"

"I can tell you how I feel about you. You're a part of me and always will be."

She backed against the counter and Roman's hands braced at her hips, enclosing her. "Your eyes are saying things your mouth isn't, honey," he murmured. "I'd have come to you, if I could."

"Why would she want to run away from you?"

"It's an adjustment for her—"

He glanced at Cindi, who had just called to them. "Hey…ah…Dad, Patty is with her mother at Mamie's Café. Can I go see her?"

Cindi paused and shyly walked to Roman. She gripped his shirt and tugged. "You'll be here when I get back, won't you?"

Roman solemnly turned to the little girl. "I will…unless I can talk Kallista into coming over and having a piece of pie with us."

"You can't talk me into anything," Kallista said firmly, distrusting herself. One look at him and she was ready to toss away her pride.

He put his hand on the girl's shoulder. "I'm not going anywhere. I'm not leaving you. When I go, you come with me. You can see the truck with Luka and Igor in it from Mamie's Café. I'll either be here, or I'll come to the Café," he repeated carefully. "Watch for cars when you cross the street, okay? Go down to the crosswalk and wait for the light to cross, and mind your manners. You belong here…you're my daughter and you're a Blaylock now, remember?"

"Come down here," Cindi said, after a quick, wary glance at Kallista.

When Roman lowered to listen to her whisper, Cindi kissed his cheek. He held very still while she wrapped her arms around him for a hug, then straightened. He placed his hand on her shoulder once more and gave her a gentle squeeze. His tender, wistful expression caused Kallista to shiver; his Michaela, another man's daughter, would have been just as loved....

After the girl had hurried off, Kallista moved away from Roman to straighten the tiny unfinished picture frames on the shelf. "When are you leaving?" Roman asked quietly.

Was he so anxious to have her leave, to take another woman with his body? The question tore a piece of her heart away. "I never stay long in one place. But you know that—it was in your file on me."

"The cameo looks good on you," he murmured, coming up behind her.

She whirled to face him. If he touched her, she'd shatter. "Don't...don't touch me. Don't put your hands on me."

Roman tensed, his hand poised to smooth her hair, lowered slowly. The incredible pain in his expression stunned Kallista.... Just then Lettie Coleman, the attractive blonde who was rumored to be husband-hunting and wanted Roman or Rio, hurried into the shop. "Why, Roman, fancy meeting you here."

Lettie hurried to him, and fluttered her lashes up at him, her hand on his forearm. "I thought you might come over tonight...you and your daughter, and have supper with the girls and me. Fried chicken and mashed potatoes and apple dumplings," she offered temptingly and rubbed her fingers over Roman's bicep. "My, you Blaylocks are fine-looking men. Those Blaylock children almost put the urge into me to become a mother again. You've been moldy, Roman, but they say Blaylock men get that way until they're stirred up. You've been stirred up lately...and you're fine-looking."

Roman's gaze never left Kallista's. "Take your hands off me, Lettie. I'm taken. Kallista is wearing my mother's cameo."

Lettie was bred of the same sturdy pioneer stock as most of the people in the valley and she wasn't easily dismissed.

"That's news to me. She may be wearing that lovely old thing, but you're not wearing a wedding ring yet, honey."

Roman looked down at her and smiled slowly, the effect devastating. "Rio was asking about you. He likes apple dumplings."

Lettie's blue eyes widened. "Rio? Asking about me?"

After she hurried out of the shop in search of Rio, Roman's hand clamped on Kallista's wrist as she took a step away from him. "You're not going anywhere.... I can't explain, but what I feel for you is true. It won't change. Come out with me tonight."

He smiled again, that slow soft smile, and Kallista's heart fluttered and melted into warm mush. "I thought you didn't play games. Poor Rio."

"'Poor Rio' can handle himself." Then Roman slowly bent his head and brushed her lips with his. "You are a soft, soft woman, Kallista Bellamy. I'll pick you up after work."

"No one lays out my schedule. I haven't agreed to—" Kallista stopped, shaken by the sight of Roman placing her hand on his cheek. The softness and hunger in his dark eyes terrified her. She jerked back, rubbing her palm against her thigh and yet the impression of his warmth, the bones thrusting into her care, remained.

"I'm not leaving here until you've given me your answer. If you keep backing away from me, you're going to knock over that shelving."

"I don't want to plant flowers...or vegetables. I am not a farmer," she managed to say as Roman's thumb stroked her jaw.

He bent to place his lips against her skin, heating it. "Uh-huh. What's that got to do with us?"

She touched the cameo at her throat; other women had worn it, had fought their needs and their hearts. The lovely old, soft pink and cream pendant told of love and courtship and she should return it to the Blaylock family. She traced the ornate gold rim, smooth with age; a selfish part of her wanted to wear the reminder of those who had loved deeply just for a little while. Families. What did she know of them? Of love and hopes and shared dreams, and black-haired little babies and... From ingrained habit, she pushed away daydreams and locked herself to her goal. "I've had time to think in this last week, Roman. You intend to wait me out, don't you? You know that I don't stay long in one place, and if you can keep—"

Roman picked her up and plopped her on the counter. His hands braced on the surface at her hips, his hips between her legs. His tone was low, deadly, like the growl of a wolf. "You think that of me?"

She wouldn't back down. "I accept your offer of marriage—with conditions. I want to know everything. If that's the only way I can get the information I need, then to speed up the process, I'll marry you. Separate bedrooms, the same as with—"

"How I feel about you doesn't compare to my relationship with Debbie. You see, I want to hold you in my arms and love you all night through. I want to wake up beside you, and to give you my babies, if that's what you want. I want to grow old loving you." Panic skittered up her nape as Roman frowned. "But if you need separate bedrooms, then that's what you'll have."

"I have to get out of here, and apparently, marriage to you is the fastest way through this. After my mother's experiences, I know exactly how to dispose of a marriage," she said, terrified by the commitment Roman had offered her. "Cindi is important. She has to be included."

The arrangement was so cold, business plopped on the table, instead of a joining of lives. Kallista mourned getting attached to the little girl, only to leave her. She firmed her defences; when the time came to leave, she would know how to soften the break—her mother's mistakes had taught her everything about what was wrong and hurtful—and

Kallista would not hurt the girl. "You made an offer, Roman Blaylock. Are you taking it back? And who is Jeremy Llewlyn?"

Roman inhaled as though she had slapped him; the defensive shields were up, his body tense and his expression hard. "Why?"

What did Roman know? What had Boone told him? "He called. He says he's my uncle and Boone's son."

As he straightened, Roman gathered his secrets around him like a cold, dark cape. He almost frightened her now, his frown fierce, a vein pulsating at his temple, his fists at his sides. "Who have you told?"

"No one. I want the answers from you."

"Then we'd better get married. I'm not breaking my word to Boone. I'd appreciate it if you'd make my family think you care a bit about me…and my daughter. We'll need time to do that, and meanwhile I'll see that Jeremy doesn't call you again. We can start with that date tonight."

He turned suddenly, his broad back to her. His body tensed and shuddered, and then he studied the floor. After a long moment, he said quietly, "A week ought to give Else enough time for that cake."

"Two weeks," she shot back, bargaining for time to think properly.

"Good enough. Two weeks then." He turned, smoothed his hand along her cheek and whispered, "You won't let Boone down, Kallista. You're a strong, righteous woman, and I'll always be faithful to you. I'll always return to you, when the day is done…because you're a part of me. I'll treat you with respect and honor you as best I know how."

"I should hit you over the head with this pot," she whispered back, when she could, her gaze filling with him. Roman's simple words could melt her bones and…

Roman chuckled and Kallista could do little but stare at him and wonder who he was and who she was and where they were going and why she wanted to launch herself upon him.

Instead she grinned back at him, and wondered why suddenly, everything seemed bright and new and exciting.

Later that night, while Cindi slept with Patty at Else's, Kallista melted beneath Roman's body on the front seat of his pickup, tiny white orchids dotting her hair. With the placing of each orchid, Roman had discussed Cindi and the wedding with Kallista. He'd moved closer, a methodical pursuit, which thrilled and disarmed her, until he'd gently eased her beneath him.

Now, Kallista looked up at Roman's rumpled hair, his tender smile as his hand skimmed her lace-covered breasts, shaping them. She'd opened his shirt, and his expression had been disbelieving and humbled when she'd placed her hands on his tanned chest, examining the textures. She couldn't resist a nibble here and there; she could have devoured him and come back for more. "You said you wanted just one kiss."

"I did," he said, bending to nuzzle her face with his. The familiar heat rose instantly between them. She parted her lips for Roman's and met the exciting play of his tongue with her own. Roman was a delight to taste, to explore, and he breathed unevenly as he took an orchid from her hair and placed it between her breasts. "Now I want more. Your mouth isn't righteous, honey. Nor the way you move beneath me, like warm silk."

"You're mashing me," she whispered as he nibbled on her bottom lip and his hand smoothed her thigh, bringing her leg around his hip, her leg tangled with his. His thumb stayed to caress the back of her knee.

"Tonight, when I saw you in this short skirt, I wanted to do this—" His hand grazed her thigh, curved slowly over it and smoothed a heated path down to the top of her boots. Roman braced slightly away, and the movement served to bring his burgeoning, thrusting heat intimately closer to her. He glanced down their tangled bodies, hungry and urgent. He placed his open hand on her stomach, a contrast of his pagan dark strength and her pale soft skin. His thumb ran over her hipbone, traced the jut of it and then the other: his fingertips lightly circled the area below her navel, and she knew he was thinking of the children he wanted.

His finger ran around the elastic of her briefs, then his hand pressed lower, searching.... "You were so hot and tight that first time, I—" He swallowed tightly as if forcing back emotion and then his mouth covered hers urgently; she held her breath, waiting, and his touch caressed, then entered gently as her fingers dug into his shoulders.

When Kallista could think again, her body floating gently back to earth, she realized that Roman probably ached, his expression taut, his body shuddering and tense above hers. That fierce glitter hidden beneath his lashes, the set of his jaw, and his fingers digging slightly into her hip told her that though Roman wanted more, he was letting her set the rules. She smoothed his cheek, drew his lips down to hers and trailed kisses along his face. "I get to you, don't I?" she asked, thrilled that he lay so humbly within her keeping. "Think how much I can torture you if this wedding goes through."

"If? It's damn well going to happen." He groaned shakily, and when he reached to pull himself up, using the steering wheel, Kallista's hand bumped the parking brake and the pickup began to roll down the hill. Roman tugged her upright, glanced hungrily at her lace-covered breasts and then tried to brake the pickup. "Hold on."

The bumpy ride down the hill was short and not dangerous, and Kallista found herself giggling as Roman cursed. The pickup smashed through a corral, tangled in barbed wire and came to a stop in the middle of the pasture, surrounded by white-faced Herefords.

"I like the sound of that," Roman murmured, easing her hair back from her cheek. "You sound happy."

She fluttered her eyelashes at him and smiled coyly. "I'm about to get what I want."

But Roman was staring at her breasts. "You're so pale and soft, so delicate, like that orchid. I could hurt you easily," he whispered unevenly, his fists squeezing the steering wheel until it creaked.

She didn't feel delicate; she knew exactly how a volcano might feel before bursting into the sky. Roman's gentle exploration along her back and the confining lace had been frustrating. "The hook is in the front."

"That's something new, isn't it?" he asked rawly.

"It's not new."

"To me, it is," he admitted shakily. "Lace isn't—"

Her finger stopped the rest of his words. She wanted Roman's chest against hers without lace barriers. She shook with the need to fit her body close to his, to feel the beating of his heart on her, within her, pulsing deeply....

Roman jerked his gaze away from her, groaned and shoved open the door. He stepped onto the pickup's bed and leaped to the moonlit ground. Holding out his arms, his order was hushed, careful not to wake Titus and Dusty in the bunkhouse. "Jump. Trust me and jump."

Kallista eased to the running board, studied the way Roman stood, his legs wide, braced upon the pasture, his shirt open and his hair rumpled. His boyish grin and chuckle surprised her. "You think I won't?" she asked, then gathered herself to leap.

"Afraid of me?"

There was Roman's old fear, never far away. "Never," she said, meaning it.

Roman caught her firmly, laughed aloud as though delighted. When she placed an orchid in his hair, he stopped, his look fierce and passionate and then he began to run to Boone's house. He didn't stop until he'd carried her up the stairs to the big four-poster bed and dumped her on it, following her down with his body. He grinned at her. "Now, Miss Sassy Mouth, what have you got to say?"

"Love me," she whispered, aching for him, to tether the restless need haunting her since she'd last touched him.

Roman's smile died, his gaze slowly taking in her body. Again, in that humble gesture, he placed her hands on his face, as though all he could be, would be, rested in her keeping as he kissed her palms. "Let's do this right this time, Kallie," he whispered unevenly and stood to undress.

Kallista stood on the other side of the bed, shaken by the depth of her emotions—not only the need to have Roman's body fill hers, but the need to hold him close and keep him safe, and deeper needs, which terrified her.

Undressed now, Roman's body gleamed in the moonlight as he eased beneath the sheet, and lay down, his head upon the pillow. "Come to bed, honey...leave the cameo on," he murmured softly, and she knew that tonight was the wedding night that Roman wanted.

She undressed slowly, aware of Roman's hunger as it pulsated around her, hurried the urgent tempo in her. When she was draped in moonlight and terror of the emotions within her, she slid Boone's moon earrings from her. She placed them on the starched doily beside a picture of the old man she had loved. She eased beneath the sheet and turned to look at Roman, a new man whom she both feared would change her life and whom she needed. "This is some first date."

He wrapped her hair around his finger, bringing it to his lips. "I want to make an impression."

Then he lay down and put his arms behind his head. Her mouth dried and her body trembled, waiting.... Roman looked at her. "I can't think about anything but you. You fit my arms perfectly, honey."

She'd heard prettier words, but Roman's affected her more deeply and again that strange, unfamiliar sense of

coming home curled around her. The night fell hushed and
warm upon them, a fragrant breeze rustling the curtains at
the window. He turned to her, his hand over hers. ''I like
how you laugh. It ripples out of you like a fresh spring
brook.''

She hadn't laughed very much in her lifetime and as she
adjusted the orchid in Roman's sleek black hair, she knew
that this man could awake passions she hadn't known, tenderness she hadn't experienced....

She closed her eyes, savoring the sweet moment, as Roman's arms went around her to draw her close to his body.
He held her gently, stroking her hair, and there in that dear,
sweet room, filled with memories of a kind old man, Kallista gave herself to Roman's gentle, trembling, sweeping
touch. He gathered her to him as if he'd found a treasure,
as if he wanted to make her a part of him forever, for the
good times and bad, as if when he loved her, he'd still love
her the same way when they were old and rocking on the
front porch. His reverence was magic, calming her restless
spirit. She opened herself to him, sighed when he slowly
filled her, stretching her and waiting until she adjusted.
Then so complete nothing could tear them apart, she held
him close. Kallista felt as though she'd fought the world to
be here, now...with Roman. She trusted him now, loved
him....

Kallista shivered, Roman's hard, bare chest dragging
against her nipples as he bent to place his mouth upon her
breast, the gentle and warm suction causing her to open, to
meet the rhythm of his easy thrusts, his hands cupping her
hips, lifting her higher, higher... Out there on that burning
plane, she burst into pieces and sensed that she would never
be the same.

With Roman resting over her, heavy, secure and warm,
she found the peace she'd been seeking all her life. When
she sensed him preparing to move away, she kept him

close, protested with a murmur, smoothing his back, his hips, his thighs resting within hers.

*Peace.* She'd found what she'd needed, she thought drowsily, as Roman nuzzled her face with his, a gentle, sweet claiming.

Twice more before dawn, they made love, with Roman protecting her as he had that first time—bodies hungry, hearts pounding, and then the heavenly, gentle release. Roman's shudder and release were leashed, his body trembling, damp, sleek, rippling with the aftershocks. That was when he came to her, and she knew the power of making love, gathering him close. He lay against her, sweet and lax and warm and sated, his heart slowing, and Kallista soothed his tense shoulders, a peace she had never known curling around her.

Again Kallista awoke, her body spooned by Roman's big one, his arms around her, his lips moving at her cheek, his body flowing rhythmically against hers, seeking entrance. Filled with the scents of their lovemaking, the room held echoes of their sounds, the racing of their hearts, the quickening of breath and tangled bodies shifting on the old bed, of pleasured sighs and Roman's quiet murmurs.

Meadowlarks trilled, Moby the rooster crowed, and men yelled. Kallista blinked, tethering Roman's wandering hands with her own. "Roman?" She sent an elbow back at him and he grunted.

"Roman?" she whispered again as the sound of buzzing saws ripped through the early morning.

"Come back here, sweetheart," he murmured drowsily, cupping her breasts.

"Stop that," she ordered as Roman began kissing the side of her throat and his thumb ran across her nipple, peaking it. "Listen."

"I want to see you, honey—uh!"

James Blaylock's voice cut through the peaceful sounds

of a country morning. "Back that digger over here. Roman's plans for the addition say the foundation starts here, and we'll need to bury the plumbing lines right here—by this red stake."

Logan shouted over the sound of the power saws. "He wants both fireplaces blocked in for now, the one in the bedroom comes first and the other we'll do comes later, but the heat and cooling vents go here. Titus, don't pick that up. Let me."

"Here come the lumber trucks," Dusty called. "Some damn fool left Roman's pickup tangled up in that barbed wire. The seat is covered with orchids. Someone mashed the tar out of them."

"Roman," Kallista managed quietly through her shock, "if we can hear them that plainly with the window open, they could hear—"

He nuzzled the side of her throat. "They weren't here when you gave yourself to me. There was no one but me to hear that sweet cry."

"Roman." Kallista swallowed, trying to find reality. "You shouted as if your life was being squeezed from you."

He chuckled, a rich rumbling sound against her ear, his tongue flicking her earlobe. "I was being squeezed all right and pretty pleased about it."

His arousal nudged her intimately and Roman groaned hungrily. "Kallie, you're so tight and hot inside, and the scent of you—"

She almost—almost—pushed against him, Roman's strong hand sliding between her thighs, opening her...

"Roman? Breakfast is ready," Else called from the kitchen. "Cindi and Patty are still sleeping, but they'll ride their bikes over when they wake up. Rio is with them. With the whole Blaylock tribe here and working this week, the addition ought to be ready for the wedding."

Kallista flipped over to stare at Roman's face, firmly

placing the sheet between them. When his head started toward her breasts, she pushed his face up to hers. "Oh, no. Not that. I can't think—and you know I can't think—when you do that nibbling, biting, suckling.... You planned all this in the space of yesterday afternoon. I thought we were going to discuss how to proceed."

"Now, Kallie," he began as she hit him with the pillow. He tore it away from her and reached out to grab her ankle as she fled, pulling her back into bed. "You're not going anywhere."

The statement was flat, hard, and unlike the gentle lover of last night. This was the man she sensed lurking beneath his leashed passions. This was a man she wanted as fiercely, one who would meet her without reserve, giving and taking everything. She grabbed the sheet between them, shy of him now. She bucked beneath his weight, his hands pressing her wrists to the bed. "I'm going to murder you, Roman Blaylock. You planned all this...and went right on without me." She tugged up the sheet that he was slowly drawing downward. "Don't you dare look at me. Don't you dare."

If he looked at her in that solemn, dark way, as though she fascinated him, and he wanted more, and the heat from his touch could burn her, and... But Roman looked at her steadily. "Once you'd agreed to marry me, I didn't see reason to waste time. There's that separate bedroom thing, you know," he thrust at her. "It's going to be damn hard to keep my hands off you, and you know it."

Roman's sudden temper startled her, that grim determination to keep her locked to him. She wasn't frightened, but she wasn't certain how to handle his sudden temper. "I could leave you at the altar...embarrass you. Then how would you look, planning a wedding and a home without me?"

"You won't. And if you did, I'd just have to come after you. I know a good thing when I see it...you're perfect."

*Perfect.* A little happy butterfly fluttered around her heart. Now how did a woman argue with that? "How do you know I won't leave you high and dry?"

He grinned boyishly and for the first time, bent to playfully nuzzle her throat. "Why, Kallie, you like to kiss me too much. You get all wild and hot and—"

While she was mulling how to deny that truth, trying not to blush under his hungry look, and holding the sheet high to her chin, Roman bent to kiss her, slow and tenderly. "There's something I—"

"I can't take any more news this morning, Roman-dear," she said firmly, meaning it.

Roman sighed slowly and eased from the bed. Kallista couldn't resist peeking at his tall rippling body as he dressed. It seemed impossible that such a strong man, tall, rawboned, all cords and muscles, could be so tender. She frowned. In lovemaking, Roman had been oddly tender, as if fearing to hurt her. She flopped over on her stomach and tried not to want him.

The edge to his voice, *"You're not going anywhere,"* should have terrified her—she'd heard those words before. But with Roman, she wanted to pit herself against him and enjoy the game, to push him to his limits and see what happened. All in all, Roman Blaylock was an exciting game.

Roman's friendly pat on her bottom stayed to become a caress, and both big hands shaped her bottom. The ragged sound of his breath filled the room and she tensed, already warming for his touch. "You're pretty when you're riled, all hot and wild like you'd like to tear something apart. When you're ready, try me—" he whispered against her ear, then nibbled it. Another pat and he was gone, closing the bedroom door and whistling as if everything was just peachy.

"Well, it isn't," Kallista muttered. In her lifetime, she'd kept her moods hidden. She walked away when situations became tense, tangled with emotions, and she never looked back. She blew away the crushed orchid in front of her nose. "'Hot and wild.' We'll see just who is hot and wild, Blaylock."

Kallista lightly ran her fingers over the crushed orchid, the bruised creamy petals dotted with deep purple. She'd intended to rip Boone's estate from Roman's keeping, and now she was tangled in long slow sultry looks and soft words, and Roman's fiercely honed, passionate expression when they made love. Life was no longer simple.

The woman wearing his shirt and starting the lumber truck wasn't happy. Roman took one look at Kallista's glare at him, and knew that if he let her get away now... He began to run after the truck, filled with bouncing boards, then hopped up on the running board. He grimaced as she shot through the field, crashing a wooden cattle loading chute on the way to her home. "Now, honey," he began, avoiding her swatting hand, and wondered where he went wrong in claiming his love. "Have you...?"

Roman groaned as she sideswiped a small wooden storage shed. It wobbled, leaned, then flopped to the ground. Unprepared for a steaming woman, he asked gently, "Ah...have you had your breakfast this morning? Do you need that morning cup of cappuccino before you make any rash decisions?"

She swatted him furiously. With her hair blowing wildly around her face, Kallista glared at him. "*You* know that I didn't sleep much last night...and everyone in Jasmine and surrounding counties knows that I spent the night with you. It's probably on the radio's morning coffee show now, right up there with advertisements for chicken feed. I'm a private person, Roman Blaylock, and I'm not used to having family everywhere. Get off my running board."

Roman tried to speak calmly. A stormy woman driving a big lumber truck, loaded with boards, didn't do a lot to preserve this morning's groom-feeling and walking-on-air delight. "Ah…honey. There's a barn straight ahead."

"I know that. You were gone for a week. No explanations. Then you…we…I'm not prepared for all this, Mr. Blaylock. Let alone facing a ranch yard full of your family this morning. And that was just the men. What would I say to the women and the children, and to…whomever?" Kallista braked quickly, and the truck skidded to a stop just inches from the barn. Before Roman could think of some morning-after niceties for the woman he wanted to marry and love his entire lifetime, Kallista had shoved open the door and bolted to the house.

Roman took one look at her hair flowing behind her as she stalked to the house, her bottom curving beneath his shirt. Oh, my, he purely appreciated that little soft quiver! His mouth dried at the sight of her long legs flashing, slight muscles above her boots, reminding him of how she'd held him, tangled him close and loved him. Roman groaned shakily. After swatting his hat on his thigh and a round of good honest cursing, he followed her.

"Unlock this door, honey," he called as sweetly as his deep voice would allow. He glanced back at the lumber truck. Someone had just started the engine, revving it.

With a wave and a grin, James was backing it, preparing to turn around and take the lumber back to the Llewlyn house. "Women," James called cheerfully. "Welcome to the land of damned if you do, and damned if you don't."

"Get lost." After that brotherly snarl, Roman turned his attention to the door separating him from his love.

*Love.* The word winded him, slammed into him sideways, and stunned all his other thoughts straight out of his mind. He'd said it before; he meant it now. "That's it, then," Roman muttered to himself. "I love her, pure and simple. I'll get this right."

"You're overconfident, Blaylock," she called to him through the door. "You stepped out there and told the world, your family, that we were getting married. Now, that is real confidence, because at this point I want to murder you."

"I'm confident this door isn't standing between us, sweetheart," he answered with determination, and reached for the key over the door frame—

"Oh, well, oh, well, oh, well. I might have known," Kallista said before she hurled a pot at him. "Everyone knew I was with you last night, Blaylock. Don't you think that's a bit embarrassing for me?"

"Now, honey…" Roman replaced the pot to the table and caught the shoe she threw at him. He placed his hands on his hips and stood there, admiring the woman he loved, all fired up and raw, glittering in honest emotion and then he closed the door.

Kallista shimmered in the morning light coming through the sheer curtains. With dignity, she lifted her chin, straightened her shoulders and walked to the bathroom door. With her hand on the doorknob, she said quietly, firmly, "I expect you to be gone when I come out."

# Nine

Roman leaned back against the bathroom wall and waited for Kallista's shower to end. Herbally scented steam circled him, and through the layers he saw his mirrored image—hard, dark and unshaven. This wary man knew how to manage acres of stock and Boone's financial kingdom, but not how to handle the woman he wanted as his wife. He studied the oval cameo, still warm from Kallista's throat, delicate against the scarred width of his palm. He ran his fingers over the tiny black velvet ribbon and traced the worn golden flowers holding the soft pink and creamy bust of a woman.

Bust. Bosom. Kallista's pale, soft—Roman swallowed and tried not to look at the shapely shadow painted on the shower curtain.

While Kallista's unique cinnamony scent curled around him, mixed with that of her soap, Roman considered his need to carry her off and make her his own. A week in bed might ease his physical needs, but he wanted more for Kallista. Women were mystical creatures; he had never tried to see into their intricacies and now he was mired in a bog of feminine sensibility. He studied the rosebud wallpaper she'd selected, the dainty array of feminine brushes and bottles upon the vanity surface. He was a plain man, with little charm to offer. He bent to collect Kallista's panties and bra and studied the fragile black lace within his hands, scarred and calloused by work. He gently placed the lace on the counter, fearing that it would distract him from making peace with Kallista. He trusted her on a level that surprised him; he knew that she wouldn't do anything to hurt Boone's memory. She wouldn't harm Cindi, or the other Innocents.

Roman ran a fingertip across a tiny, delicate fern and it quivered beneath his touch, just like Kallista. Would she walk away when she had learned all she needed?

Would she tear a part of his heart away and throw it into the dust? None of that would change his love for her.

Roman inhaled unsteadily and tensed as the shower water stopped and the soft green curtain was pulled back. After a slight wince, Kallista stepped from the steamy enclosure. She lifted her arms to smooth back her wet hair, and her eyes locked on him. Grabbing a lush jade towel, she pulled it in front of her as her face began to flush.

Roman Blaylock believed in magic at that moment. She looked like a woodland nymph, caught stepping from her flower petal, dew beading, glittering on her skin like diamonds. With a tenderness that far exceeded anything he'd ever felt, ever allowed himself to feel, Roman studied her shy blush, her gleaming shoulders and let his eyes wander appreciatively down to the thighs that had cradled him last night. He wanted to touch her there, feel that silky moist warmth and soothe her. "You're moving like you hurt. Deep inside. Are you all right?"

"I am. I just found a few new muscles, that's all. I'm

an athletic woman...a power swimmer. I'll adjust. Now get out of my bathroom.''

"I want this settled," Roman said quietly and damned himself for wanting her when she was already aching. "Are you going to run away from me every time you get mad?''

"No." She blew a drop of water from her lip. "I'm going to throw things at you. But don't worry, Cindi won't see me destroy you.''

"Last night was..." Roman floundered and smoothed his thumb across the drop of water on her eyebrows. "Special," he said for lack of words to suit the depth of his emotions.

She shivered, glaring up at him, her fists locked in the jade toweling. "You know, don't you? You know about—''

"The stepfather who tried to rape you? Yes. Boone told me. He told me that you were afraid of being held too tightly.''

"So you didn't. You took me so softly I thought I'd dreamed each time. That wasn't fair, Blaylock.''

He took a matching towel and patted the moisture from her face, her throat and shoulders. "I mean well," he said simply and tried to avoid looking at the mirror behind her. He could almost feel her back in his hands, the curve of her waist between his hands, those soft hips undulating against him—he shivered and realized that moisture beaded his forehead and upper lip.

"Why are you building that addition?''

"Boone's things need to remain as they are, for now. I wanted something you could claim for your own, the way women like to do...and I'm not certain if I can keep from carrying you to my bed." He wanted a new home for Kallista, something untouched by his past life, or by his obligations to Boone. He wanted to be a part of the home, the making of it, helping Kallista make it her home, too. He had visions of that grand old furniture, refinished and gleaming in the firelight, while he held his wife, his love, close and safe against him. But lying next to her a futon would seem like heaven.

"That's a lot of house for you when I leave."

"That it will be. But I'll have you to remember…and last night." Roman eased her wet hair aside and reached to tie the ends of the ribbon at her nape.

When Kallista placed her hand on his cheek, Roman kissed her palm. "You're all I want, that I'll ever want for the rest of my days," he said simply and drew the towel away from her, easing her into his arms.

"You…I…the way you talk is—"

"Exactly how I feel about you." He breathed unsteadily, holding her close, her hair fragrant against his lips.

"You were so careful last night," she whispered against his throat.

"I was. It's a powerful feeling I have for you, sweetheart. I was afraid I'd hurt you."

She shivered as his hands caressed her back. "I don't know what to do. I like Else and your family. It's wrong to deceive them."

"They know you make me happy." Roman brushed her face with his, lightly, so as not to scrape her soft skin with his morning beard. "I haven't had time to shave."

"I want the truth from you, Roman Blaylock…when you tell me about Boone and when you hold me in your arms. Promise me that."

"I do." Roman stared down at the twin damp spots, left from her breasts, on his shirt and his body jolted into hardness.

She followed his gaze before he could look away, shield the desire within him, and slowly Kallista moved her hand lower, covering him. She'd been timid in their lovemaking and he'd tried to be gentle.

In his lifetime, Roman Blaylock had not been intimately caressed. He jerked, stunned by the fierce need to enter her, lock their bodies together and fly into the heat. "Damn it, Kallie, you can't just reach out and touch a man."

"Why not? You touched me."

Roman ran his shaking hands roughly over his face. At this point, he wasn't certain of his control with Kallista. When she unzipped his jeans, staring at him, Roman groaned. The sight of his body, heavy with desire, spilling into her inquisitive hands, almost took him over the edge.

"Be careful with me," he said and then fought the wave of heat rising up his throat. He felt outdated and pure country, or like a lonely old wolf.

She smiled, and the impish curve to her lips delighted him. "Why? Are you delicate?"

"Damned delicate," he admitted rawly and fought a shudder as the tip of her finger slid across him. "Where you're concerned."

The steamy mirror revealed her tapering back, her lush hips and before Roman knew his intent, he'd lifted her, bracing her back against the wall.

"Roman!" Her cry was startled and pleased him even as he entered her. Kallista's legs held his hips tightly, and she curled her arms around his shoulders and kissed him as if nothing could stop her. He opened her lips with his tongue, his body thrusting heavily into her warmth, and with a muffled shout as his passion poured out of him, Roman realized that Kallista's pleasured cry had mated with his own.

They stared at each other, breathing hard, hearts racing. "If you put me down, I can't stand," Kallista whispered unevenly. "What was that?"

He sounded dazed, "I don't know.... I should have— I just look at you and I—"

"You are an exciting man, Roman Blaylock. Don't you dare say you're sorry."

He grinned, feeling as if all the years had been lifted away from him. "I'd like to try that silly futon."

"You wouldn't fit."

He lowered her feet to the floor, still wondering how they could come together so fast and hot like a summer lightning storm.

Her eyes were cool, shielded, reminding him of the lush grass in a woodland meadow. "That first time—I closed my eyes after one look at you. Then last night was in the dark, and it wasn't enough and that terrifies me. But I'm not afraid of you, Roman Blaylock. I can't make promises to stay. I wasn't bred to home and hearth and families, like you."

Roman straightened his clothing, a little embarrassed that he'd been so hungry for her. "Else said I ought to be ashamed of myself for moving too fast with you. She hit me with her wooden spoon this morning—"

Kallista smoothed his hair, and he was encouraged by her soft look. Was it for him? But maybe that was her goodbye look? Her fingers flowed down his hair to his nape, caressing his skin, and Roman resisted the urge to shiver as he said, "She said I'd better marry you, and that I should have asked you about the addition. I'm used to making decisions for myself, and haven't had time to consider how to make a woman feel good. You have her for a friend when you need—"

He looked down at her soft breasts snuggled close to him and his throat dried. "I don't think we'd better..."

"You're frightened of me, aren't you?"

Frightened? He was terrified. "I'm scared stiff of myself...how I feel about you. Think of what just happened, there against that wall. Kallista, I'm afraid that I...I could hurt you when I'm...making love to you. Inside you is so sweet and close and tight that I—"

"You didn't hurt me."

"I could have—I did that first time." The admission was raw and painful, that in his passion he feared he'd release his terrifying need of her. The knock that had just sounded on the bathroom door startled Roman. "What?"

A cultured Southern male voice asked, "Would a Miss Kallista Bellamy happen to be in there?"

"Channing! It's you! How wonderful! I'll be right out," Kallista called and hurried to replace Roman's borrowed shirt.

"Not like that you're not," Roman said as she wrapped a towel around her hair, turban-style. The delight in her voice nettled him. He studied the damp shirt over her breasts and reached to drape a large dry towel around her shoulders.

She reached to smooth his hair. "I've worked for Channing for years, but he's my friend. Now you just be nice to him."

When Roman showed his teeth, Kallista pushed a firm finger against his chest. "You...be...nice."

"I always am, honey," he stated grimly, already planning to evict the intruder who delighted Kallista.

She stood on tiptoe to kiss his cheek, surprising him. "Not always, and that's when I like you best. When everything is pouring out of you and you're not holding anything back. I do like that," she repeated.

In the living room, Channing Boudreaux the Third's well-cut hair ran in dark waves to his silk collar, his tan revealing a man who spent time in the sun. Carrying a filled grocery sack, he was dressed in an elegant three-piece suit and wearing a grin as Kallista and Roman entered the living room. "Your shirt is wet, whoever you are," he drawled in amused Southern tones and placed the sack on a table.

Kallista glanced at the two wet spots on Roman's shirt and stepped in front of him. Faced with a man from Kallista's past life, a man she thought of as a friend, Roman placed his hands on her shoulders. For just that heartbeat, she leaned against him, her soft body comforting him. The other man noted the action, eyes narrowing.

"You look…wonderful." Channing bent to kiss Kallista and Roman tensed. Channing looked up with just enough amusement to cover the dangerous narrowing of his eyes. "Are you going to introduce us, Kallista?"

"We're getting married next week. I'm Roman Blaylock." Roman met Channing's gaze over Kallista's head, and drew her back to him.

"Two weeks," Kallista corrected. "If his manners improve."

"That's fast. And explains the orchid in your hair. You carry that off quite well, old man. But then Kallista is like that, once she's made up her mind she wants something. I hate to lose my best resort troubleshooter. She did a wonderful job at Nassau.… Darling, I've been worried about you," Channing said, his cool eyes locked with Roman's. "You didn't come home last night and I made myself at home on your futon."

"'Futon,'" Roman heard himself mutter and grimaced as Kallista's elbow jarred his ribs.

"Wonderful! You're staying here, of course, with me. I'll make coffee and we can talk. Sorry, not a biscotti around." Channing's "darling" was beaming up at the two men, obviously delighted.

Roman wasn't in the mood for catch-up talk between Kallista and a man who looked as though he matched her. Biscotti weren't ham and eggs and he was country to Channing's polished good looks. Together, Kallista and Channing looked as if they suited each other. A lonely chill sank into the heart of Roman Blaylock. "I have work to do. Trying to get ahead of the wedding. I'll want my bride to myself, you know," he added pointedly to the man who had slept on Kallista's futon.

"Nice meeting you, Mr. Blaylock." Channing's tone held just enough warning to lift Roman's hackles.

Kallista crossed her arms and eyed Roman. "I think you

could stay, if you wanted. After all, everyone is at your place building that addition, aren't they?''

"Now, darling, I'm certain Roman has something he needs doing—''

Roman asked the question that had just slammed into him. "Is he staying here? At night?''

Kallista's expression was cool; her tone was a challenge. "He certainly is. You don't have a problem with that, do you?''

"Not a bit,'' he lied tightly. He tried the word "darling'' on his lips and it wouldn't fit. Channing had used "darling.'' *Darling*. What kind of a real man would say words like that?

The rumpled futon mocked him.

"Shake hands, sweetheart,'' Kallista ordered. One look down at her set face and Roman stretched out his hand. He didn't find it easy to extend a friendly greeting to a man Kallista adored, who made her voice lilt with delight and made her eyes light—but if she wanted...

Channing lifted his hand to meet Roman's, amusement in his honey brown eyes. "You're an unusual choice for Kallista. She's very...cosmopolitan,'' he said quietly, "but I think you'll do. You look like a man who gives his word as a solemn promise. You'd die for her, wouldn't you?''

"I would.'' Roman caught the slender hand that Kallista had just placed in his and brought it to his mouth. He retrieved his hat and summoned his pride to leave his bride-to-be with a man she adored.

"*Adieu,* sweet prince—uh!'' Channing's dashing farewell was cut short by Kallista's sharp elbow.

It was crystal clear to Roman Blaylock as he stalked across the field back to Boone's house that he'd never before been jealous, and that jealousy wasn't an emotion he enjoyed. But he hadn't loved a woman, either, and he could take whatever she gave him. She'd given him everything in that steamy bathroom, shattering, clenching him, her desire as immediate as his own. He settled into a determined mood—the woman he loved was living with another man...a good-looking, smooth mannered, continental play-boy type. In the next two weeks, he didn't have time to be sweet. He had a house addition to build and he was behind on Boone's business. He wanted to hold Kallista in his arms, but if he did, he'd want more. He glared at Rio, who was grinning, and because his brother needed a taste of humility, Roman leaped upon him.

A rap from Else's wooden spoon didn't feel like a caress and after rolling on the dirt, Roman and Rio began laughing.

"She'll either show up for the wedding, or she won't," Roman said to Else, who knew everything about him.

"She'll show. You two are a match."

Roman clung to that small bit of information, until he caught Else alone later. "What do you mean, we're 'a match'?"

"I changed your diapers and watched you grow up. Watched you hurt and bleed, and now you're glowing, Mr. Roman Blaylock. She lights up when she looks at you, and you can take that to the church."

For the two weeks, Roman grabbed that glimmer of hope with both fists, repeated it to himself as if it were a litany, and ached for Kallista. It was then that he discovered that telephone calls from an intended bride could be torturous...and erotic.

He'd come for her five times, waiting for her in the night, waiting to carry her to his sleeping bag. Only the soft surprised cry of her delight, her body clenching his, her arms and legs and mouth fusing their passion, kept him sane. Then the dawn would come too soon, and lying in his arms, Kallista would turn to him, already soft and warm and hungry....

# Ten

**K**allista held tightly to Channing's arm as they walked slowly down the flower decked aisle to the altar, where Roman waited. As best man, Rio stood next to him; Dan, Logan, James, and Tyrell stood all in a row, equally tall and dark, black hair gleaming in the light from the stained-glass windows.

Panic ran through her in an icy stream; what was this traditional wedding leading up to? She wasn't used to traditions; content to fly in her own world, free from tethers, she had lived so differently from Roman's sisters-in-law. There would be expectations of a Blaylock wife—could she meet them?

She touched the cameo at her throat. Other women had worn it, loved it. Blaylock women. Mothers of Blaylock children, the matrons in charge of keeping a family safe and strong. *A Blaylock wife. She'd be Roman's wife. What did "wife" actually mean—in assigned duties...?*

At the altar, Roman waited solemnly, the white collar of

his shirt a contrast to his deeply tanned skin. With his hair neatly brushed, he looked like someone she didn't know—couldn't...couldn't...

*You'll be fine, Kallie-girl.* Big Boone's voice curled gently around her and she faltered, shaken. *I'm right here beside you.* But Boone wasn't here, not to hold her and keep her safe, and she had to run away.

"You're crushing my best Armani," Channing whispered.

"What am I doing here?" she whispered, the veil over her face fluttering with her breath. She tried to smile at Cindi, who was hurling flower petals at the Simpson boy, rather than the carpet. This was a church meant for families, for marriages that lasted, and...

Roman was wearing a new suit—Else had just hurried to him and snipped a price tag from under his arm. A new suit and a new life...new...new...new...

Channing was steady as always, unflappable. "You're here showing off my sister's designer wedding gown for one thing—though she never would have thought of white combat boots—and for another, you're marrying that cowboy. Do you want to?"

Kallista gripped the rose-and-bleeding-heart bouquet in her fists. "Yes, I do. I'm going to make him pay. You have no idea what he said to me on the telephone."

Roman's deep uneven descriptions of how he felt when he was inside her, how soft she was against him, and the fragrance she emitted when she... Kallista swallowed tightly. "He can look innocent—he isn't. He's quite predatory. He looks slow and easy, but he pounces. Channing, the man is a taker."

"Whatever he's doing, you look wonderful, darling. I appreciated the extra futon he sent to your house, after I declined the offer to stay at Llewlyn House. The man has class and good taste. Now don't worry about a thing. Your precious Bisque Café will be safe in my hands." Channing chuckled and with a flourish lifted her hand to Roman's. "Good luck, old man. She's in a snit," Channing purred as he stepped back and sat by Else.

Else smoothed Channing's collar, straightened his tie and patted the little cowlick at the back of his head—he looked wary and edged slightly away from her. She smiled brightly and studied his cowlick as though searching for an idea to hold it in place. A blush began to rise beneath Channing's tan.

Kallista looked up through the lace to Roman. The message that his eyes were telling her dried her throat and trembled sweetly around her heart. She held his hand tightly and Roman looked down at her sharply. Then he reached to place his arm around her and to draw her to his side. "This will do," he told the minister quietly.

Roman's vows were given in a strong, solemn tone, and Kallista heard herself speaking as firmly. When the minister pronounced them married, Roman gently lifted back her veil and bent to kiss the tears from her eyes. Because she saw his eyes mist, she reached to place her hand on the back of his head, tugging him down so that she could kiss his damp lashes. She hadn't comforted a man before, hadn't been touched by his tears. As he had before, in that strangely humbling, wonderfully endearing gesture, Roman held her hand, lifting it to his lips before resting his face within her palm. "I will remember you like this, for all the days of my life," he whispered unevenly. "I'll see my bride coming toward me."

He straightened and smoothed her hair, the style old-fashioned and piled high, with tendrils along her face and nape. "My wife."

The impact of those quiet words and Roman's tender smile jarred Kallista. She parted her lips to speak, then his mouth brushed hers lightly.

In the rush after the ceremony, Kallista couldn't spot Roman. Cindi held her hand and grinned up at her impishly.

"He's got things to do."

"He's run off, leaving me to face this...all this. When I get my hands on him—"

"Time to change clothes," Else said, pushing Kallista into a small room and following her. The Blaylock women were waiting, hurrying to remove her wedding dress and leaving her veil intact, no small feat. Kallista was hustled into a red shirt with billowing sleeves, skintight tan pants— at which point a royal debate occurred among the women if the bride's garter should go on the outside or inside. They settled for outside, then Kallista was pushed into a chair. Bernadette relaced Kallista's white combat boots. They tugged her to her feet and adjusted the veil while kissing her. Else swung a broad leather belt around Kallista's waist and tucked a long musket pistol into it. She straightened the cameo at Kallista's throat and wiped the tears from her eyes. "It's the best we could do, princess," she said before gently pushing Kallista out of the room.

"Well, hello, pirate princess." Channing and Rio came up behind her, swooped and carried her between them out the church and down the stairs.

There in the early September sunlight, Roman sat on Massachusetts, dressed in pirate gear. His loose white shirt billowed in the early September breeze, an eyepatch covering one eye, and a long scarf tied rakishly around his head, the red cloth fluttering. His Western jeans and moccasins added to the fascinating image.

She caught her breath and felt as if the world were spinning in golden magic and all her dreams were coming true....

"Hello, princess," he said quietly, holding out his hand to her. There was just that heartbeat of wary hesitation that told her of his uncertainty and yet he'd given her a sense of freedom, of dreams coming true.

She'd dreamed of being a pirate princess, of freedom to

choose her own oceans, to raise her own flag. Roman's outstretched strong hand offered her the excitement and the calm she'd needed for years.

She glanced at his family. Else held by Joe, was dabbing tears from her eyes, and all the Blaylocks had the same soft expression. In that moment, she felt a part of them, the family she'd never had. With delighted laughter that came from her heart, Kallista took Roman's hand and stepped on his moccasin covered foot. When he lifted her up in front of him, she threw her arms around him and gave him the kiss she'd been wanting. She opened her heart to him, slanted her lips to his and gave him everything in the sunlight. When the kiss was finished, Roman looked down at her tenderly. "Ready?"

"Not yet." Kallista found Cindi, huddled against Else, and beckoned to her. "Avast me, matey. Cindi, want a ride on my pirate ship?"

"You bet, I do, pirate princess. I haven't sailed the seven seas for years, haven't lopped off any heads, either." Rio lifted Cindi, placing her in front of Kallista, and after placing his eye patch on Cindi, Roman nudged the gelding into an easy trot. As the horse circled in front of the church, Cindi giggled and waved at the crowd. She glowed as she turned to Kallista and Roman. "Thanks, Dad. Thanks...er...Mom."

"We'll be back in two days. If you need me, Rio or Tyrell will get word to me and we'll come back," Roman stated carefully as Rio lifted Cindi from the horse.

"I'll be just peachy," she said. "I get to stay at Patty's the whole time. She's got lots of kittens."

Amid the falling confetti thrown by the crowd, the hoots and cheers, Kallista held Roman tightly, her arms around his waist, as he urged Massachusetts onto the trail behind the church.

Roman had been too silent, intent upon their journey. Loves Dancing had been saddled and waiting, and they rode silently up the winding mountain trail leading to Boone's cabin. In early September, the trembling aspens had turned to gold and fire, their trunks brilliantly white against the foliage. A mule deer, a doe with her fawn, turned to watch the passing riders.

For Kallista, it was a strange, fearsome journey to answers Roman would give her and to a life she could easily leave or enter. He hadn't asked for promises, and she studied her hand, resting on the saddle horn. The wide gold band gleamed, the design simple and strong, and terrifying in the shadows of the pine and fur. She hadn't thought to buy him a ring; she hadn't known she'd be so terrified. *Easy, girl,* Boone's voice slid along her nerves and she could almost catch his familiar scents of leather and earth and love. She glanced at a doe, a white mottled fawn against her side. Kallista was alone now, without her defenses, without Boone....

At the cabin, Roman lifted her from Loves Dancing and she placed her hand on his cheek. Was she so sensitive to Roman Blaylock that she knew his needs without words? Her terror soared; what did he know? What made him look so concerned, his dark face turned to her palm?

*Whatever lay in store, she trusted him.*

"I want to know now. Everything," she whispered as Roman unsaddled the horses, tethering them to a fallen pine.

Roman turned slowly and bent to pick her up in his arms, carrying her to the old cabin's porch. His throat worked, his jaw tensed and she knew Roman was thinking of how to tell her.

"It's cold up here...winter coming.... You've been my wife since that first time," he said slowly, emotion running beneath his deep tone. He held her hand, toyed with the wedding band. "But today was the sweetest moment in my life and when I saw you coming to me, to our marriage,

I—'' His voice broke and Roman gathered her closer. "I didn't believe it was possible to be this happy, to feel like this, as if I'm complete.... The cabin is cleaned and stocked. I thought we'd stay here a couple days, for appearances. I'll sleep on the porch. The cabin is nice and clean for you...Else, Hannah, and the rest of the women wanted to do this for you, Mrs. Blaylock.'' He spoke as if testing the words reverently upon his lips.

She stroked his hair, aware of his tense body, and whatever he feared to tell her. The very nice thing about Roman Blaylock, she decided, was how he responded to her touch...as though something calmed within him. The comforting of Roman Blaylock, her new husband, soothed the restlessness within her. "Thank you for today, for the pirate outfit.''

"It seemed right. Boone would have liked that, his pirate princess. That's what he called you, his pirate princess. Else liked being in charge of the shirt sewing and the wedding. There wasn't time before the wedding, but she's planning some big shower-reception thing after we return. If you're uncomfortable with that—''

"Tell me now.'' She wanted to know, to sort out her emotions and push away whatever troubled Roman.

He lifted his head, tracing the woods, the rippling stream. His hand smoothed her hair, bringing her head upon his shoulder and rocking her. "Jeremy Llewlyn is your uncle. Your father, Michael, was killed in a wreck nine years ago, leaving his current wife pregnant.''

"Why—'' she began only to be hushed by Roman's finger on her lips.

"Let me tell the story...Boone's story. It isn't sweet, dear heart....'' He took a deep breath and continued, "Boone didn't want either of his sons to return to the land. He knew they'd destroy it and the honor of the Llewlyns. They were his shame, born to a cold wife while he was making his kingdom away from Jasmine. Both sons were bigamists, marrying under different names. But the children that they produced were Boone's grandchildren, and he loved them."

"That's why there were always other—"

"Children. Their parents left them with Boone." Roman brushed his lips upon her temple. "Kallie, Boone's sons and their illegal wives receive monthly payments to keep them away from Llewlyn land. But Boone's will provides for those grandchildren—The Innocents, he called them."

Kallista's heart raced as quickly as the rabbit scurrying under the brush. She sat up to look at Roman. "I'm Boone's granddaughter? Why didn't he…?"

"Because he loved his sons, too, and he thought that children belonged with their mothers. I differ on that—"

Kallista froze. A gentle burst of cold September wind sent a spray of leaves to the earth. They rustled against the old board porch as she asked, "Is Cindi his granddaughter?"

Roman nodded solemnly. His black gaze traced her face. "She is. She's also your half sister. You look exactly like Boone's maternal grandmother and mother."

"You knew all this. You allowed people—me—to think that you were taking advantage of Boone."

Roman looked as if he'd traveled too many miles, weary to the bone, the lines deepening around his mouth and on his forehead. "The man needed his pride to die, honey, and it was the least I could do. He wanted the Llewlyn name to remain good, at least here where he was raised. I intend to keep it good…and there are more grandchildren to reclaim."

"My father and my uncle were bigamists. Boone cleared the legalities to keep them from jail, isn't that so? He wiped out all records."

"He did. He wanted to keep the children away from his shame, his sons' cruelty."

Kallista eased from Roman's arms to stand. He looked

wary, as though he'd been battered and couldn't fight anymore. She ached for him. "He must have paid a terrible price, keeping this secret. But you've paid, too, Roman."

"Boone was a wealthy man and building his kingdom cost him what he wanted most—family to live on the land. You're to have this—" Roman reached into his pocket and placed a gold doubloon in her palm. "And one thousand acres. And there's a fat Swiss bank account with your name on it. Boone wanted to keep his financial affairs very private. You're a wealthy woman, Mrs. Blaylock, and I'll help you do whatever you want."

Kallista gripped the gold doubloon in her hand, tears welling to her eyes. "I have to think about all this."

"Yes, you do. I thought it best to come here, where you were happy with Boone. You can think without distractions…and make decisions…about your life. But Boone doesn't want the land to go to outsiders. I am to buy out your portion at market value if you don't want it."

"*You think I'd sell my grandfather's family land?* Think again, Mr. Roman Blaylock. One thousand acres… Boone has ten thousand acres of fields and rough land. Roman, there's Cindi and me. Does that mean there are eight more grandchildren?" Overwhelmed, Kallista waited, her heart pounding.

"Yes," he answered quietly. "I have to contact eight more."

"Who are they…my…brothers and sisters and cousins?"

"Most of them are adults, some older than you. The files are at Boone's place." Then Roman stood slowly and looking older than his years, took an ax from a stump and began chopping. His movements were experienced and methodical, those of a strong man pitting himself against a mountain of wood. Kallista glanced at the high stacked woodpile and knew that Roman fought the frustration he'd hidden for so long.

She longed to comfort Roman, to hold him close and wipe away his burdens. Trembling, fighting the past and overcome by the new knowledge of Boone's relationship to her, she fought tears. Because she couldn't bring more hardship to Roman, because she had to tend her wounds, to mourn Boone in a new way, Kallista forced herself to enter the cabin. When the door closed, she released a lifetime of tears—

# Eleven

In the cold September night, a light spray of snowflakes fell on the old cabin. Roman sat on the front porch and hungered for his bride.

He wanted to hold her and to cherish her, and to take her burdens upon himself. Kallista had the information she needed now, and— Roman inhaled sharply, pain slamming into him. She could leave. Kallista wasn't a woman who liked tethers, and the extensive Blaylock family was certainly one of those ties that bind.

He'd married Debbie to protect her; he'd married Kallista because his desire for her was greater than his pride...and he loved her, this other part of his heart.

She hadn't eaten the simple meal he'd prepared; she'd been too quiet, too pale, her expression shattered as she'd wandered by the stream and the woods, traveling through her memories with Boone, trying to adjust. He'd followed her, to keep her safe from the mountain, and when Kallista turned to him, she seemed so vulnerable and small. One look told him that she needed to meet this emotional passage alone. Wearing his revolver and his sheathed hunting knife, he'd kept his distance, letting her roam amid the fir and pine and aspen, but he never lost sight of her. If anything happened to her...

His heart and soul would simply pour out of him.

Roman scanned deer moving across the clearing as they had done for centuries. He shouldn't want her now, giving her time to think, but he did, his body ripe with the need to love his wife on his wedding night. Roman rubbed his forehead, the pounding headache brewing there. He scanned the cold snowy mist surrounding the mountain and curled his hand into a fist.

He glanced at his sleeping bag, spread on the porch where he could hear Kallista if she needed him. Then Roman slowly stood. He'd kept his promise to Boone, but he'd made Kallista marry him to get the secret; she'd protect Boone and the Llewlyn legacy. Would she remember what they'd shared? Would she remember how she fit into his body and his heart?

Roman swallowed and eased open the door to the dark cabin, the small stove casting firelight upon the rough-board room. He smiled tenderly at the white combat boots she'd worn with her elegant gown. He frowned at the basket sent from Channing, loaded with champagne and snacks and a small battery-powered radio. Concerned with the information he would give to Kallista on their wedding day and the addition, and the man staying at her house, Roman had not thought of fruit, or champagne. Instead, when he couldn't sleep, hungering for her, listening to echoes of her breathing, her passion, Roman had worked on Mrs. Llewlyn's walnut wardrobe and had confronted Jeremy Llewlyn, no small chore. Llewlyn, when threatened of being stripped of any income, had retreated—for now.

Roman ran his hand through his hair—he wasn't a champagne man or a model of charm and elegant manners. He could only give Kallista what was in his heart and soul; he found his bride, lying small and curled up on Boone's massive cot. He shut the door, fearing she would take chill, added more wood to the fire as quietly as he could, then turned to his wife. In the firelight, her eyes were on him, and he sat slowly on the cot, smoothed back the long swath of hair that circled her throat. He placed his hand on her head, his fingertips rubbing her scalp. "Tired?"

"Exhausted."

"You'll work it through. Boudreaux's best troubleshooter is tough when it counts. I'll be right outside if you need me." He ran his thumb across the silvery, damp, smoothness of her cheek.

"Tough. I feel as if I've been mauled." Her voice was no more than a quiver in the shadows, the sound of tears laced through it. "You looked like a hunter from the Old West today, following me through the woods. Every time I looked back, you were there, that six-shooter strapped low on your hip, and that huge, evil knife on the other side."

"I wanted you safe." He smoothed the big collar at her throat. "You're wearing my shirt, the one you wore that morning when you drove the lumber truck.... I look—I am tough because I come from a long line of mountain men, honey. Trappers and hunters, and there is that Blaylock Apache blood..."

Her hand caught his wrist, turning his hand to examine his palm. "Oh, Roman..."

Roman noted the gleam on her hand—Kallista still wore his wedding ring. It was enough that she hadn't removed the symbol of their wedding, of his love for her.

She bent to kiss the raw skin, the legacy of his hours with the ax, when she'd hid in the cabin and cried. She hadn't wanted him to see her pain and that had hurt. Then her soft gaze lifted to his. "Get undressed, Mr. Blaylock. Come lie beside me."

"That might not be a good idea—" Roman heard his

indrawn breath hissing through his teeth as Kallista sat up and began unbuttoning her borrowed shirt.

When the edges were open and revealing the soft curves of her breast, she placed her hands on his chest. "Come lie by me," she repeated in a whisper. "I need you to hold me."

Roman hesitated, then tugged off his moccasins and stood to undress. "Don't look at me like that, Kallie," he whispered, when she studied him intimately and reached out to smooth his body with her fingertips.

He was aroused, thrusting, aching, and shivered when her fingers curled curiously around him. Kneeling on the large, sturdy bed, Kallista eased out of the shirt and wrapped her arms around his waist, her head resting against his chest.

Roman groaned shakily, uncertain of how to hold her, what to tell her. Could he restrain his need for her now?

The softness of her breasts brushing sweet and low on his body caused him to tremble and Roman eased her back on the bed, sliding into the covers beside her.

She turned to drape her arm across his chest, toying with the hair there; her slender thigh slid between his rougher ones, caressing him. Kallista raised slightly to look down at him. "Thank you, Roman, for keeping Boone's land safe...for keeping his secret."

"You don't owe me," he said roughly, uncertain and wary of her mood.

"No, I don't. But I want you to know that I realize I was wrong—you are a good man, Roman Blaylock."

"I want you," he murmured, giving in to the blunt truth that had always been his way.

"But the decision is mine, right? What if *I* want *you?*"

"Want me?" He flattened to the bed as Kallista moved over him, his hands immediately locking to her hips.

"I'm not making any promises, Roman. But you are a beautiful, sweet man, and you're mine—at least for now."

She would always be his—in his heart. Roman turned her

slowly, ran his trembling hand down her soft body, and brushed her lips with his. He could tell her with his body how much he loved her, how deep she went in his heart— then he realized he was speaking aloud.

"You say the most beautiful things." Kallista's slender hands smoothed his back and hips and Roman thought he was floating. Then she looked up at him and locked her legs with his, rubbing his calves with her soles.

The burning moist entrance to her body beckoned to him, and with a reluctant groan, Roman slid fully into her. The fire came quickly to them, bodies pounding, hunger blazing, mouths fused, heat pouring from them; then Kallista's tight body clenched his intimately and Roman cried out, both in pleasure and in devastation.

The incredible softness of Kallista beneath him soon caused Roman to lift his head, to find her breasts with his mouth and to nibble gently—she twisted against him, bucking, her nails digging in. In her eyes, he saw the desperation that rode him, and for once in his life, Roman cut his leashes and began loving her again, thrusting deep, lifting her hips, feeding upon her skin, tasting her...

She pushed him back and Roman shook his head, startled that he'd pushed so deeply into her tight body, that he'd taken greedily. Then Kallista flung herself at him, turned him, and lay upon him. "You're so traditional," she whispered with a grin.

"What do you know about it?" he returned, grinning up at her.

Her body clenched his tightly and he released the breath he'd been holding. "You're shockable, Mr. Roman Blaylock."

"Am not." He barely kept himself from pouring into her, fighting to be gentle, fearing to unleash his passion for her.

Her dive to his nipple, suckling it, proved that Roman Blaylock had much to learn about her body and his. He laughed aloud and turned her to her stomach, lying over her, nibbling on her ear. "You taste good."

She turned to smile up at him. "You're better than a blanket—in fact, you're burning…and you're definitely not a soft man."

"That I am…for you." Roman studied the long black swath of hair across her sleek back and eased it aside. He bent to trail kisses across her shoulders and down her back, sliding his hands beneath her to capture her breasts. "You're so sensitive here—" Then he turned her to taste her, the dark mauve tips cresting within his mouth. She shivered, her nails digging in his shoulders each time he licked and bit gently. "You're shaking, burning—"

Her hips bucked against his, the slap of heated damp flesh startling him as she asked, "Is that me burning in this hurricane—or you?"

Roman—her new husband—braced himself over her, his face as dark and fierce as his Native American and Spanish ancestors, and as passionate, his hair rumpled from her hands. Kallista quivered as his hands ran down her, locking to her hips, those hard, rough, callused hands, drawing her knees gently higher. Then he came to her, strong, wild, fighting the passion she fought, climbing with her, and Kallista cried out, panted, her teeth biting his shoulder, her nails digging in—holding Roman, holding his strong, rippling body within hers.

He breathed as if air had been torn from him, as if he were fighting to claim eternity, and yet leashing his strength.

She held him tighter, flung herself at him, and his teeth caught her lip tugging at him, his mouth found hers and ravished, pounding her as she lifted to him, retreat, dive and retreat, the race taking her soul, the pleasure building.

He took her breast in his hand, suckled until she cried out, cords of pleasure tightening until she thought she'd found fire and melted—then the rhythm began again, Roman's big hands sweeping over her, his face feverish upon her skin, his words rough and dear and sweet against her ears, her skin. Locked to her, Roman was hers...hers...and they were flying across the fire, until...

She held him fiercely, poised on that ultimate crest of rippling pleasure. With a shout, Roman followed her, as though he'd flung all that he was, all that he would be into his passion for her. In the silence later, his heart pounding against her, his skin damp beneath her palms, his body tense, she fought to keep him close, and suddenly Roman turned, keeping their bodies locked as she lay over him.

Because she could almost sense his thoughts—berating himself for dominating, for the power he'd used with her in the eternal struggle, male and female, locked in sensual battle, Kallista whispered against his chest, "Don't you dare let me go now, Roman Blaylock."

He shivered, a huge, strong man in terror that he'd hurt or frightened her. She couldn't have him in pain, and slid her hand to where they were joined at the same time she nibbled on his neck. She smiled when his big hands tightened on her hips, molding them, his body growing hard within her now, stretching her and instantly she caught him again.

The interesting thing about Roman Blaylock, she thought with pleasure, was that his passion matched hers. When she hurled herself against him again, the movement took them off the bed and Roman landed on his back, catching her amid the heavy patchwork quilt. She braced herself above him and studied him. "I should have told you I wanted you badly. You're shy in your way."

"Me?" he asked, clearly astonished.

A half hour later, after her bath in the old tin tub, Roman lifted her to the floor and dried her. His bath was hurried, his eyes never leaving her as she nestled on the old bed. When he came to her, she saw what he wanted, knew that already his desire leaped for her, needed her.

There in the wildfire, the hurried sweet mating, their bodies joined, slick with sweat and trembling with the storm, Roman began to explore her carefully, and she cried out as he touched her delicately, found that sensitive spot and then she was lost, locking him to her so tightly that they were one, flying again and she found herself lying on his broad chest, heart racing and bones melted. Then Roman began to lift her hand, to kiss her ring, and to hold her close as the fire crackled in the old stove and a gentle calm came over Kallista Blaylock, as though she'd known all her life that she was meant for this one man.

He smoothed her hair, turned her face up to his for a kiss and covered her bare shoulder with the heavy patchwork quilt.

She awoke to Roman thrashing in his nightmare, his face damp with sweat, and his mournful cry. Kallista hurried to place her hands on his face, to soothe him as he had shown her. Strange, she thought, how her touch meant so much as he began to still. His lashes fluttered open and bending over him, she saw into his hell, his nightmare, his grief. "Roman?"

"I'm sorry." He was trembling now, his deep voice streaked with pain. "It happens sometimes when I—I let go. Did I hurt you?"

"It's Michaela, isn't it?"

He shuddered, sitting up, his bare back to her, as he held his face in his hands. "I see her facedown in that damned swimming pool. She was so tiny."

"It wasn't your fault. Debbie should have—"

"Leave me alone," he said and quickly jerked on his jeans and moccasins, leaving her.

The instant the door closed behind Roman, Kallista was out of bed, hurrying to dress. She grabbed Roman's jacket and stepped out into the chilling wind. He stood amid the snowflakes, hands on his head, his unbuttoned shirt blowing in the wind. The pain in his eyes tore at her, and Kallista shoved his arms into his jacket, then hurled her arms around him. He held her tight, then in the next instant, bent to pick her up and hurry back into the cabin.

They met in passion, falling onto the bed, Roman's hands already upon her body, finding her beneath her jeans. She tugged open his jeans and came down on him, her body filling with his as she pushed him back, straddling him and rocking. Roman twisted beneath her, hips bucking, meeting hers. He ripped off her jacket, flinging it away, then his met the same fate. His hand pulled open her blouse, just as she tore open his shirt, buttons popping as the fever blazed between them.

Kallista gloried in Roman's unbridled need for her, in the wild pounding of his body, the race they shared, the heat and storms burning away the past.

Lying on her now, because she wouldn't let him leave her, Roman shuddered, and eased to one side. He smoothed her hair and gathered her close. "You are a strong woman, Kallie," he murmured softly before falling into a deep sleep.

The depth of his pain startled her, and it was a long time before Kallista slept, twined with Roman's hard, warm body.

The man cooking breakfast bacon and potatoes on the old stove looked delicious—freshly bathed, worn jeans his only clothing, his powerful back rippling as he moved... Kallista slid from the bed and walked to Roman, sliding her arms around his waist, and kissing the long red streaks her nails had made.

Roman tensed. "You've got my marks on you, Kallie. I'm sorry."

"I didn't mean to—" When Roman turned, her eyes widened; the red marks on his dark skin. "I actually bit you. I bit you," she repeated, stunned.

"I did some biting of my own," he whispered gently, and slid the skillet aside. He began backing her to the bed, then stooped and picked her up and plopped her on it. With a dive, Roman came down on her, already hungry.

"You've shocked me," Kallista murmured later over their breakfast of champagne and bacon and freshly baked sourdough biscuits.

"I've wanted you a long time. You're a passionate woman, a strong woman, Kallie Blaylock. And still shy of me," he added, running his fingertip down her hot cheek.

"You should see yourself, Mr. Blaylock, rising up like some warrior, all fierce and hungry and—mmm." Kallista stopped talking and gave herself to the man who had just plucked her from her chair and held her high in the air, laughing up at her. She wrapped her legs around him and dived into the man she wanted more than freedom.

The next night, they lay in the huge empty room of his addition, still hungry for each other. "Is this what you want?" Roman asked as he lifted his lips.

"I make noises," she muttered and realized she barely had the strength—after Roman's devastating lovemaking—to lift her hand.

"That you do. The purrs knock me sideways, but that high keening sound as if you're flinging away your soul. That is a lovely sound and I feel like I'm in the middle of thunder and lightning."

"I'm not alone in the noise business," she said to defend herself. "You shout as if you're dying."

"I purely do die, just that bit after your lightning bolts sizzle the holy soul out of me. Or that nice sweet surrender when everything comes calm and gentle upon us."

She could have listened to him talk forever, his simple words easing her past and what she would find in Boone's records.

The flickering light from the fireplace traced Roman's hard face. He hadn't shaved tonight, hadn't had time. He'd carried her into the new addition and kicked the door closed behind him. "It's for you to decide if you want to live here.

But if you could find it in your heart, I'd like to share our bedroom with you.''

The rooms were barren, scented of new wood, the wood floors gleaming. The living room led into a family kitchen, sprawling countertops and cupboards waiting to be filled. One large bedroom viewed the mountains, with a door to a smaller one.

Kallista snuggled close to Roman and studied Mrs. Llewlyn's refinished walnut wardrobe. ''Thank you. I haven't given you anything.''

Roman's grin was wicked, boyish and tempting. Then his hand found her breast and the passion ripped through them again.

When Cindi rode her bike to The Llewlyn the next morning, she crossed her arms, tilted her head and studied Kallista in the bright September midmorning. ''You look different. There's marks on your neck. Roman looks like he's come unglued and only his silly smile is pasting him together.''

This was her little sister, and Kallista bent to hug her. Bristling, Cindi pushed away, but then she smiled slowly, shyly. When she was old enough to know, Kallista would tell her that they were sisters. ''There's a present for you in the house,'' she said now.

''For me?'' she asked before racing to the house.

Kallista turned to Roman and with a grin, patted his backside. He straightened, stunned and wary. ''That's a familiar thing to do, Mrs. Blaylock.''

She fluttered her lashes at him, fascinated with the quick leap of desire in his eyes, his body humming instantly with it. ''You're so easy, Mr. Blaylock.''

''Are you staying?'' he asked bluntly, in one of those quick turns that sent her reeling.

''It would be too easy to do,'' she answered truthfully.

''Then we'd better get a bed today, a good strong one… you're sleeping with me.''

* * *

"That sure is a big bed," Cindi remarked looking out the pickup's rear window to the furniture in the back. "We had to drive to two towns to get it. Mine is better. Mom, you look like you'd like to murder someone—"

"I would." Kallista managed a sweet tone although she really wanted to leap the man driving the pickup and burn him.

Roman lifted that one innocent eyebrow as he looked down at her, his hand tightening on her knee. "Whatever it is, I didn't do it."

She took his wrist and placed his hand on the steering wheel. "You can't just walk into a furniture store and tell them that you just got married and you want the biggest, strongest bed in stock...and say 'now' as if you can't wait to get it home."

His look at her sizzled. "I can't wait to get it home, dear."

"I like my new combat boots. I said thanks," Cindi said worriedly, reminding Kallista of the girl's experience with battling adults.

Kallista held her hand, and ignored Roman's thumb caressing her own nape. He'd braided her hair that morning; then while Titus and Dusty showed Cindi the new barn kittens, Roman had closed Boone's office door. One look at him took Kallista toward him, matching his passion with her own.

There in the pickup seat between the safety of Roman and her young sister, Kallista fought tears. Her grandfather had suffered so much, his shame burdening him, his sons hurting him, and yet he'd wanted to keep Llewlyn land for his grandchildren.

Suddenly Roman's arm came around Kallista, and he gathered her close.

"Why's she crying?" Cindi asked in hushed, worried tones.

"Her heart is aching, honey. But she'll be just fine."

# Twelve

Two weeks later, while September's wind brushed the aspen leaves upon the old cabin's wooden shakes, Roman forced himself to lift his head from his wife's soft breasts. He brushed back the silky black hair from her damp, flushed cheek; he traced her swollen lips with his as the big bed creaked beneath them and the fire crackled in the stove. "I'm glad you like the combs."

The huge, old silver combs, embedded with bloodred garnets, gleamed in Kallista's hair. "I love the man who gave them to me...who put them in my hair and who loved me last night and every night. Boone chose the perfect man to bring his grandchildren back to the land."

He brought her hands to his face, nuzzling them in that tender, humbling way. "You've given me so much. I should have had a special something for you on our wedding day."

"Well, there was that pirate thing. How many brides can have their wishes come true? You were gorgeous, darling looking like a pirate and a mountain man—so romantic," she teased, loving this dear man she had captured.

"I want all your wishes to come true, Kallie," Roman said sincerely against her palms.

"Come here," she whispered, sliding her fingers through his hair and drawing him down for her kiss. "I want you again, now and always...."

For a man who had had little loving in his lifetime, Roman Blaylock quickly made up for lost time....

October covered the jutting Rocky Mountains with snow. Cindi was adjusting to being a member of the extensive Blaylock family, and to her new school, and the addition was warm with Kallista's touch. Roman smiled as he repaired the barn's stall; the uses of a futon were many. Kallista's fiery temperament set off his own, but the advantages of a genuine relationship also had the benefits of making up after quarrels. He treasured each day now, and Rio had agreed to help with the ranches because—Roman's smile grew—because his bride wanted more of him.

He had more in his life than he'd ever expected, ever dreamed...

"Roman!" Kallista's curt tone raised the hair on his nape, and he straightened slowly. The offenses of a husband were many and frequently defined by his bride, he'd discovered, and Kallista was still shy of him, and the large Blaylock family.

At the sight of her black shiny jacket, jeans, combat boots and big bag slung over her shoulder, Roman's body went cold. There in the shadows of the barn, she would tell him she was leaving. He'd expected this somehow, feared it.

"Do you like my outfit?" she asked in none too sweet tones.

"No, I don't," he returned and stripped away his leather

gloves. It was her traveling gear and soon she'd be leaving....

She came closer, eyeing him, the huge silver combs gleaming in her hair. He quickly checked her hands, tension easing as he noted her wedding ring. He braced himself for the pain; she would tear herself from him.

"You should be wearing a wedding ring, Roman. You've been in our bed without one. In fact, you've made love to me in this barn, in the cabin, in the woods, and in the kitchens and various other places without one."

"There's a framed marriage certificate over the bed, sweetheart," he reminded her and waited for her to say how easily a marriage paper could be torn apart, just like happiness.

She placed the flat of her hand on his chest and pushed him back a step, her green eyes gleaming up at him. Wary of this new mood of his bride, Roman let himself be pushed back into the haystack. He caught her jacket and she toppled over him. "What's this about, Kallie?"

She braced her hands on his chest and began unbuttoning his shirt. She kissed his chest and Roman groaned unwillingly, already aroused beneath her. "Kallie?"

She eased a gold band onto his third finger, left hand and kissed it. "There. I love you, you're wearing my ring, the certificate is over the bed and, dear heart, I'm going to have a baby—and I won't be able to wear this outfit forever, so I might as well make use of it while I can...and I've got flower bulbs for next spring in my bag and seeds, too, and I like potted plants, but I thought next year a flower bed, or a vegetable garden and—"

She rummaged in her bag and plopped a ceramic bassinet splayed with flowers on his chest. "This is for you, Dad."

While she fought tears of happiness, Roman stared at her and swallowed heavily. "All I want to know is if you're happy."

"Very. I've found what I've wanted all my life. I'm

home, Roman…with you. I…am…finally home," she repeated, her heart filling happily with the words.

Fifteen minutes later, Kallista watched her newly showered husband slide into their bed.

She welcomed him into her arms and smiled as Roman whispered, "Now tell me everything again and we'll take each item, one by one."

"My, you're such a thorough man." Kallista fluttered her lashes at him; she loved to flirt with her husband. He reacted so wonderfully—all steamy and hungry. That was one of the many reasons she loved Roman Blaylock, who was peeling back the sheet to reverently fit his hand over the new life within her, tears glistening in his soft dark eyes.

\* \* \* \* \*

*Don't miss the exciting, dramatic stories in*
*Cait London's upcoming continuation of*
*her popular miniseries THE BLAYLOCKS:*
*RIO: MAN OF DESTINY in August 1999,*
*TYPICAL MALE in December 1999*
*—only from Silhouette Desire.*

# FORTUNE'S Children™

### The Fortune family requests the honor of your presence at the weddings of

Silhouette Desire's scintillating new miniseries, featuring the beloved Fortune family and five of your favorite authors.

### *The Secretary and the Millionaire*
#### by Leanne Banks (SD #1208, 4/99)

When handsome Jack Fortune asked his dependable assistant to become his daughter's temporary, live-in nanny, Amanda Corbain knew almost all her secret wishes had come true. But Amanda had one final wish before this Cinderella assignment ended....

### *The Groom's Revenge*
#### by Susan Crosby (SD #1214, 5/99)

Powerful tycoon Gray McGuire was bent on destroying the Fortune family. Until he met sweet Mollie Shaw. And this sprightly redhead was about to show him that the best revenge is... falling in love!

### *Undercover Groom*
#### by Merline Lovelace (SD #1220, 6/99)

Who was Mason Chandler? Chloe Fortune thought she knew everything about her groom. But as their wedding day approached, would his secret past destroy their love?

**Available at your favorite retail outlet.**

# COMING NEXT MONTH

**#1213 LOVE ME TRUE—Ann Major**
*Man of the Month*
Why did international film star Joey Fassano ache with longing for
a woman he couldn't forget? Heather Wade's parents had finally
succeeded in transforming his lovely, free-spirited ex-girlfriend into a
cool socialite. But now that Joey knew about Heather's little boy, even
her powerful family couldn't keep him from seeing her again....

**#1214 THE GROOM'S REVENGE—Susan Crosby**
*Fortune's Children: The Brides*
He was out to destroy the Fortune name! Nothing was going to stop
Gray McGuire from avenging his father's death, except maybe beautiful
innocent Mollie Shaw. But was exacting his revenge worth the price of
losing the love of his life?

**#1215 THE COWBOY AND THE VIRGIN—Barbara McMahon**
Well-bred Caitlin Delany had no business falling for sexy cowboy
Zach Haller, especially since he was a one-night kind of man and she
was a virgin! But the irresistible bachelor made her want to throw
caution to the wind. And how could Caitlin say no to the man who
could just be her Mr. Right?

**#1216 HAVING HIS BABY—Beverly Barton**
*3 Babies for 3 Brothers*
When Donna Fields returned from her trip out West, she brought home
more than just memories. Nine months later, Jake Bishop was back in
town and determined to make a family with Donna and their baby. If
only he could convince sweet Donna that even a brooding loner could
be a devoted dad—and a loving husband.

**#1217 THE SOLITARY SHEIKH—Alexandra Sellers**
*Sons of the Desert*
Prince Omar of Central Barakat was looking for a woman. To be
precise, he was looking for someone to tutor his two young daughters.
But one look at Jana Stewart and Omar was beginning to believe that *he*
was the one in need of a lesson—in love.

**#1218 THE BILLIONAIRE'S SECRET BABY—Carol Devine**
He had vowed to always watch over his child, even if he had to do it
from the shadows. And when tragedy struck, billionaire Jack Tarkenton
knew it was time to take care of Meg Masterson and their child himself.
Even if it meant marrying the only woman who had the power to bring
him to his knees....

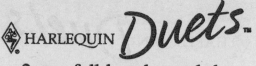

# HARLEQUIN *Duets*™

2 new full-length novels by
2 great authors in
1 book for 1 low price!

**Buy any Harlequin Duets™ book
and SAVE $1.00!**

# SAVE $1.00

when you purchase any

HARLEQUIN

*Duets*™ book!

**Offer valid May 1, 1999, to October 31, 1999.**

**Retailer:** Harlequin Enterprises Ltd. will pay the face value of this coupon plus 8.0¢ if
submitted by the customer for this specified product only. Any other use constitutes
fraud. Coupon is nonassignable, void if taxed, prohibited or restricted by law. Consumer
must pay any government taxes. Valid in U.S. only. Mail to: Harlequin Enterprises Ltd.,
P.O. Box 880478, El Paso, TX 88588-0478 U.S.A.

**Non NCH customers**—for reimbursement submit coupons and proofs of sale directly
to: Harlequin Enterprises Ltd., Retail Sales Dept., 225 Duncan Mill Rd., Don Mills
(Toronto), Ontario, Canada M3B 3K9.

**HDUETC-U**

HARLEQUIN®
*Makes any time special.*™

**Coupon expires
October 31, 1999.**

5 65373 00051 9 (8100) 1 06254

Look us up on-line at: http://www.romance.net                HDUETC-U

### HARLEQUIN *Duets*™

2 new full-length novels by
2 great authors in
1 book for 1 low price!

**Buy any Harlequin Duets™ book
and SAVE $1.00!**

# SAVE $1.00

## when you purchase any

### HARLEQUIN

## *Duets*™ book!

**Offer valid May 1, 1999, to October 31, 1999.**

**Retailer:** Harlequin Enterprises Ltd. will pay the face value of this coupon plus 10.25¢ if submitted by the customer for this specified product only. Any other use constitutes fraud. Coupon is nonassignable, void if taxed, prohibited or restricted by law. Consumer must pay any government taxes. Valid in Canada only. Mail to: Harlequin Enterprises Ltd., P.O. Box 3000, Saint John, New Brunswick, Canada E2L 4L3.
Non NCH customers—for reimbursement submit coupons and proofs of sale directly to: Harlequin Enterprises Ltd., Retail Sales Dept., 225 Duncan Mill Rd., Don Mills (Toronto), Ontario, Canada M3B 3K9.

### HARLEQUIN®
*Makes any time special.*™

**HDUETC-C**

**Coupon expires
October 31, 1999.**

Look us up on-line at: http://www.romance.net          HDUETC-C

at the two approaching. Mandy moved to the opposite side of Sam and they stood, waiting, forming a welcoming committee of sorts.

"Look!" Merideth whispered, trying not to laugh. "She's blushing."

"Who wouldn't?" Sam muttered. "With the three of us standing here gawking at them like they're some kind of carnival sideshow."

"Hi!" Mandy called cheerfully when the two were within hearing range. "We were on our way to Alayna and Jack's house to give it a quick cleaning before their return tomorrow and thought we'd stop in and say hello."

"Well, that's mighty neighborly of you ladies," Travis replied amiably.

Lacey's face heated another degree or two. She was sure there was a banner across her forehead that read, *I just made wild, passionate love with Travis Cordell on a rowboat out on the middle of a lake, and, oh, what it ride it was.* She gave herself a shake, telling herself that there was no way her half sisters could know how she and Travis had spent the afternoon.

"Catch any fish?"

One look at Merideth's smug smile and Lacey's assurance wilted away. She knew. How she knew, Lacey wasn't sure. But she knew.

"No," Travis replied with regret as he propped his rod and reel against the porch railing. "They just weren't biting today."

"Oh, that's too bad," Merideth said and shot Mandy a knowing wink. "But there's always tomorrow."

"Yeah," Travis agreed with a confident nod. "There is that to look forward to." He looked from one sister to the other, his smile growing. "So, y'all are going to give Jack and Alayna's house a going over, huh?"

"Yes," Mandy replied. "We thought we'd freshen things up a bit, so they could enjoy their homecoming."

"Why don't you come with us, Lacey?" Merideth suggested impulsively.

"Oh, I don't know," Lacey hedged. "I really need a shower. I probably smell like…fish," she finished feebly.

"Come on," Mandy urged. "It'll be fun. We were thinking of shortchanging their sheets, and maybe putting some petroleum jelly on the commode seats. You know," she said, wrinkling her nose impishly, "giving them a *real* welcome home."

Before Lacey could think of another excuse to offer, Merideth had her by the elbow and was hustling her toward the car. "I just knew we could count on your help."

Lacey looked back over her shoulder at Travis in a silent plea for help. He just laughed and waved. "Don't tear up things too much," he warned. "Remember—paybacks are a bitch."

Lacey stood in the kitchen, her hands shoved in her back pockets, feeling like a fifth wheel, while Sam, Mandy and Merideth stood on chairs and hung a banner across the wall.

"Would you hand me that roll of tape, Lacey?" Mandy asked.

Lacey snagged the tape from the table and held it up.

"Thanks."

Merideth glanced at Lacey, then whispered something to Mandy that had both women laughing uproariously.

"What's so funny?" Lacey snapped irritably.

"Nothing," the two sisters chorused, then collapsed in a fit of giggles.

Sam stole a look over her shoulder, then turned her face

to the wall to hide a smile. "It's your shirt," she said, then burst into laughter, too.

Lacey looked down and her face turned flame-red when she saw that she was wearing her shirt wrong-side-out and the buttons were fastened incorrectly. Mortified, she turned her back to them and started jerking frantically at the buttons. "Why didn't somebody tell me?" she cried in embarrassment.

Mandy immediately climbed down from her chair and went to her. "I'm sorry, Lacey," she said, trying her best not to laugh. "We should have said something." She helped Lacey out of her shirt and pulled the sleeves through, turning it right-side-out...then pressed the blouse against her mouth to smother her laughter.

Lacey jerked the shirt away from Mandy and shrugged it on. "It isn't funny," she said furiously.

"Oh, but it is!" Merideth cried, laughing hysterically. "If you could see your face right now, you'd be laughing, too."

Shooting Merideth a glare over her shoulder, Lacey pushed buttons through holes. "Yeah, I'm sure I would," she said sarcastically.

Dressed again, she turned to face her half sisters. Merideth and Sam still stood on chairs and were laughing so hard, they were having to hold on to each other to keep from falling to the floor. Mandy stood in front of them, her hands clamped tightly over her mouth, tears of laughter streaming down her cheeks.

"And I suppose none of you has ever been caught in a questionable situation?" Lacey demanded indignantly.

Mandy looked up at Merideth, her eyes glittering mischievously. "Do you remember the night we caught Sam?"

Sobering instantly, Sam looked from one sister to the other. "What night?"

"The night Nash went to the smokehouse looking for you?" Mandy prodded helpfully.

It was Sam's turn to blush. "Oh, that night," she mumbled in embarrassment.

Merideth hooted at the ceiling. "And your shirt wasn't buttoned correctly, either."

"Well, that was nothing compared to the night Mandy came home wearing John Lee's shirt."

"What!" Merideth cried in outrage.

Sam chuckled, relieved to have the spotlight taken off her.

"It wasn't John Lee's shirt," Mandy said, turning to frown at Sam. Then she laughed. "It was Jesse's. And if Sam had returned home at a decent hour, she wouldn't have caught me sneaking back into the house at dawn."

As Lacey listened to the exchange, she gradually became caught up in the wild tales and totally forgot her own embarrassment.

Merideth climbed down from the chair and sat on it, crossing her legs and swinging a foot. "I can top that one," she said airily and held out a hand to admire her diamond ring. "One morning John Lee's housekeeper came into his bedroom and caught John Lee and I in bed together." She dropped her hand and laughed, remembering. "You should have seen the look on the poor woman's face. Of course, at the time, John Lee and I weren't married, and his housekeeper was convinced that I was Charise, the schizophrenic character I played in the soap opera I starred in, and that I was cheating on my husband with John Lee. Took days for John Lee to straighten out that mess. Then there was the time..."

The stories went on and on, with each sister trying to

op the other's tale. Mandy raided the refrigerator and poured drinks for everyone, while Sam dug through the pantry until she found some pretzels and chips. Lacey simply sat and soaked it all up, never having experienced anything like it before.

"What about you, Lacey?" Merideth asked, nibbling on a pretzel. "Did you ever get caught before?"

Lacey blushed again at the reminder. "No, today was my first time."

Anxious to hear details, Merideth scooted to the edge of her chair. "So, tell us. What's Travis like in bed?"

Lacey looked from one expectant face to the other. "He's—" She cleared her throat and tried again. "Well, he's—"

"That good, huh," Sam said, laughing.

Lacey laughed, too. "Yeah, that good."

By the time Lacey returned home, it was nearly midnight. Travis had left the lamp on beside the bed, but was sound asleep.

Accepting the light as an invitation, Lacey quickly showered, put on a clean T-shirt and crawled into bed beside him.

He rolled over and draped an arm around her, pulling her close. "Have fun?" he asked sleepily.

"Yeah, I did," she replied, and was surprised to realize that the evening with her half sisters *had* been fun.

"That's good," he murmured and pressed a kiss to the end of her nose. "G'night," he said, yawning as he tucked her head beneath his chin.

Content, Lacey snuggled against him and closed her eyes, still feeling a little dizzy from the evening shared with her half sisters.

# Six

---

"**M**andy just called. They're having a Welcome Home party for Alayna and Jack tonight."

Halting his razor mid-swipe, Travis glanced at Lacey's reflection in the bathroom mirror. She stood in the doorway behind him with her shoulder propped against the door, watching him shave. "You don't sound too excited," he said, looking at her curiously. "Don't you want to go?"

"No."

"Why not?" he asked in surprise.

"I don't have anything to wear. She said that everybody's dressing up, and all I've got with me are boots and jeans."

Chuckling, he shook his head, then drew the razor to his chin. "Women," he muttered and swished the razor in the sink, cleaning it, before lifting it to his face again. "Nobody's gonna care how you're dressed."

''That's what you think,'' she replied miserably. ''Didn't you see all the strange looks I got at Jack and Alayna's wedding? Me dressed in jeans, and everyone else all gussied up.'' She shook her head and turned away. ''I'm going to check on Buddy. See you later.''

Surprised by the dejected slump of her shoulders, Travis watched her until she disappeared from sight. Hearing the front door close, he grabbed a towel and wiped the shaving cream from his face as he headed for the phone. He punched in Mandy's number then waited for her to answer. ''Mandy? It's Travis. We've got a little problem.''

''What's wrong?'' Sam asked as Mandy hung up the phone.

''Lacey's not coming to the party tonight.''

''Why not?'' Sam asked in surprise.

''Travis said that she doesn't have anything to wear, that all she has with her are boots and jeans.''

''That's ridiculous,'' Merideth said with a huff of disgust. ''Of course, she's coming. We don't care what she wears.''

''That's what Travis told her, but she still insists that she's staying at the cabin.''

''She's coming,'' Merideth replied stubbornly. ''She can borrow something from one of us to wear.'' She glanced sharply at Mandy. ''She's about your size,'' she said, frowning as she studied her sister's figure, then she snapped her fingers and smiled. ''And I know just the outfit.''

''Uh-oh,'' Sam said, her voice heavy with dread as Merideth hurried from the room.

''Uh-oh, what?'' Mandy asked, looking at her sister in puzzlement.

"Remember the last time Merideth played wardrobe mistress with someone?"

Mandy chuckled, remembering. "Yes. It was with Alayna, and as I recall, the outfit Merideth chose for her was what awakened Jack's feelings for Alayna."

Sam snorted. "Awakened? I'd think *turned on* would be a more accurate term."

Mandy laughed. "It'll be interesting to see what Merideth comes up with for Lacey."

Sam headed for the back door.

"Where are you going?" Mandy asked in surprise.

"I'm getting out of here before Merideth decides to play wardrobe mistress with *me*."

"Coward," Mandy chided.

"Past victim," Sam corrected and stopped in the doorway to look back at her sister. "Remember what she made me wear to your wedding? Cut to here," she said and slashed an imaginary line from her neck to her navel. "And she even made me wear one of those stupid padded bras that make a woman look two sizes bigger than she really is."

"You looked beautiful," Mandy argued, then waved a hand, silencing Sam before she could argue further. "I just wish our lawyer had the paperwork ready," she said with regret. "Then we could have made this more than a welcome party for Alayna and Jack. We could have made it a welcome to the family party for Lacey, too."

Lacey glanced up as Travis stepped from the bedroom. Dressed in charcoal-grey slacks and a black collarless shirt, he looked as if he'd stepped off the cover of *GQ*. She closed the magazine she'd been reading. "Well, don't you look nice," she said, unable to hide the surprise in her voice.

He shot her a wink as he crossed to her. "Being a twin has its advantages. I went over to Jack's and raided his closet." He braced a hand on either side of the chair she sat in, then leaned over and closed his mouth over hers.

The heat was instantaneous and debilitating. Weakened by it, Lacey had to force open her eyes in order to meet his gaze when he withdrew slightly.

"Sure you won't come with me?" he asked hopefully. "I hear there's going to be dancing."

She smiled wistfully and rubbed her thumb across his bottom lip, removing the moisture she'd left there. "No, but thanks for asking."

With a disappointed sigh, he straightened. "Without you there to protect me, I'll probably have to beat off all the women with a stick."

Lacey laughed. "I'm sure you'll manage just fine." She waved him toward the door. "Go on and have a good time. Oh, and, Travis," she called after him. When he turned to look at her, she wagged a warning finger at him. "No fighting with your brother."

Though the decision not to attend the welcome home party was hers, it didn't stop Lacey from feeling a bit blue after Travis left. She moped around the cabin, looking for something to do to fill the hours until he returned.

She'd just gone into the bedroom in search of a book or another magazine to read when she heard the sound of an engine outside. Thinking Travis had forgotten something, she headed for the living room to greet him.

"Did you forget your stick?" she teased as she opened the front door. She stepped back, her mouth sagging open when she saw that it was Mandy, Merideth and Sam stepping up onto the front porch, and not Travis. "What are you doing here? You should be at the party."

''We're playing fairy godmother,'' Mandy said, laughing as she swept past Lacey and into the cabin followed quickly by Merideth and Sam.

She dumped a garment bag on the couch, then turned, rubbing her hands together with glee. ''Okay, Cinderella, let's get busy.''

Still dizzy from the whirlwind of activity created by her half sisters when they'd appeared unexpectedly at her door, Lacey stepped out onto the patio where the party was already in full swing, flanked by Merideth, Mandy and Sam.

Decorated much as it had been for the wedding reception less than a week before, the patio looked more fantasy than reality to her. Strands of miniature lights woven through the vine-covered lattice ceiling twinkled like stars on a dark sky, while tiki torches set strategically along the patio's perimeter added their own golden glow. Two banquet tables heaped with what seemed standard fare for a McCloud party—barbequed brisket, potato salad, baked beans and bread baked a rich, golden brown—stood along the patio's low wall.

''You made it!'' Alayna cried and rushed over and grabbed Lacey's hands, squeezing them within hers. ''I'm so glad they were able to persuade you to join us.''

Lacey scowled. ''Coerced would be more like it.''

Alayna wrinkled her nose. ''They can be rather overpowering at times, can't they?''

Lacey glanced over at her three half sisters, then rolled her eyes when she found them peering at her innocently. ''Bulldozers, the lot of them.''

Alayna took a step back, still holding Lacey's hand, and looked her up and down. ''Merideth couldn't have been a part of this,'' she murmured, frowning, then laughed, squeezing Lacey's hand in hers. "You're dressed much too conservatively."

"I'll have you know I coordinated the entire outfit," Merideth cried, insulted. She gave an indignant sniff, then added, "She just didn't require as much embellishment as you."

Laughing gaily, Alayna tugged on Lacey's hands, drawing her with her. "She's right, you know," she admitted confidentially. "I was rather a sad case. Covered myself from neck to toe, sure that no man would find what was underneath in the least bit interesting." She scrunched her nose impishly. "But Jack did." When Lacey's cheeks turned pink in embarrassment, with a laugh, Alayna draped an arm around her cousin's shoulders. "I'll bet you're starving," she said. "I know I am."

Within minutes, Lacey held a laden plate in one hand and a frosty margarita glass in the other.

"Mom, do I have to wear this stupid tie?"

Lacey glanced down at the little boy who had asked Alayna the question and tried not to laugh at the pained look on his face.

Alayna set her plate on the buffet table and knelt in front of him. "But you look so handsome, Billy," she said, adjusting the knot of his tie. "Why do you want to take it off?"

He wedged a finger between his neck and his shirt collar and stretched, trying to give himself some breathing room. "'Cause it's choking me to death."

Alayna laughed and tweaked him on the end of his nose. "You're as bad as your father."

Lacey watched the boy's chest swell a bit, and knew the comparison pleased him. But it obviously didn't dissuade him from his goal to receive permission to remove the hated tie.

"Uncle Travis isn't wearing one," he complained, trying to build a stronger case for himself. "So why do I have to?"

At the mention of Travis, Alayna frowned and pushed to her feet. "Okay. Okay," she said, with an impatient wave of her hand. "Take it off." With a whoop of victory, Billy wrenched the knot of his tie loose and ripped it over his head.

"Put it in your pocket so you won't lose it," Alayna called after him as he dashed away, happy again. She reclaimed her plate. "Children," she said with a heavy sigh, then laughed. "Aren't they wonderful?"

Lacey took a sip of her margarita to hide her smile. "I'll have to take your word for it."

"Word for what?" Travis asked, joining them.

Alayna whipped her head around to look at him, then away again, fixing her gaze on her son. "That children are wonderful," she replied reluctantly, obviously resenting his presence, then cried, "Billy!" and quickly shoved her plate back onto the table. "Don't you dare put that ice down the back of your sister's dress!"

Chuckling, Travis draped an arm around Lacey's shoulders as they watched Alayna race away to prevent a sure tragedy. "Cute kid," Travis said. "Reminds me of myself at that age."

Concerned by Alayna's obvious resentment of Travis, Lacey looked up at him. "You haven't been fighting with your brother, have you?"

Travis shook his head. "Haven't so much as said a word to him. I think we're in what's called a Mexican standoff."

"What's that?"

He laughed and kissed the end of her nose. "It means

we're avoiding each other." His smile softened as he looked down at her. "I'm glad you came."

Leaning into him, she returned his smile. "Me, too."

He ran his hand from her shoulder to her elbow and back, sending shivers dancing down her spine. "You look beautiful."

She glanced down, holding the skirt of her dress out to admire it. "It is pretty, isn't it? It's Mandy's," she said, then frowned. "Or maybe it's Merideth's and the shoes are Mandy's. I can't remember which."

He crooked a finger beneath her chin and tipped her face back up to his. "I wasn't talking about the dress. I was talking about you."

"Oh," she said, flustered.

He laughed, then dropped a kiss on her lips. "Wanna dance?"

She held up her plate. "I'm eating."

He took the still full dish from her and set it on the table next to Alayna's abandoned plate. "You can always eat," he said as he pulled her into his arms, "but how often do you have the chance to dance with a man as handsome as Travis Cordell?"

Laughing, she slipped an arm around his neck. "Your ego has got to be as big as the state of Texas."

"Bigger," he said proudly and guided her into a waltz.


"That shirt looks damn familiar."

Travis glanced up and saw Jack standing not a foot away, his hands planted on his hips. As happened nearly every time he looked at his brother, Travis felt as if were caught in the middle of a tractor pull and was being slowly but viciously ripped in two. One part of him wanted to grab his brother up in a big bear hug and the other part wanted to slink away in shame because of the secret he kept from him. He turned his gaze back to his beer mug and finished filling it, then shut off the spigot on the keg. "It ought to," he said, then forced a smile as he turned to face him. He lifted the beer in a silent toast. "It's yours."

"Damn right it is," Jack replied and plucked a mug from the table. "And it looks a hell of a lot better on me than it does on you," he added as he gave Travis a nudge away from the keg. He filled his mug, then turned to stand beside his twin, both looking out over the people crowding the patio.

"How was the honeymoon?" Travis asked after a minute or two of silence.

"Good. Real good, as a matter of fact. How was the cabin?"

"It was okay," Travis replied with a shrug.

"Do any fishing?"

"Some."

"Catch anything?"

"A few."

Jack turned to frown at him. "You're a talkative son-of-a-gun, aren't you?"

Travis smiled, but kept his gaze on the crowd. "I'm told that my brother and I are a lot alike in that way."

Laughing, Jack hooked an arm around Travis's neck and hugged him hard against his side. "Yeah," he said as he turned his gaze back to the patio, "but I'm the good twin and you're the bad one."

The truth in the lightly made comment robbed Travis of his smile. You don't even know the half of it, he thought sadly.

Narrowing his eyes against the emotion that burned behind them, Travis stared out at the crowd. "Do you love her?" he asked quietly.

Jack dropped his arm from Travis's shoulders, and sighed heavily, obviously having feared that the conversation would eventually lead to this topic. "Yeah, I do."

"You couldn't have known her for very long before you proposed."

"About a month."

Travis whipped his head around to stare at his brother. "A month! Hell, that's hardly any time at all."

Jack lifted his chin, but refused to look at Travis. "Long enough for me to fall in love with her."

Travis fought for patience, knowing that losing his temper would serve no purpose. And he had to make sure Jack wasn't making another mistake. He owed him that much, if not more. "I know you were hurting, Jack," he began. "Losing your son, and all. That was tough. But—"

Jack turned, singeing Travis with an angry look. "Yes, it was tough. Tougher than anything I've ever had to face in my life. But Josh's death has nothing to do with Alayna, and it has nothing to do with my reasons for wanting to marry her, and I resent you inferring that it does."

"I'm sure you do," Travis replied agreeably, "but you need to look at this rationally, and I'm not sure that you can. It would be only natural for you to want to fill the void Josh left in your life. People do it all the time. Hell, they've even got a name for it," he said gesturing wildly with his beer mug. "Rebounding. You see cases of it every afternoon on those TV talk shows. But it's nothing to be ashamed of, Jack. Those kids of Alayna's are cute, and considering how they're orphans and all, it would be only natural for you to want to adopt them, so you could replace—"

"I'm not trying to replace Josh."

Sighing, Travis laid a hand on his brother's shoulder and squeezed. "I know you don't think you are, but—"

Jack shook the hand off his shoulder. "You can't replace something that is still there, Travis. Josh will always have a place in my heart. No matter how many kids Alayna and I decide to bring into our home and into our lives, Josh will always be right here," he said thumping a hand hard against his chest. "He's my son. I could never replace him."

"I know you couldn't, but—"

Jack tossed up his hands in frustration. "Damn it, Travis! Are you hearing anything at all that I'm saying to you?"

"Well, sure I am, Jack. I'm hearing every word. But what I think you need is some counseling. We can set you up with—"

Jack turned on his heel and stalked away.

"Where are you going?" Travis called after him. "I'm not done talking to you, yet."

"Yeah, you are," Jack tossed over his shoulder. "You ruined my wedding. I'm sure as hell not going to let you ruin my welcome home party, too."

Travis glanced at his watch then looked around again in search of Lacey. He was ready to head back to the cabin and hoped she was, too. He didn't want to ruin Jack's welcome home party, but if he hung around, he was afraid they'd come to blows again. His brother's unwillingness to talk to him frustrated him that much.

Wondering where Lacey had slipped off to, he headed for the house. Just outside the powder-room door, he bumped into Sam.

"Have you seen Lacey?" he asked.

"No. Is she lost?"

Travis chuckled. "No, or at least, I don't think she is."

Sam pointed down the hallway. "There's another bathroom off the master bedroom. You might check there."

With a nod of thanks, Travis headed down the long hall. At each room he passed, he peeked inside to make certain he didn't miss her. When he approached the third door on the right, he noticed a light was on. He stuck his head inside and saw Lacey standing in front of a portrait, her arms folded beneath her breasts, staring up at it.

He glanced at the picture and decided that it must be of her father. Though faint, there was a resemblance between the two. He shifted his gaze to her. Tears glimmered in her eyes and her expression was one of longing, yet he was sure he saw regret there, too. He recognized the look because he lived with it himself everyday.

With a sigh, he slipped quietly into the room. He eased up behind her and wrapped his arms around her, resting his cheek against hers. "Is that him?" he asked softly, looking up at the picture.

She folded her arms over his and nodded.

"You've got his eyes," he said and pulled her a little closer against his chest.

"So does Mandy," she murmured. "Odd, isn't it? That we would have the same eyes, yet different mothers?"

Sensing her need for a connection to the man who had sired her, he lifted a shoulder. "Not really. In fact, you share a few traits with all your sisters."

Intrigued, she angled her head to look at him. "Really?"

He smiled and bumped his nose against hers. "Yes, really. You walk like Sam and you've got Merideth's figure."

She laughed and turned back to the picture. "I do not."

"Yes, you do," he insisted, "although the walk may be due to the fact that you and Sam both ride horses."

"Maybe," she said doubtfully, "but I certainly don't have Merideth's figure. Heavens!" she said and laughed. "She's—well, she's—"

"Stacked?" he suggested helpfully.

She swung her head around to look at him, then turned back to face the picture, frowning. "I'm not stacked, and what are you doing looking at Merideth's figure, anyway? She's a married woman."

"No harm in looking," he said in his defense, then laughed when she turned to glare at him. "And you are stacked," he said when she turned to face the front again. He lifted his hands to cover her breasts and squeezed gently. "And in all the right places," he added, nuzzling her ear.

Sighing, Lacey relaxed back against him and rested her head beneath his chin. "I wish I knew why he didn't want me," she said sadly as she stared up at the picture.

"Why is knowing so important to you?"

"You wouldn't understand."

"I might."

"No, you wouldn't."

"Try me."

Frustrated, she pushed from his arms and turned to face him. "You can't possibly understand because you have parents who love you," she said, her voice rising. "And you know them. Their likes and dislikes. Their faults, as well as their strengths." She whirled back around to gesture at the picture. "But I never knew my father, and I have no idea what he was like. I only know that he didn't want me."

She turned to him then, tears flooding her eyes, and

drew her hand into a fist against her heart. "And that hurts," she said, her voice raw. "That hurts really bad."

Travis followed Lacey into the cabin's bedroom, unsure what he could say to make her feel better. He watched her tug off the borrowed earrings and step out of the borrowed shoes, then turn, stretching a hand over her shoulder to fumble for the dress's back zipper.

Wanting to give her what comfort he could, he crossed to her and placed his hands on her shoulders and his mouth against the side of her neck. "Here. Let me," he murmured. When she dropped her arms to her sides in defeat, he caught the zipper's small flap and slowly pulled it down. He felt her shiver as his knuckles scraped across her bare skin, then the swell of her sigh as she dropped her chin.

Slipping his hands beneath the dress's shoulder straps, he leaned to press his lips between her shoulder blades, then slowly pushed the dress down her arms. It fell in a pool of black around her bare feet.

Slowly, he turned her around and drew her into his arms. "I wish I had the power to give you the answers you want," he said, holding her close.

She gulped and wound her arms tightly around his neck. "Don't be nice to me, Travis," she said, fighting back the tears. "If you are, I'll cry."

He chuckled and caught her beneath the knees and swung her up into his arms. "You don't have anything to worry about, then," he said as he crossed to the bed, "because I couldn't be nice even if I tried." He sat down, kicked off his shoes, then swung his legs up onto the bed, shifting her more comfortably across his lap. "I've told you, my heart is as black as cast iron and twice as hard."

Smiling wistfully, she drew his face down to hers. "Liar," she said before touching her lips to his.

He rolled, turning her against the mattress beneath him. "A liar, huh?" he growled playfully, hoping to draw her from her blue mood. "Nobody calls Travis Cordell a liar and gets by with it."

Lacey reached for the top button of his shirt. "Oh?" she said coyly, knowing full well his intent, and grateful to him for offering her the distraction she needed. "And what do you plan to do about it?"

"Make you beg for mercy," he threatened, and was relieved to see her smile.

She laughed softly and released another button. "We'll see who begs who for mercy," she chided. She opened another button and another until she reached the waistband of his slacks where she tugged his shirttail free. Placing her hands high on his chest, she drew them down, scraping her nails lightly over his flesh. At his waist, she unbuckled his belt and let it fall open while she went to work on his waistband hook.

After freeing it, she lifted her gaze to his and held it as she slowly pulled down his zipper. Her smile turned smug when he shuddered and then groaned. "Ready to beg for mercy, yet?" she asked.

"Not on your life," he said, then sucked in a breath when her fingers grazed his quickly hardening arousal.

Smiling confidently, she gave his chest a shove and succeeded in rolling him to his back. Before he could move, she was climbing on top of him to straddle him. "I'm going to enjoy listening to you beg," she whispered as she raked her tongue over his nipple.

He jerked instinctively, then groaned as her clever mouth worked its way down his chest. He felt her fingers close around his arousal and could have easily begged for mercy then, but his pride wouldn't let him. And Travis did have his pride.

She sat up and worked his slacks and briefs over his hips, then dipped her face over him, running her tongue along his length.

"Damn, Lace," he grated out through clenched teeth, wondering how long he could hold out before she had him screaming for mercy.

She glanced up at him and smiled. "Ready to beg, yet?" she teased.

"No," he said and squeezed his eyes shut, steeling himself against whatever torture she had planned.

Smiling, she took him in her mouth and flicked her tongue against his tip. "You will," she promised. "It's just a matter of time."

Travis ground his teeth together as pleasure ripped through him and left him gasping. Perspiration popped out on his forehead and upper lip while she teased him with her mouth and tongue, and still he managed to remain silent. Knowing he couldn't hold out much longer though, he reared up, caught her beneath the arms and drew her to him as he lay back down.

"Think you're pretty clever, don't you?" he said as he nipped at her lower lip. "Well, we'll see who's going to do the begging." He closed his mouth over hers, stealing her reply, then began his own form of torture, running his hands up and down her body, stroking, petting, teasing, lighting one fire only to abandon it to start another.

Wanting him more at that moment than she'd ever wanted anything in her life, Lacey pushed away from him and rose to her knees, positioning herself over him. He looked up at her, his eyes burning into hers. "Mercy," she whispered and held his gaze as she lowered herself onto him. She gasped as their sexes met and arched, instinctively taking him deeper. "Sweet mercy," she said on a ragged sigh and slowly began to ride him.

# Seven

With her head tucked beneath Travis's chin and her cheek resting on his chest, Lacey stretched, purring her contentment.

"I won, you know," Travis reminded her smugly and pressed a kiss against the top of her head.

She laughed and smoothed her palm across his chest. "This round," she conceded prudently, not willing to give him the full victory.

"This round!" he cried, feigning indignation. "I suppose now you're going to demand the best two out of three?"

She glanced up at him and teased him with a smile. "Or the best three out of five. Whatever it takes."

He shifted her on top of him, cupping his hands around her buttocks. "You don't scare me. My endurance is exceeded only by my good looks," he said, grinning.

As Lacey looked at him, she couldn't remember ever

being more happy, more totally or supremely content. And it was all due to Travis. Laughing, she dropped a kiss on his mouth. "Oh, I love you."

The hands on her buttocks tensed, and the body beneath her went rigid. "Don't say that," he said flatly and shifted her off him.

Startled, she watched as he rolled from the bed and to his feet. "Say what?"

"That you love me," he said, jerking on his jeans.

Lacey stared at his back, her eyes wide in horror. She hadn't said that, had she? She didn't love him. She couldn't possibly be in love with him! She was much too wise to allow herself to fall in love with a charmer like Travis Cordell.

But as badly as she wanted to deny his claim, insist that he'd misunderstood, she couldn't seem to push the words past the knot of emotion that clogged her throat. She did love him, she realized, feeling the panic tighten her chest. She hadn't meant to fall in love with him, hadn't planned to. She wasn't even sure at what point her feelings for him had grown that strong. Yet, she did love him. With all her heart.

And obviously, he didn't share her feelings.

Angry with herself for falling in love with him, she pushed off the bed. "Well, don't let it go to your head or anything," she snapped and snatched his shirt from the floor and stuffed an arm through a sleeve. "It wasn't a marriage proposal."

Hearing the hurt in her voice, as well as the anger, Travis braced his hands against his hips and hauled in a deep breath. He didn't want to hurt her. But he didn't want her to love him, either. Inevitably, he hurt the people who loved him. And he didn't want to hurt Lacey.

He turned slowly and watched as she furiously pushed

buttons through the holes of his shirt—or rather, Jack's shirt. He sighed, thinking of the irony in that. It was one of Jack's shirts that had destroyed the close relationship he'd always shared with his brother.

"I'm sorry," he said quietly. "I didn't mean to hurt your feelings."

She snapped up her head to glare at him, her cheeks flushed with anger. "Hurt my feelings?" She hooted a disbelieving laugh. "There goes that ego of yours again, killer. I'm amazed you can even carry that head of yours around, it's so big." She snatched a high-heeled shoe from the floor and tugged it on.

"It isn't you," he said, his voice heavy with regret. "It's me."

She straightened, and swept her hair back over her shoulder. "I think we've already established that, haven't we? I love you, but you don't love me back. End of story."

"Lacey—"

When he started toward her, she pushed out a hand, stopping him. "Don't touch me," she warned him angrily.

He stopped and shoved his hands deeply into the pockets of his jeans. "Okay. I won't touch you. But you have to listen to what I have to say."

She snorted a laugh and headed for the door. "I don't have to do anything I don't want to do."

He grabbed her arm before she'd taken two steps and whirled her around. She braced her hands against his chest to keep from slamming against him.

"You're going to listen," he grated out and gave her a hard shake.

Fearing she wouldn't be able to hold back the tears much longer, she jerked up her chin. "All right, fine. But make it fast, killer. My patience is wearing thin."

He let her go so fast she stumbled back a step, unaccustomed to the height of the heels she was wearing. "I don't deserve you," he said, and turned away.

Stunned, she stared at his back. "Don't *deserve* me?" she repeated, then laughed. "I've heard a lot of excuses before, but that one wins the prize."

He spun again to face her, his face tight with barely contained fury. "You asked me why I wasn't close to my family and I told you it was because I'd committed the unforgivable sin."

Frightened by the fury she saw in his eyes, she took a step back. "Yeah, you did. So what? My family and I aren't very close, either."

He took a step toward her. "But you deserve your family's love. I don't deserve mine." He took another step and she could feel the heat of his anger radiating from him. "I slept with my brother's wife the night before their wedding."

Her eyes went wide. "Alayna?" she gasped.

Frustrated, he sliced a hand through the air and turned away from her. "No, not Alayna. His first wife, Susan."

"Why?" she whispered, shocked by his confession.

He dragged his hands down his face, then dropped them to his sides, his shoulders slumping beneath the weight of his guilt.

"I didn't know she was Jack's fiancée until the next day at the church when I saw her walk down the aisle toward him." He dropped his chin to his chest, shamed by the memory. "But that doesn't make me any less guilty. The fact is, I slept with my brother's fiancée."

"What did Jack do?"

"Do?" He turned to look at her over his shoulder, then snorted a humorless laugh. "He didn't *do* anything. He never knew." He snatched up a T-shirt and tugged it over his head, needing to escape, to get as far away from her as he could. "And I didn't have the guts to tell him," he said, pushing his arms through the sleeves.

"Oh, my God," she whispered.

He angled his head to look at her. The disgust he found in her eyes didn't surprise him. Hell, he disgusted himself. "I'm a coward, Lace. Nothing but a yellow-bellied coward who hurts the people who are foolish enough to trust me with their love." Stalking past her, he stormed through the door.

Lacey stood, staring at the spot where he'd been, too stunned to move.

He'd slept with his brother's fiancée?

The slam of the front door made her jump and she whipped her head around to see Travis walking away from the cabin, his hands stuffed deeply into his pockets, his shoulders hunched beneath the weight of his guilt.

He loved his brother, she argued silently, staring after him, her eyes wide, her heart thundering against her ribs. Hadn't he come to the wedding to try to stop Jack from making another mistake? He'd stood before a room full of strangers, surely a humiliating experience, and tried to persuade his brother to leave with him. And when Jack had refused, hadn't he tried to bodily remove him, even fought with him, in an attempt to save him from what he was sure was another mistake?

She pushed to her feet and ran to the front door, watching as Travis disappeared into the woods beyond the cabin. She pressed a hand against the screen's coarse mesh, fighting the need to go after him and comfort him. He'd hurt her, she told herself, even as she strained to see him in the darkness. He didn't deserve whatever comfort she had to offer him.

He'd broken a heart already scarred by those whose love she had foolishly yearned for.

Cognizant of the pain that she was subjecting herself to, Lacey pushed through the screen door and went after him.

Travis hurled the rock, watching as it skipped along the ribbon of moonlight on the lake's glassy surface before sinking below the murky water.

He wasn't sure why he'd felt compelled to tell Lacey his sordid story. He'd certainly never told anyone else. Not his brother. Not even his parents. But when he'd seen the hurt in her eyes and known that he was responsible for it, he knew she deserved to know the truth about him. It was his guilt that had alienated him from his family, a just punishment for his sin, to his way of thinking. He didn't deserve their love. Not after what he had done. And he didn't deserve Lacey's love, either.

Angry, he picked up another rock and hurled it, watching until it disappeared from sight...and wished he had the courage to dive beneath the dark water and put an end to the guilt.

"What are you thinking?"

He tensed at the sound of Lacey's voice, then forced his shoulders to relax. "That I wish I could sink like that rock, and end it all."

"Why don't you?"

Sure that his honesty would have sent her running in the opposite direction, he turned to look at her. She stood on the dam just above him, still wearing Jack's shirt, watching him. With the moon behind her, her face was in shadows, making her expression unreadable. "Because I'm a coward," he replied bitterly and turned his back on her.

"Really?"

"Yeah, really," he muttered and folded his arms across his chest. He heard the crunch of her footsteps on the crushed rock that lined the dam's wall as she started down the embankment, and wished with all his heart that she would go away and leave him alone with his misery.

"How do you know?" she asked as she stopped beside him. "Have you considered suicide before?"

"Once," he said, hoping if he proved to her how cowardly he was, she would run screaming from him. "I even went so far as to load my rifle."

"What stopped you?"

"Jack called."

"Jack called," she repeated thoughtfully and turned her face to peer up at him. "Did he talk you out of it?"

"No," he said, frustrated by her persistence. "He didn't know what I was planning to do. He called to ask me to go into partnership with him in the building business."

"And you did?"

He angled his head just enough to frown down at her. "Yeah, I did."

"Why? I thought you didn't like the building trade?"

He heaved a frustrated breath, wanting to end the conversation, wanting her to leave. "I don't. But Jack's wife was putting pressure on him to move to Houston and start his own company, and he didn't have the start-up money required to go it alone."

"And you did?"

"I had my savings."

"And you were willing to sacrifice your savings and work at a job you didn't enjoy just to appease Jack's wife?"

He whipped his head around, his eyes filled with fury.

"I didn't do it for *her*. I did it for Jack. He loved her and would have done anything to please her."

"And you love Jack."

"He's my brother."

And for Travis, Lacey thought, that was reason enough. She couldn't imagine the depth of that kind of love, had never experienced it herself. But she'd had a sample of it over the past few days, the barest taste, and discovered it left her hungry for more. Having experienced Travis's warmth, his comfort, made looking at him now even more difficult, knowing he didn't share her feelings.

But he'd offered her comfort when she'd needed it the most, she reminded herself, and she'd give him the same. Even if it killed her.

As he himself had once said, she thought sadly, paybacks were a bitch.

Knowing this, she shook her head slowly as she turned her face toward the water. "You're really eaten up with it, aren't you?"

He angled his head to look at her again. "Eaten up with what?"

"Guilt."

Stunned by her simple pronouncement, he could only stare.

"Know what, Travis?" she said and turned to meet his gaze. "I think you're probably the bravest man I know."

He barked a laugh and stooped to pick up another rock. "Yeah, right," he said sarcastically, and hurled the rock out across the water.

"No, really," she insisted. "Not many people would have been willing to make the sacrifices you have made for your brother."

"It wasn't a sacrifice. I did it because I owed him."

"No. You did it because you loved him, and that just proves that you *do* have a heart."

He grabbed her by her wrists and jerked her up hard against his chest. "Don't fool yourself, Lacey," he warned darkly. "I don't have a heart."

The hands that gripped her wrists were strong and bruising, and the eyes that bored into hers dark and threatening. But the heart that throbbed against hers was real and warm.

"Yeah, you do," she said, remembering what he'd said to her not so long ago about her finding her place in the McCloud family. "You just haven't found it yet." Easing from his grasp, she turned and walked away.

Desperate to leave before Travis returned, Lacey didn't take the time to change clothes, but threw her belongings in her bag and left the cabin. By the time she reached Mandy's house, the party was over and the guests were gone. She parked her truck and trailer on the driveway and headed for the patio where lights still burned.

Hearing her approach, Merideth straightened, holding a plate with a half-eaten cake. She sputtered a laugh when she saw Lacey. "Well, look who the cat dragged up."

Lacey glanced down, her face heating when she realized that she had on the black shirt that Travis had worn to the party, the hem of which hit her just below mid-thigh, borrowed high heels...and nothing else.

"Shut up, Merideth," she growled and stepped onto the patio.

Merideth tossed back her head and laughed. "You couldn't stand it, could you? You're determined to beat my record for getting caught most often in an embarrassing moment."

Not in the mood for Merideth's digs, not after the conversation she'd just had with Travis, Lacey crossed to her half sister, scooped icing from the cake plate, then slapped it on Merideth's forehead and dragged her fingers down her face.

Merideth's mouth dropped open. "Why you—you—" she sputtered indignantly as she swept the icing from her face. Then, sucking in a furious breath, she firmed her lips and pushed the cake plate into Lacey's cheek.

"Merideth!" Mandy and Sam cried in horror.

But Lacey didn't even hear their cries. She was spoiling for a fight, and she'd just found one. Snatching a bowl of chocolate sauce from the table, she whirled on Merideth.

"You wouldn't dare," Merideth said, backing away, then squealed, covering her head when Lacey upended the bowl over it. Chocolate ran over her fingers, through her blond hair and dripped off the end of her nose and chin. Seething, she wiped chocolate from her eyes. "You've done it now," she warned dangerously and made a wild grab for Lacey. Within seconds they were rolling around on the patio, smearing chocolate and creamy white icing all over each other.

"Do something, Sam!" Mandy cried helplessly.

"Like what?" Sam asked, unconcerned by it all.

"I don't know. But *something!*"

With a shrug, Sam turned away.

"Stop it, you two!" Mandy shouted, trying to separate them. "Stop it right this instant!"

Sam returned, dragging the water hose. Calmly, she turned it on all three.

"What—!" Mandy whirled and caught the spray full in the face.

Sam laughed, then shrieked when Mandy jerked the hose from her hand. She turned to run, but slipped on the wet patio and fell against Merideth and Lacey who were

rying to scramble to their feet…and managed to pull
Mandy down with her.

The hysterical laughter of all four of Lucas McCloud's
daughters filled the night as they held on to each other,
slipping and sliding as they tried to stand, their efforts
hampered by the slick mixture of water and chocolate and
creamy icing that coated the stone floor.

Jesse, Mandy's husband, opened the patio door and
stuck his head through the opening. "Mandy?" he called
uncertainly. "Are y'all all right?"

"We're fine, sweetheart," she called, laughing, holding
on to Lacey as they both struggled to stand. "We're just
cleaning up the patio."

He gave them all a funny look. "Whatever you say,"
he said doubtfully and went back inside.

Laughing, Merideth offered Lacey and Mandy each a
hand and helped them to their feet. Lacey immediately
tugged off the borrowed shoes. "Dang heels," she muttered. "I'd have whipped you good, if not for them."

Merideth slung an arm around Lacey's shoulders and
headed her toward a nearby grouping of chairs. "Oh, I
don't know," she said offhandedly. "You seemed to be
holding your own just fine in spite of them." She dropped
her arm from around Lacey and sank down into a chair.
"In fact, if I had any doubts you were a McCloud, they're
gone now. You fight just like one." She held up a hand,
palm facing out.

Not wanting to put too much stock in Merideth's comment, Lacey slapped her hand against her half sister's in
a high-five. "You didn't do too shabby yourself," she
said as she took the chair next to hers.

"I think this calls for a celebration," Mandy said, and
set a tray of margaritas on the table. Pulling up a chair,
she reached for a glass, then sat down, gesturing for the

others to take one, too. She lifted her own glass in a toas
"To the McCloud sisters," she said proudly.

"To us," Merideth and Sam chimed, lifting the
glasses. They all three turned to look at Lacey expe
tantly.

Stunned that they were including her as one of th
McCloud sisters, she slowly raised her glass. "To us,
she said hesitantly and clinked her glass against theirs.

"To us!" they echoed, laughing.

Feeling the warmth of their acceptance, Lacey san
back against her chair, a slow smile building.

Mandy took a sip, then propped her feet on the edg
of Merideth's chair. "Now don't take this wrong," sh
said to Lacey, "but why exactly are you here?"

Reminded of the purpose of her visit, Lacey curled bot
hands around her glass and clung to it as tears pushe
their way into her throat. "I was hoping you could pu
me up for the night."

Merideth cocked her head to look at Lacey. "Don't te
me you and Travis have had a fight?"

Lacey shook her head. "N-no. Not a fight, really. Wel
I guess it was a fight. You see, he— It's just that—" T
stop the tears that brimmed, she tipped back her head an
groaned, frantically trying to blink them back. When sh
thought she could control them, she lowered her chin an
tried again to explain. "I thought he loved me. I reall
did. But when I told him I loved him…he—he didn't sa
it back. In fact, it made him mad."

Merideth jumped to her feet, her face flushed with fur
"I'll teach that Travis Cordell a thing or two. Nobod
messes with a McCloud. When you hurt one, you take c
the whole bunch."

Though touched by Merideth's willingness to go to ba
tle for her, Lacey caught the hem of her skirt and pulle

her back down. "It's not his fault," she said, then added miserably, "I guess I'm just hard to love."

"Bull hockey," Sam groused. "There's nothing wrong with you. If there's a problem, it's with him."

Thoughtfully, Lacey studied her glass. "Maybe," she said slowly, thinking of the guilt he lived with. Then she glanced up, moving her gaze from one McCloud sister to the other. "It really doesn't matter whose fault it is. The fact is, I can't stay at the cabin any longer." She turned to look at Mandy. "Would you mind if I stayed here until Buddy is ready to haul?"

Mandy leaned forward and laid a hand on Lacey's knee. "Of course you can," she said and gave the knee a reassuring squeeze. "This is your home. You'll always be welcome here."

This is your home.

Even as Lacey thought about what Mandy had said the night before, a lump formed in her throat. Her home. And a home where she was assured she'd always be welcome.

She stepped out onto the patio and breathed deeply of the early morning air. A home, she thought again. How long had it been since she'd felt as if she had one?

With a shrug, she strode in the direction of the barn. Didn't matter, she told herself. She had one now, and that was what was important.

And that was what she would turn her mind to. She wouldn't think about Travis or the pain that currently filled her chest.

She had a home to come to and sisters who cared for her. That's what she would focus on.

With dawn turning the sky pink behind him, Travis pulled open the cabin's screen door and stepped across the threshold. He turned and held the door until it closed completely behind him, not wanting it to slam and wake Lacey. Then, keeping his tread light, he crossed to the bedroom.

One step inside and he stopped, his heart seeming to stop, too.

She was gone.

He knew it without even looking around. But he did look, needing the validation. The bed was empty, the covers tangled as they'd been when he'd bolted from the bed the night before. The borrowed dress he'd helped Lacey out of wasn't on the floor where he'd dropped it either. And the dresser top was bare but for a thin layer of dust and the smear of fingerprints she'd obviously left when she'd reclaimed the earrings she'd placed there.

With his heart thudding in his chest, he headed for the bathroom. The vanity where she'd stored a small assortment of toiletries was clear, and only one toothbrush lay on the back of the sink.

He sagged against the door, the wood frame digging painfully into his shoulder.

She was gone.

It's best, he told himself and forced himself to turn away. If she'd stayed he would've only hurt her more. Crossing to the bed, he shucked out of his jeans and ripped his T-shirt over his head then fell face first across the mattress, dragging a pillow beneath his cheek.

Her scent, though faint, rose to choke him. Or was it the tears? On a dry sob, he rolled to his back to stare blindly at the ceiling.

It's what you deserve, Cordell, he told himself miserably. You aren't worthy of anyone's love.

Travis grunted when a boot hit the side of his leg, then rolled, blinking open his eyes to a squint to find his brother standing at the foot of his bed.

"What the hell did you kick me for?" he grumped irritably.

"It's noon," Jack said and pulled up a chair. "Past time for you to be up and moving."

Travis pushed himself to an elbow and raked a hand through his hair, making it stand on end. "I'm on vacation," he grumbled sleepily. "I don't have to get up at any special time."

"And how long is this vacation of yours going to last?"

Travis glanced up sharply, his eyes narrowing. "How long is *yours* going to last?" he shot back.

"Yeah, we need to talk about that," Jack said with regret and propped his boots up on the bed. "You can have the business."

"I don't want the business. I never did."

Jack lifted a shoulder. "So sell it and do what you want."

Moaning his frustration, Travis dropped his face onto his palms, slowly counted to ten, then dragged his hands down his face to look at his brother. "You're the one who wanted the business, Jack," he said carefully, "not me."

"True, but Alayna and I have talked about it and we've decided we don't want to live in Houston. We want to stay here. I'm going to start a business here."

"You and Alayna," Travis repeated, his anger rising in spite of his determination to remain calm. "Why is it that you can talk to her and not to me?"

Jack grinned. "Because she's prettier than you."

Scowling, Travis fisted a hand in his pillow and chucked it at his brother's face. Jack caught it, laughing. "Sorry, but it's true."

Travis decided to give it one last shot. "Jack, you need

counseling. I can make you an appointment with a psychologist who can—"

"I live with a psychologist."

"—help you come to terms with your grie— What did you say?"

Jack's grin widened. "I said I live with a psychologist."

Travis's eyebrows shot high on his forehead. "The hell you say!"

Jack held his hands up. "It's the truth. I swear. Alayna has a degree in psychology. Had a practice for several years in Raleigh, North Carolina, before she sold it and moved here. If you don't believe me, ask her."

Travis's scowl returned. "I doubt she'd talk to me."

"Can you blame her? You crashed her wedding and turned what was to be the happiest day of her life into a barroom brawl."

"I was only trying to keep you from making another mistake."

Jack arched a brow. "If you were worried about me making a mistake, you should've stopped me from marrying the first time around."

Travis tried to discern if there was something in Jack's tone that suggested he knew something that he wasn't sharing. When he couldn't detect anything he heaved a sigh. "Okay, so maybe I went about it all wrong," he said, willing to concede a little. "But I'm still not convinced that you should've married so soon after Susan's and Josh's death. What are you doing?" he cried in frustration when Jack drew the pillow to his nose and sniffed.

"Since when did you start wearing perfume?" Jack asked, narrowing an eye at his brother.

Travis launched himself off the bed and snatched the pillow from Jack's hand. Turning his back on him, he tossed the pillow back to the bed. "It's not mine, it's Lacey's."

"Lacey's!" Jack exclaimed, rising to his feet. "You've been shacking up with Alayna's cousin?"

Travis whirled and threw a punch at Jack's jaw. Jack ducked, barely missing the blow, then slowly straightened, looking at his brother in surprise. "You're in love," he said, an incredulous smile building.

Growling, Travis lunged again, but this time Jack was ready for the attack. He caught the fist aimed for his face and twisted it up and around until he had Travis's arm pinned behind his back. He gave it a sharp tug, making Travis bow his back, grunting in pain. "So my little brother has finally fallen in love," he said, chuckling.

"I'm not in love," Travis snapped, then ground his teeth together when Jack gave his arm another tug.

"Sure are acting like a man in love," Jack replied, unconvinced.

"Let go of me, damn it!" Travis demanded angrily.

"I'd be willing to do that if you'll make me a promise."

"What?" Travis grated out, glaring at the far wall.

"You being around makes Alayna kind of uneasy. She knows how you feel about our marriage and she's uncomfortable. She's afraid you're going to start trouble again."

"Bullsh—" Travis started to say, then sucked in air through his teeth when Jack gave his arm another tug, making pain shoot up his arm and across his shoulder.

"Look," Jack said patiently, "Alayna...well, she's my wife, and a man needs to keep the peace in his family, you understand?"

"Just spit it out, Jack," Travis said in frustration. "What do I have to do?"

"Talk to her. Just talk to her," he said, grinning. He

released his hold on his brother. "Now that's not so hard to do, is it?"

Travis could fill a book with the reasons why he found the thought of talking to Alayna difficult. First, she was a woman, and women, in his experience, tended to get emotional over the slightest little thing.

Second, she was Jack's wife, a fact that Travis himself had tried to prevent from happening, which he knew didn't endear him to his new sister-in-law.

And, third, she was a psychologist, and Travis had always felt a little uneasy talking to psychologists or psychiatrists or anyone else who had studied the subtleties of the mind. He'd dated a psychiatry major for a while several years back, and had finally broken it off because he'd discovered that after being with the woman for an hour or more, he was a nervous wreck. Always worrying about what he was saying, how he was saying it, what his expression or body language was when he was saying it. Hell! It got to where he couldn't put two words together and make any sense.

But he'd talk to this psychologist, he told himself as he made his way to her house. And he'd do it as much for his own sake as Jack's. He had to be sure that this woman was the right one for his brother. He couldn't stand by and watch Jack make another mistake.

Not again.

# Eight

**A**layna opened the back door at Travis's knock, her eyes guarded as she peered at him suspiciously. "Jack's not here," she said and would've closed the door in his face if he hadn't stuck his foot in the opening, preventing her from doing so.

He frowned when her gaze snapped to his, her eyes wide in alarm. "I know where he is. I came to talk to you."

"Me?" she asked in surprise and hastily stepped back out of his way as he brushed past her.

"Yeah, you," he said peering around. "Jack seems to think we need to talk."

Clasping her hands nervously at her waist, Alayna followed him into the kitchen. She unwound her hands to gesture at a chair at the table. "Please, sit down," she said politely.

"Thanks," he muttered dryly, infuriated as much by

her formality as he was by her obvious discomfort around
him. He flopped down in the chair and hooked a thumb
in the waist of his jeans. Rocking the chair back on two
legs, he studied her. It pleased him when she lifted her
chin and met his gaze squarely, even if her chin did quiver
just a bit.

He dropped his chair down to all four legs and scooped
up a saltshaker to hold between his hands. "Jack tells me
that you don't like me."

She was quick to deny it. "I never said that to Jack."

"Maybe not in so many words. But it's obvious you
don't want me around."

Alayna dropped her hands to her lap and nervously
pleated the skirt of her apron between her fingers. Aware
of the nervous habit, she dropped the fabric and flattened
her palms against it, smoothing it over her thighs. Rather
than deny the accusation, she chose to qualify it. "I love
Jack," she said firmly. "And I won't see him hurt."

"I love him, too."

Startled by the depth of emotion in his voice, Alayna
stared. "You love Jack?"

He scowled and avoided her gaze by slumping down
in the chair and focusing his attention on the saltshaker.
"He's my brother. I don't want to see him hurt, either."

"It's not my intention to hurt Jack," she returned. "I
think he's suffered quite enough, don't you?"

"Too much," he muttered, then set the saltshaker aside.
He planted his forearms on the table and leaned toward
her, leveling his gaze on hers. "More than any man de-
serves to be hurt," he added, "which is why I think it
was a mistake for him to marry you so soon after Susan's
and Josh's death."

Alayna heard the accusation in his voice, felt it in the
intensity with which he looked at her...but wasn't of-

fended by it. If anything, it made her curious to know why he considered her a threat to his brother. "And what would you consider an adequate amount of time for Jack to wait to remarry?"

He snorted and reared back, picking up the saltshaker again. "Longer than he did," he said dryly.

"Would a year have made it easier for you to accept?" she asked pointedly. "Or perhaps two?"

He tossed the saltshaker up in the air, watching its slow fall. "Maybe."

"Do you have a problem looking at a person when you talk to them?"

He slapped his hand around the saltshaker, catching it in midair, and snapped his gaze to hers. "Don't pull that psychological bullshit with me," he warned her. "It won't work."

She surprised him by smiling and even visibly relaxing a little. "Jack said something similar in a discussion we had once."

"Yeah," he replied bitterly. "Jack's had some experience on a shrink's couch, too."

"Yes, he told me. An unpleasant experience for him, as I recall. But he didn't mention that you'd seen a psychologist also."

Travis continued to toss the saltshaker but glanced her way. "Not professionally," he replied and turned his gaze back to the saltshaker. "Though I did sleep with one for a while."

"Slept with one," she repeated slowly, studying him. "Not in love with one, nor dating one, but you *slept* with one."

"Yeah," he said and caught the saltshaker, closing his fingers around its neck as if strangling it. "You got a problem with that?"

She arched a questioning brow. "No, do you?"

He slammed the saltshaker down on the table. "Damn it," he swore, dropping his elbows to the table and raking his fingers through his hair. "I hate psychologists."

"Why?"

He peered at her through the frame created by his arms. "Because they're always twisting a person's words around and making something out of them that they're not."

"I don't believe I twisted your words around. You said you'd slept with one. I merely repeated your words."

"Yeah," he said, anger burning through him. "But you made it sound as if I don't have any feelings. That I'm a user."

"Do you consider yourself a user?" she asked.

Glaring at her, Travis reared his chair back and stuffed his fingertips into the waist of his jeans. "See!" he cried, freeing a hand to gesture wildly at her. "You're doing it now. You're twisting my words all around. I never referred to myself as a user."

"You inserted the word into the conversation, not I."

All four legs of the chair hit the floor with a loud thump. "Okay, I'm a user," he said, his voice tight with barely controlled fury. "I sleep with a woman and I take from the relationship what I want, what I need. And when, and if, I think the woman is getting too serious or she starts making little nesting noises, I split. But," he said emphatically, "and this is important, so listen carefully," he warned, leveling a finger at her nose. "I give her what she wants while I'm there. I know how to satisfy a woman and how to make one happy."

"So you consider yourself a good lover."

"I don't consider myself a good lover, I *know* I am."

"You sound awfully sure of yourself."

He leaned across the table and placed his face inches from her own. "I am."

Though she tried to school her expression, to keep it free of the suspicions that suddenly spun through her mind, it was difficult, and Alayna could only pray that she succeeded. "Why do you feel that you have to prove yourself?"

He shoved to a stand, knocking over his chair, his face red with a rage that had been building since he'd first stepped into her kitchen. "Because women demand of it of me," he shouted angrily, gesturing wildly with his hand. "They throw themselves at me, wanting to see for themselves if I'm as good as they've heard. To see if they'll be the one to tame me, to force me to my knees." He whirled away from her and braced his hands against the wall as if he could shove his way through it and escape her probing questions, using nothing but his bare hands to bust his way free.

As suddenly as it had appeared, the rage drained from him, and he dropped his forehead into the crook of his elbow, his chest heaving.

Alayna rose slowly and crossed to him, laying a hand on his back. He shuddered at her touch and pressed his forehead deeper into the curve of his arm. "I didn't know she was his fiancée," he murmured, his voice trembling. "I swear, I didn't know."

"Susan?" she asked, suspecting from the guilt she heard in his voice, that it was Jack's first wife to whom he referred.

"Yes," he said and slowly pushed himself away from the wall. He drew his hands to his hips and inhaled deeply, tipping his face to the ceiling. Then he turned to look at her, and released the breath on a shuddery sigh. "Yes, Susan," he murmured.

"Does Jack know?" she asked quietly.

"No. I never told him."

She watched him roll his lips inward, gripping them between his teeth, his guilt obvious in his ravaged look, in the haunted depths of his brown eyes. A face, she noted absently, whose features matched almost perfectly those of her husband. Eyes the same shade and shape of her beloved Jack's.

Knowing somehow that his heart was just as warm and pure as that of her husband, Alayna opened her arms to him. "Come here," she said softly.

Travis hesitated only an instant before he stepped into her embrace and wrapped his arms tightly around her. He felt the steady beat of her heart against his chest, the tenderness in the hand that stroked his back, and buried his nose against her hair, filling his senses with her sweetness and absorbing the comfort she offered.

"What are you doin' to my mother?"

Travis tensed, then slowly released Alayna and stepped from her embrace. "Stealing all her hugs," he said, holding on to her arms a moment longer as he searched her eyes for the condemnation, the disgust, he feared he would find there. Seeing only forgiveness and understanding, he released her and turned to look at Billy, one of Jack and Alayna's foster children. "Jealous?" he asked, ruffling the boy's hair.

Billy ducked from beneath his hand, scowling. "No, but my dad might be," he warned, eyeing Travis suspiciously.

"Jealous of me?" Travis asked, then looked at Alayna and smiled. The warmth and openness of the smile she offered back to him freed him of his fears for his brother and made him realize that his brother was right this time. Jack had found the perfect woman as his mate. "No reason to be jealous of me," he said and shifted his gaze back to the boy. "Jack's the better twin."

"You're darn right he is," Billy replied, his chest swelling a bit. "My dad's the best dad there is."

"Won't get an argument out of me," Travis said easily. He turned and looked at Alayna. "About what I told you…"

She smiled softly. "That's your secret and not mine to share."

Relieved, he heaved a deep breath. "I guess I better be going then. I have a feeling that Jack's probably waiting for me to help him finish up the repairs on the barn roof."

"We're getting a horse," Billy said and fell into step beside Travis.

Travis held the door open and waited for the boy to pass through. "You are?" he said, feigning surprise. He shot Alayna a wink. "I bet he'll buck you off."

"Will not," Billy said smugly. "I ride real good. Jaime taught me."

Alayna stood at the door, her hand pressed against the screen and listened to the two argue as they walked together toward the barn, Billy hurrying to match his step to Travis's longer stride. She saw Travis toss his head back and laugh and was warmed by the rich sound of his laughter. Then she watched, her heart skipping to her throat, as Travis bent and scooped Billy under his arm and carried him like a sack of potatoes to the barn. With a sigh, she turned back to the kitchen, knowing that though she and Travis had resolved their differences, he had a long way to go before he was freed of the guilt that held him in its clutches.

Travis watched Billy skip off, trailed by his little sister Molly. "Cute kid."

Jack looked up from the board he was measuring, then back down, smiling as he scraped a pencil across the wood, marking his measurement. "Yeah, he is. They all are."

Travis picked up a level and held it across his open palm, watching the bubble move from side to side before settling. "I talked to Alayna."

"Hoped you would." Jack clipped the tape measure to his belt and grinned. "I sure didn't want to have to wrestle you down again."

Travis snorted. "Like you could."

"I did, didn't I?"

"Pure luck. You caught me at a weak moment. Hell, I was still half-asleep."

Biting back a smile, Jack picked up a handsaw and aligned it over his mark. "Women'll do that to you."

"You ought to know. Personally, I avoid 'em every chance I get."

Jack lifted his head slightly to peer at his brother from under doubtful brows. "Sharing a bed with a woman for almost a week is what you call avoiding?"

"She's not there now, is she?" Travis replied arrogantly.

"In the cabin?" Jack asked as he pushed the saw across the board, making the first cut.

"Well, yeah." Travis looked at his brother curiously. "Where else would she be?"

"At Mandy's. Saw her over there a while ago when I went to talk to Jesse about buying the kids a horse."

Travis's breath locked up tight in his lungs. He'd thought she was gone. As in all the way gone. When he'd returned to the cabin and hadn't found her there, he'd assumed she'd packed up and left. He hadn't thought about her just relocating. He turned to stare at the fields that lay between the barn and Mandy's house.

"You don't have to hang around here," Jack said. "You can go and talk to her if you feel the need to."

Travis whipped his head around to glare at Jack. "And why would I want to do that?"

Jack shrugged a shoulder and spun the board around, preparing for the next cut. "It was just a suggestion."

"She did the leaving," Travis said defensively. "Not me."

"And you didn't give her a nudge toward the door?"

Travis felt the guilt seep into him, remembering the look on her face when he'd bolted from the bed after she'd told him she loved him. "She said she loved me," he said absently, staring blindly at the board Jack had marked.

"Do you love her?"

Travis snapped his head up. "I care for her, but I didn't encourage her, if that's what you're thinking."

"I'm not thinking anything."

"Well, you have that look in your eye, like you don't approve of what I did."

Jack chuckled and shook his head. "What you do is your business." He picked up the saw again. "But if you hurt her, I'm going to have to beat the tar out of you. After all, she is Alayna's cousin."

"I didn't do anything to her," Travis insisted. "It isn't my fault she fell in love with me."

"I doubt that it's her fault, either." Holding the saw in place against his thumb, Jack glanced up at his brother. "Not everybody can keep as tight a rein on their emotions as you can. You'd do well to remember that the next time you invite a woman to share your bed."

"What do you think, Sam? Is he ready?"

Sam walked slowly around Buddy, pinching her lips

thoughtfully between thumb and finger as she looked the horse over. Squatting down beside his left foreleg, she murmured softly to him as she smoothed a skilled hand over his wound. Pleased with the way it was healing, she pushed to her feet and lifted his hoof, bending his leg at the knee and watching for any resistance to the movement. Satisfied, she dropped his hoof and straightened.

"Well?" Lacey asked anxiously. "Is he ready?"

Sam laid a hand against the horse's neck and squinted against the sun as she looked up at Lacey who was squirming nervously in the saddle, awaiting her report. "He looks good," she said carefully, afraid to build Lacey's hopes up too much before she was sure. "But why don't you run a pattern of barrels and let's see what he does under stress?"

"Okay," Lacey said uneasily as she gathered the reins in her hand. "But watch him on the second barrel," she warned as she trotted away. "He really digs in and spins on that one."

"Just breeze him," Sam called out, hitching a foot on the arena fence and climbing to sit on the top rail. "We don't want to push him too hard."

Lacey tipped a finger to her forehead, acknowledging she'd heard the warning, then turned Buddy into the narrow alleyway that led into the arena. She drew in a deep breath, feeling the energy building in him as he strained at the bit. "Okay, Buddy," she whispered. "Let's show her what you can do."

She took a deep seat when he began to prance, set her boots firmly in the stirrups and tightened her fingers on the reins, knowing what would happen once she pointed his nose toward that first barrel. Buddy was a competitor and loved nothing better than to run. The alleyway that led into a rodeo arena was to him his own personal launchpad.

"My God," Sam whispered as she watched Buddy burst from the alleyway and out into the arena, his hooves flying over the plowed ground, his tail streaming out behind him. In the blink of an eye, he was sitting down on his haunches and spinning around the first barrel. Impressed, Sam sat up straighter and strained to watch as Lacey raced Buddy for the second barrel.

"Is he doing okay?"

At the sound of Travis's voice, Sam frowned and patted the air beside her, signaling for him to be quiet. She squinted her eyes, focusing her attention on the horse's left foreleg as he wrapped the second barrel. "He took it a little wide," she noted uneasily as Lacey headed him toward the third. "But that's okay," she said as if reassuring herself. "This is his first time out since his injury, so she's probably not pushing him too hard."

Travis propped his arms along the arena wall and peered through the rails, watching. It was the first time he'd seen Lacey ride…and it was the first time he'd seen her since the night she'd told him she loved him and he'd turned her away.

He wasn't sure which of the two circumstances to blame for his heart suddenly crowding his throat.

"Couldn't she get hurt doing that?" he asked in concern, then winced as the horse brushed against the third barrel and made it rock.

"Sure she could," Sam replied, beginning to smile as the barrel righted itself and Lacey leaned forward in the saddle, giving the horse his head as they raced for home.

Once the two disappeared into the alleyway, Sam looked down at Travis and her smile disappeared. "But not any worse than you could hurt her." She jumped down from the arena wall and dusted off the seat of her jeans. "In fact," she added, turning to frown at him from the opposite side of the fence. "I'd trust that horse with her before I would you."

"How'd he do?" Lacey called as she trotted Buddy back into the arena.

"Fine," Sam replied as she crossed to her, still frowning. She glanced up and saw the fear in Lacey's eyes and forced a smile. "Better than fine," she quickly amended. "Y'all are going to look good at the nationals."

Relief washed through Lacey. "Oh, Sam," she said, wilting in the saddle. "You scared me there for a minute. Judging by the look on your face, I thought for sure you were going to say he wasn't—" At that moment, she saw Travis standing beside the arena, and her throat closed up.

"Ignore him," Sam said quietly, seeing the tears fill Lacey's eyes. "Or, if you want me to, I can tell him to leave."

"No," Lacey said, shaking her head and forcing her gaze back to Sam's. "It's okay." She inhaled deeply and forced a smile. "So you think he's ready, huh?"

"Ready as he'll ever be," Sam replied confidently. "You're planning on leaving tomorrow, right?"

"Yeah, there's a rodeo in Houston."

Sam gave the horse a last pat then stepped back out of the way. "No more running today, then. Cool him down and you might give him some more water therapy on that shoulder."

"Will do. And thanks, Sam." With a wave to her sister, Lacey reined Buddy toward the far side of the arena, hoping that Travis would leave before she reached the spot where he stood.

He didn't. In fact, by the time she'd lapped the arena, walking Buddy to cool him down, he'd climbed to the top rail and was sitting, watching her and waiting. She kept her gaze focused straight ahead, refusing to look his way.

"Lacey?"

She closed her eyes, steeling herself against the entreaty in his voice, then opened them and glanced his way. "What?"

He waved her toward him. Reluctantly she guided Buddy alongside the rail.

He leaned over and rubbed a hand on the gelding's face. He smiled when Buddy nickered. "What'd he say?" he asked, glancing up at her.

"He said, keep your hands to yourself."

Travis heard the resentment in her voice, but stubbornly kept on rubbing, determined to try to make things right between them.

"Doesn't it scare you to go that fast?" he asked, hoping to draw her into a conversation.

"That wasn't fast. That was just a breeze."

"Looked fast to me." He jerked his hand away when Buddy nibbled at his fingers, and drew it to his knee, rubbing it along his thigh.

"Don't worry," Lacey said spitefully. "He doesn't have any communicable diseases." She saw the hurt flash in Travis's eyes before he ducked his head and wished she could take back the sharply spoken words.

She watched his hand move slowly along his thigh and remembered that hand smoothing across her own skin. Soothing, comforting...seducing. She felt a knot of yearning curl low in her gut and glanced away just as he raised his head to look at her.

"Can't we at least be friends?" he asked softly.

Friends? Was that all he wanted from her, friendship, when she wanted so much more than that from him?

More, obviously, than he was willing to offer her in return?

She hadn't known that a heart could break twice. But it could, she realized, feeling the fissure rip through her chest.

"I don't know why we should be," she said, fighting back the storm of tears that threatened. She dug her spurs into Buddy's sides. "See you, killer," she called over her shoulder as she loped toward the barn.

Lacey didn't allow herself to cry. She couldn't. If she did, she was afraid that she'd never be able to stop. Instead, she focused her mind and her attention on her horse, rubbing him down and grooming him, then giving him the water therapy as Sam had suggested.

By the time she was finished, she was hot, wet and bone-dead tired. The heat was due to the intensity of the unrelenting Texas sun. The wet was due to Buddy deciding that she needed a shower too, and bumping up against her hand and making her soak herself with the hose.

But the tired she could blame only on Travis Cordell.

She hadn't had a decent night's sleep since she'd left the cabin and his bed.

A nap, she told herself firmly and quickened her step toward the house. That's what she needed. Once she had rested, she knew that she'd be able to look at his rejection in a whole new light. She might even be able to laugh about it.

Maybe.

Seeing a strange car in the drive out front, she frowned as she headed for the back door, hoping to avoid having to meet whoever was inside. It seemed there was always someone coming and going at the Double-Cross, but she wasn't in the mood to suffer through any more introductions. Not today.

Using the metal bootjack by the back door, she jimmied off her boots, then stooped to roll up the hems of her wet jeans before stepping inside the kitchen. The scent of bread baking teased her nose, making her realize that she'd skipped lunch.

She grabbed a banana from a bowl on the counter, then turned for the rear hallway and the guest room that Mandy insisted on referring to as "Lacey's room." She'd just taken a bite out of the banana when she heard a voice raised in anger. The sound seemed to come from Mandy's office, just ahead of her. Hoping to slip by the office unnoticed, she tiptoed quietly down the hall.

"We have our rights, you know. I won't stand by and do nothing while my daughter is denied what's hers."

Lacey froze at the sound of the voice, then had to flatten a hand against the wall to keep from sagging to her knees.

*Her mother? Here? At the Double-Cross?*

"Our lawyer will take this case to the Supreme Court if necessary," JoAnn Cline raged on. "Lucas may have refused to claim her, but she's his and I have the proof right here to substantiate our claim."

Fury built slowly, starting low in Lacey's gut and climbing to swell in her chest until she could barely breathe. She tossed down the banana and stormed into the office, her eyes blazing as she glanced quickly around, noting its inhabitants.

Sam sat on the couch and Mandy behind the desk, her husband Jesse standing behind her. Her mother sat in the wingback chair that Lacey herself had sat in a week ago when she'd had her first meeting with her half sisters.

Had it really only been a week ago? she thought wildly, then shoved the thought aside.

Beside her mother sat a man Lacey didn't know. She ignored him and turned to her mother. "What are you doing here?" she demanded furiously.

JoAnn Cline stood and glanced nervously at Mandy before turning back to her daughter and lifting her chin. "I came to protect your rights. Something that you'll thank me for later," she added with a pointed look that Lacey was sure was meant to cow her into going along with whatever plan she'd concocted.

"You're not wanted here, Mother," Lacey said bitterly.

"No, I'm sure I'm not," her mother agreed, turning to look pointedly first at Sam, then at Mandy. "But you have as much a right to Lucas's estate as they do. And I'm here to see that you get it."

"I don't want anything that was his."

JoAnn's nostrils flared at Lacey's open defiance, but she recovered quickly. "She's high-strung," she said to the man beside her as she sat again. "Like her father in that way, I'm afraid," she added, sending a damning look Lacey's way. "And bitter, too," she continued, turning her attention back to the stranger, "which is understandable, considering that her father refused to acknowledge her while he was living." She turned to face Mandy, once again in control. "And that's why I'm here. To keep Lacey's anger and her bitterness from robbing of her of what is rightfully hers. She's entitled to a fourth of Lucas's estate," she said, daring anyone to disagree with her. "And not a penny less."

"I can understand your concern for your daughter and her welfare, and your desire to see that she gets—"

"I don't want a fourth!" Lacey screamed in frustration, cutting Mandy off. "I don't want anything that was Lucas's. I've already told you that. All of you. Including you," she cried, swinging around to thrust an accusing finger in her mother's face. "It's *you* who wants his money, not me. You always have.

"It infuriated you that Lucas didn't give you control over the trust fund he set up for me when I was born, and it made you even more angry when I refused to give you the money when I turned twenty-one. So angry that you kicked me out of your house and told me never to come back." Tears streamed down her cheeks, and she dashed a hand beneath her eyes, not wanting her mother to think she had the power to hurt any longer. "Well, you aren't getting your hands on any of Lucas's money," she warned. "Not the trust fund, and certainly not the Double-Cross. I won't let you."

"Now, Lacey," her mother began, shifting uncomfortably in her chair.

"My, my, my," Merideth drawled as she strolled into the office and came to a stop in front of JoAnn's chair. "You didn't mention that you were expecting visitors, Mandy," she said, though she kept her gaze focused on Lacey's mother.

"I didn't know she was coming," Mandy murmured from behind her.

JoAnn gave Merideth an assessing look, and, judging by her expression, obviously didn't deem her a threat. "I'm JoAnn Cline," she said arrogantly. "Lacey's mother. Who are you?"

"Mother?" Merideth repeated and turned to look at Lacey. "It seems as if I do remember you mentioning having one of those." She turned a cat-like smile on JoAnn. "And a loving one, as I recall." She shifted a briefcase-style purse to tuck it beneath her arm and extended her hand to JoAnn in greeting. "I'm Merideth, Lacey's sister."

"Half sister," JoAnn snapped and brushed the offered hand aside.

Merideth tossed back her head and laughed, the sound echoing in the suddenly quiet room. Then she turned and slung a companionable arm around Lacey's shoulders and drew her to her side. "Well, we don't get hung up on those little details around here, do we, Lacey?" Not waiting for an answer, Merideth gave Lacey a fierce hug, then turned to Mandy, who was sitting behind the desk, trying her best to hide a smile.

"While I was in town, I stopped by the lawyer's office as you requested," Merideth told her and slipped a large envelope from her purse and dropped it on the desk. She shot Mandy a wink. "But before we discuss what he's sent us, I think we need to bid farewell to our company." She turned to look at JoAnn, one eyebrow arched expectantly. "You *were* leaving, weren't you?"

Glaring at Merideth, Joann stubbornly remained in her chair.

Undaunted, Merideth turned to the man sitting beside her and extended her hand. "I don't believe we were properly introduced. I'm Merideth McCloud Carter."

He rose, all but salivating. "Merideth McCloud? The movie star?"

She laughed gaily and clasped her hands around his and squeezed. "Why, yes!" she exclaimed, and drew his arm to her side as she led him to the door. "Have you heard of me?"

"Lord, yes, Miss McCloud!" he gasped, obviously starstruck. "I watched you—what I mean to say is, my *wife* watched you on that soap opera for years. She's a big fan. And we *both* have enjoyed your movies."

"Well, I declare," Merideth simpered, batting her long eyelashes at him flirtatiously. "I'll have to arrange for you and your wife to have tickets to the premiere of my new movie. It opens next month, you know.''

With her hired gun now seemingly camped with the enemy, JoAnn snatched up her purse. ''You haven't heard the last from me,'' she threatened as she stormed from the room.

Lacey sagged into the chair her mother had vacated and dropped her face into her hands, moaning.

Sam and Mandy burst into laughter.

Slowly Lacey lifted her head and looked from one to the other. ''What's so funny?''

When they continued to laugh, Jesse sighed and dropped a hip onto the corner of his wife's desk. ''It's Merideth. They fall apart every time she gives one of her performances.''

''That was an act?''

Merideth swept back into the room and took a bow. ''My best,'' she said, and winked at Jesse. ''In fact, that one will probably win me an Oscar.''

''Or another ardent admirer,'' Sam added wryly. ''Merideth attracts men like a hay barn attracts mice,'' she explained to Lacey. ''It thrills her no end when they start drooling all over her.''

Merideth dropped gracefully onto the sofa beside Sam and waved away her sister's comments, sending the gold bracelets on her arm clinking musically. ''Ignore her,'' she said to Lacey. ''She's just jealous. Besides,'' she said, and gave Sam a smug look. ''I got rid of them, didn't I?''

Not sharing their feeling of elation, Lacey pushed herself wearily from the chair. ''I'm sorry,'' she said, shamed by her mother's greed. ''I had no idea she was planning on coming here and demanding a part of Lucas's estate. I'll pack my things.''

''Sit down,'' Mandy ordered firmly.

"But—"

"Sit," Mandy repeated and pointed to the chair.

Lacey glanced at Jesse, but he merely lifted a shoulder. "When she gives an order, I've learned it's easier to comply than to argue. Saves time, too," he added, and smiled at Lacey.

Stunned that they were insisting she stay rather than hustling her toward the door after what her mother had tried to pull, Lacey sank back down into the chair.

"Now," Mandy began and reached for the envelope Merideth had dropped on her desk. "We have a little business to take care of." She opened the envelope's flap and pulled out a sheaf of papers. "Earlier this week—Monday to be exact," she clarified, glancing up at Lacey and smiling "—Merideth, Sam and I paid a visit to our attorney.

"We know that you've said that you don't want anything that was Lucas's and we all respect your reasons for feeling that way. But you *are* a McCloud and our sister, and we want you to always consider the Double-Cross as your home." Rising, she paused a moment as tears filled her eyes. She pressed a finger beneath her nose as she stared down at the papers she held, then looked back up at Lacey, inhaling deeply. "We instructed our lawyer to—" She held up a hand then pressed it to her lips. "Just a minute," she murmured tearfully, then sniffed and dabbed at her eyes, struggling to get control of her emotions.

"Oh, for heaven's sake!" Merideth snapped. She rose, snatched the papers from Mandy's hands and turned to Lacey. Tears filled her eyes as she met Lacey's gaze. Squaring her shoulders, she drew in a deep breath. "We discussed this at great length," she began, then had to stop and firm her lips. She huffed a breath, then tried again. "And after careful consideration, we instructed our lawyer to draw up papers giving you—'' She held up her hands in defeat, tears streaming down her face. ''I can't do it, either,'' she wailed.

''Geez,'' Sam muttered as she pushed herself to her feet. ''Do I have to do everything around here?'' She jerked the papers from Merideth and shoved them into Lacey's hands. ''We had the lawyer draw up these papers making you a full partner in the Double-Cross.'' She dashed a finger beneath her nose and sniffed. ''It's not from Lucas,'' she said before Lacey could refuse them. ''So you don't have to feel as if you're accepting anything from him. It's ours to give, and we want you to have it.''

Numb, Lacey stared at the papers in her hand, then looked up at Sam. ''W-why?'' she stammered.

''Don't you get it?'' Merideth cried, sweeping her hands across her cheeks to wipe away the tears. ''You're family! Our sister.''

Mandy rounded the desk and placed an arm around Lacey's shoulders, hugging her to her side. ''You were already our sister here,'' she said softly and placed a hand over her heart, ''where it counts most. The papers just make it official.''

# Nine

Jack glanced over at his brother then down again at the sheet of tin he was hammering into place. "Heard Lacey was leaving today."

"Yeah," Travis muttered as he crawled along the roof to push a new piece of tin into position. "That's what I heard, too." And hearing that bit of news had kept him up all night, which was the only explanation he could come up with for his current dark mood.

"Have you told her goodbye?"

"I talked to her yesterday."

Jack rocked back on his heels to look at his brother. "Well? What did she have to say?"

"That she'll see me around."

Jack dropped back down to his hands and knees and positioned a nail over the tin. "Sounds pretty vague to me. But I guess that's what you wanted."

"No, it's not what I wanted," Travis snapped. He lifted

the hammer and pounded the nail home in three angry strokes.

"But I thought you said you didn't care for her?"

"I never said that."

Puzzled, Jack scratched his head. "I could've sworn that yesterday when you told me that she was in love with you, you didn't mention anything about loving her back."

"I said I *cared* for her. I didn't say anything about loving her."

Jack scowled and picked up his hammer. "Semantics," he muttered under his breath. At Travis's quizzical look, he added irritably, "Choice of words."

"I know what semantics means," Travis cried, "I just didn't know that you did."

"I'm married to a psychologist. I *have* to know these things. Self-preservation."

Jack's pained expression drew a smile as Travis remembered his own conversation with Alayna. "I bet she's hell to fight with."

Jack snorted. "You don't know the half of it. Everything I say, she has a comeback. 'And why do you feel that way, Jack?'" he said mimicking her. "Or, my personal favorite, 'Though I can understand why that might upset you, have you considered...'" He shuddered just thinking about it. "Now I ask you," he said, shaking his hammer at his brother, "who can fight with a woman like that? Especially one who never loses her temper?"

"Not me," Travis said. "That's for sure. There's nothing like a good heated argument to get the old blood pumping and the bedsprings squeaking." He chuckled and bumped a new piece of the tin with his knee, edging it into position. "Take Lacey for instance. Now that woman's got a temper." He shook his head as he positioned a nail over the tin. "Can't stand to let anybody see her cry, though."

"You made her cry?"

Travis glanced over to find Jack watching him carefully. "Not exactly. Well, no," he said with more conviction when Jack started crawling toward him, his eyes narrowed dangerously. "She just had a lot to deal with while she was here."

When Jack kept coming, Travis started backing toward the ladder, knowing that if it came to a fight—and it was bound to because Jack had always felt the need to protect those weaker than himself—his brother had the advantage on a roof. Travis never had been any good at negotiating an incline, whereas Jack could dance a jig on a tightrope. "You know what I'm talking about," Travis said, stalling for time, "all that stuff about her father. That was pretty heavy. And I think Merideth was giving her a pretty hard time."

"I'll take care of Merideth later," Jack growled. "What I want to know is, did *you* make her cry?"

Travis dropped a foot over the side of the barn, fishing for the ladder. "I'll have to give that some thought," he said, and all but sagged with relief when his boot struck a rung. He was sliding down the ladder like a monkey before Jack had reached the edge of the roof.

He hit the ground running, but skidded to a stop when he heard Jack cry for help. He glanced over his shoulder and saw the ladder swaying back and forth and Jack clawing at the barn roof, trying to get a grip so that he could pull the ladder back against the wall.

His heart in his throat, Travis lunged for the ladder and put all his muscle behind it, forcing it back into position. Dipping his forehead in the curve of his shoulder to wipe the perspiration from his face, he held the ladder steady while Jack climbed down.

"Whew! That was a close one," he said and released the ladder to wipe his hands across the seat of his jeans as Jack stepped to the ground.

"Did you make her cry?"

Travis froze, his palms cupped around his rear end. He glanced up at the roof, then back to his brother, his eyes narrowing. "You faked that whole thing, didn't you? Just so I couldn't get a head start on you?"

"I'll do whatever it takes to make you admit that you love her."

"Love her!" Travis tossed up his hands. "Didn't you hear what I said up there?" he asked, stabbing a finger in the air toward the roof. "I said I *cared* for her."

"And I say you love her."

Travis huffed a breath and turned away. "You can say anything you want. It doesn't change a damn thing."

"It's still eating at you, isn't it?" Jack called after him.

Travis froze, his heart shooting to his throat. Jack couldn't know, he told himself. There was no way he could know. Unless Alayna had told him. But she'd promised she wouldn't, and Travis would swear on his life that Alayna was a woman who honored her promises.

He forced himself to take a step, then another. "You're the only thing that's eating at me," he tossed over his shoulder, trying to bluff his way out of what he feared was a confrontation with his past.

"She told me, Travis. Susan told me what y'all did."

Travis stumbled to a stop and squeezed his eyes shut, praying that he'd heard Jack wrong.

"She wanted to hurt me," Jack continued. "Thought that by telling me what y'all had done, she could turn me against you. She succeeded for a while."

Though he had to dig deep, Travis found the courage to turn and face his brother. "I didn't know who she was, Jack. I swear, I didn't know. Not until the next day at the wedding when she walked down the aisle."

"She said you knew. She said that you told her we shared everything, including our women."

Travis fisted his hands at his sides as rage poured through him. "She lied. I never said that. Hell," he said, tossing up his hands as he turned away to pace. "I didn't even know who she was, or why she was in your apartment! I'd just stepped out of the shower and was putting on one of your shirts, getting ready to go to your bachelor party, when she came in." He raked a hand through his hair, sickened by the memory of Susan stripping off her clothes and luring him back into the shower. But he wouldn't tell Jack that. No man deserved to hear the details of his spouse's infidelities, especially when those infidelities were committed with his twin brother.

"She never even told me her name," he continued miserably. "All she said was that she was a member of the wedding party." He lifted his hands helplessly. "I wanted to tell you the truth, Jack, I swear I did. After the wedding I even told Susan that I intended to tell you. But she insisted that it was all a huge mistake, that she'd seen the shirt and mistaken me for you. She swore that she loved you, and that if I told you what happened, it would break your heart."

"And you honored her request."

It wasn't a question. It was a statement. But Travis felt his brother deserved an answer. "Yes," he said, bowing his head with regret. "I honestly thought that it was for the best. I was afraid if I told you it would screw up your marriage, and I didn't want to ruin your life."

"So you let it ruin yours, instead."

Travis looked up at Jack in surprise and saw that his brother was bearing down on him. He braced himself, knowing he deserved whatever punishment his brother decided to mete out.

"It was my fault, Jack," he said, feeling the full weight of the guilt he'd carried for over five years. "Not yours. There was no need for you to suffer because of something I had done."

Jack stopped in front of him and braced his hands on his hips. "You're a damn fool, Travis."

Travis puffed his cheeks and blew out a long frustrated breath, wishing Jack would just slug him and get it over with. "Yeah, I guess I am."

"Susan made my life a living hell the entire time we were married."

"I know that, Jack, and I'm sorry. A hundred times I've wished that I had told you, and maybe spared you all that pain."

"How long are you going to let her ruin yours?"

Travis gave his head a shake as if it to clear it. "What?"

"I said, how long are you going to let Susan ruin your life?"

Travis angled his head, looking at his brother suspiciously, wondering if he'd been right all along about Jack's mental state. "Susan's dead, Jack," he said carefully. "She can't hurt either one of us anymore."

"I not only *think* she can, I *know* she can," Jack said and folded his arms stubbornly across his chest. "Maybe not me, but definitely you."

Travis shook his head and released an unsteady breath. "I think you've been out in the sun too long, brother. Susan can't hurt me. She never could."

Jack stepped closer, his face livid, and shoved his hands

against Travis's chest, knocking him back. "Can't she?"
he said closing the distance he'd created right back up
"Then tell me why you have avoided the family for the
past five years? And while you're at it, why don't you
explain to me why you tense up every time I get near
you? Why you can't look me in the eye?"

Wanting it over, Travis stood his ground. "Guilt," he
replied matter-of-factly. "I couldn't bear to face any of
you, knowing what I'd done."

"Bingo," Jack said. "Now we're finally getting somewhere."

"I'm glad you think so," Travis said, his frustration
growing by the minute. "Because I sure as hell don't."

"Oh, but we are," Jack said. "In fact, now we're getting to the good stuff."

"What good stuff?"

"Like why you've never married? And why you're letting a woman like Lacey, a woman you obviously care
deeply for, walk away?"

Travis took a step back and held his arms out at shoulder level, offering his brother a wide target. "Hit me,"
he demanded angrily. "Take your best shot. Just hit me,
for God's sake, and get it over with."

"Oh, I'm gonna hit you all right," Jack threatened even
as Travis braced himself for the blow. "I'm going to hit
you right square between the eyes with the truth." He
gave Travis a shove, sending him staggering backward
again, his arms windmilling wildly. "The truth is, you
won't allow yourself to get serious about a woman because of Susan. You're so damn afraid that you'll end up
getting hurt as badly as I did you won't even give yourself
a chance to fall in love."

Furious with his brother for striking so near the truth,
Travis gave him a shove back. "So what's wrong with a

little self-preservation?'' he demanded angrily and gave Jack another shove. ''Just because I'm not a glutton for punishment doesn't mean I've allowed Susan to ruin my life.''

''Doesn't it?'' Jack stared at him a long moment, then shook his head and turned away. ''You're a damn fool, Travis. You're not living your life, you're just existing.''

''Where are you going?'' Travis shouted after him. ''We're not through discussing this yet!''

Jack flapped an arm behind him in dismissal. ''Yeah, we are. Until you're ready to pull your head out of that hole you've stuck it in and take a chance on living, I don't have anything more to say to you.''

Travis stormed around the cabin, throwing his gear into his duffel bag and burning off the anger his brother had left him with.

*Head stuck in a hole. Not living his life. Just existing.*

Each of his brother's accusations burned through him, feeding his anger.

Well, he was doing a hell of lot more than just existing, he thought furiously. He may not have suffered through a lousy marriage, survived an ugly divorce or grieved over the loss of a son, as Jack had done, but, by God, he had a life! He was living.

He stuffed his shaving equipment into his duffel and jerked the zipper closed. ''Damn your sorry hide,'' he swore and tossed the duffel in the direction of the front door.

''Who you cussin'?''

Startled, Travis whirled to stare at the door. Billy stood on the opposite side, his nose pressed against the screen.

''Your daddy,'' Travis muttered, embarrassed at being caught talking to himself. He picked up his rod and reel.

Billy opened the door and stepped inside. "You leavin'?" he asked, nudging the duffel with the tip of a high-top tennis shoe.

"Yeah."

"Where you goin'?"

"Back to Houston."

"Is that where Lacey lives?"

Travis set his jaw at the mention of Lacey, and put a little more strength than was required in securing the lid on the case that held his rod and reel. "I don't know where she lives," he snapped and moved to prop the case by the door.

"I just wondered, 'cause that was where she was headed, too."

Travis turned to look at the boy in surprise. "Houston?"

"Yep." He hopped up on the couch and began to jump up and down on the cushions as if they were a trampoline. "She's riding in a rodeo there tonight."

Scowling at the boy, Travis braced his hands on his hips. "Get down off that couch before you fall and break your neck."

Grinning, Billy bounced once more and landed on the floor. "I never fall," he said confidently, and began to nose around the room.

Travis arched a brow, watching him. "Oh, really? I would've sworn you were the one who busted his head open the night your mother and daddy left on their honeymoon."

Billy tossed a scowl over his shoulder. "Yeah, but that was an accident."

Travis bit back a grin. "That's what most falls are."

"Geez," the boy said, rolling his eyes. "You sound just like my dad."

"We're brothers, so I guess that's only natural."

Billy stuck his head up the fireplace, examining the opening. "You got any kids?"

Travis choked on a laugh. "No. Did you think I might be hiding some up there?"

"No," Billy said, his voice muffled. He was grinning when he pulled his head back out. "I'm just naturally curious." He hopped down from the hearth, then sat on it, propping his elbows on his knees and his chin on his fists as he watched Travis pack up his fishing gear.

"Is everybody gonna cry when you leave?"

Travis looked at the boy in surprise, then snorted a laugh. "I doubt it."

"Man, you should have heard all the blubbering going on over at Mandy's when Lacey left this morning."

Travis didn't reply, hoping the boy would change the subject. He didn't want to talk about Lacey any more, or hear about her either.

"Even Sam teared up," Billy continued, obviously not taking the hint, "and she hardly ever cries, unless she's hurt or something."

"Women are emotional. Might as well learn that now."

"Dad says that, too."

Travis lifted a shoulder. "Smart man, your daddy."

"You think so? He said you were a dumb ass."

Travis whipped his head around and frowned. "He did, did he?"

"Yep. Said he ought to have knocked some sense in that thick skull of yours while he had the chance."

Travis dropped the jeans he was folding and turned to peer at the boy, his eyes narrowed in suspicion. "He said all that to you?"

Billy grinned sheepishly. "Not exactly. I heard him telling it to my mother."

"You shouldn't be listening in on other people's private conversations."

"Wasn't too private. I'm surprised you didn't hear him. He was yelling it at the top of his lungs."

"He was yelling at Alayna?"

Billy squinched his mouth to one side and considered the question. "Not *at* her, exactly. Just to her. Kinda like blowing off steam, you know?"

"Yeah," Travis replied dryly, knowing he was the cause of the steam. "I know."

"He said he'd changed his mind about leaving you alone and was gonna come over here and knock you around some more, but my mother wouldn't let him. She said a person couldn't *make* another person do something, they just had to love 'em and support 'em and hope they eventually saw the light."

"And what did your daddy say to that?"

Billy rolled his eyes. "Nothing. They just started hugging and kissing. Nearly made me puke."

"Billy!'

Billy jumped at the sound of his mother's voice, then ducked his head guiltily when he saw her standing on the other side of the screen door, her mouth squeezed up like a week-old prune. "Uh-oh," he mumbled. "Busted."

Travis tried hard not to laugh as Alayna whipped open the door and marched inside, stopping in front of her son. "Billy Cordell, you ought to be ashamed of yourself, repeating conversations that you had no business listening to in the first place."

"Well, shoot, Mom," he complained, digging the toe of his tennis shoe against the hardwood floor. "I'd've had to be deaf not to hear. Besides, I didn't tell Uncle Travis anything he doesn't already know. Heck, he and Dad beat up on each other all the time."

She pointed a finger at the door. "Out," she ordered. "And don't stop until you reach your room."

His chin bumping his chest, Billy headed for the door. "See ya, Uncle Travis," he mumbled, then pushed through the door.

Travis waited until the boy was out of earshot then burst out laughing. "How do you do it?" he asked incredulously.

"Do what?" Alayna asked, looking at him in confusion.

"Keep a straight face. The kid's a pistol."

Alayna bit back a smile. "I know. And it's hard. *Very* hard," she added, glancing out the window to watch Billy shuffle his way back to the house. She turned back to Travis, her expression softening with regret. "I'm sorry he told you what Jack said. He shouldn't have."

Travis lifted a shoulder and picked up the jeans again, folding them in half. "The kid's right. He didn't tell me anything I didn't already know."

"But still…"

He stuffed the jeans into his suitcase. "Don't worry about it, Alayna. Jack and I have been butting heads for years."

"More than just heads, if what all he's told me is true."

Travis closed the lid on his suitcase. "We've had our share of fights, but that's how we settle our differences." He lifted the suitcase and set it by the door with his other gear. "Isn't that what all you psychologists preach? Express it, don't suppress it?"

"I hardly consider fighting expressing one's self."

"Well, sure it is," he said. He hooked an arm around her neck, and pretended to sock her jaw. "You ought to try it sometime. In fact, I can even give you a few pointers. I know all Jack's weak spots. Spent years studying them so that I could keep the upper hand. His left side is his weakest, so always—''

She turned from beneath his arm and looked up at him. "He loves you, Travis, and he's worried about you."

Though he wanted to, Travis couldn't ignore the concern in her eyes or the seriousness in her tone. He heaved a sigh. "I know he is, but there's no cause for him to worry. I'm fine."

"Are you?" she asked and reached up to lay a hand on his cheek.

The tenderness in her touch was almost his undoing. He closed his hand over hers. "No, I'm not fine. But I'm going to be. I promise."

"And what are you going to do to make yourself better?"

He drew her hand from his cheek, but continued to hold it, squeezing his fingers around hers. "Are you playing doctor with me again?" he teased, hoping to lighten the mood.

"I will if I need to."

"Whoa!" he said, and fell back a step in mock horror. "Is that a threat?"

She bit back a smile. "No. It's a fact." She squeezed his hand, her expression softening again. "Oh, I wish that you could see what we see when we look at you."

"And what do you see? A mirror image of Jack?"

"No," she said, refusing to allow him to distract her from what she wanted to say. "I see a man. A wonderful man, who is sensitive and warm and loving. But I also see a man who is hurting."

He pulled his hand from hers and turned away. "I'm not hurting."

"Then why did you pull away just now? Why won't you look at me?"

He turned to scowl at her. "Is the clock running, Doc? Am I going to get a bill for this session?"

She arched a brow. "No. This one's on the house."

He chuckled ruefully and shook his head. "Listen, Alayna, I don't want to argue with you."

"You'd rather fight with Jack? If so, I'll be happy to go and get him for you."

He huffed a breath. "No, I don't want to fight with Jack."

"Then talk to me. Tell me what you're feeling."

"Why is what I'm feeling so important to you?" he asked in growing frustration.

"It's not so much to me as it is to you. When a person vocalizes his feelings, he must first identify them, and he does that by looking inward. If you'll do that, Travis, I think you'll discover things about yourself that you weren't even aware of."

"Okay," he said, planting his hands on his hips. "We'll play your little game. Right now I'm feeling a strong case of frustration."

"Why?"

"Because everybody keeps pushing me in a direction I don't want to go."

"And what direction is that?"

"You know where."

"Tell me."

"Toward Lacey!" he shouted angrily.

"And why don't you want to go in that direction?"

He sucked in air through his teeth, feeling as if he was being nudged toward the edge of a cliff. But he wouldn't take that last step. He knew the fall would kill him. "I don't know," he snapped and turned away.

"Yes, you do."

When he turned to glare at her, she smiled softly in

understanding. "You don't have to talk to me if you don't want to. But if you want to find the answers, you need to look here," she said placing her hand over her heart. "That's where the answers are." She brushed a kiss on his cheek, then cupped her hand over it as she looked up at him. "Listen to your heart, Travis. Then follow where it tells you to go."

Highway 290. The road that led to Houston. The road that led home. That's where Travis's heart told him to go.

Or so he kept telling himself as he barreled down 290, headed for Houston and home.

The only problem was, the road led to Lacey, too.

Or it did at the moment.

But by tomorrow, Lacey would probably be long gone. The rodeo would be over, and she'd hit the circuit again. And which road would she take out of Houston? North? South? East? West? There were a hundred or more possibilities, and the closer Travis got to Houston, the more the panic set in that he didn't know which way she would go when she left or where to find her when she did.

He told himself it didn't matter, that she'd been nothing more to him than a nice distraction, a pleasant way to pass the time until Jack returned home. She'd been a one-night stand that had stretched into five. But so what? As far as he was concerned, no matter how long the duration, she was still a one-night stand, and that was the type of relationship he liked best. No strings. No commitments. Just good, hot sex.

*Oh, I love you!*

He tightened his hands on the wheel, hearing her voice again as clearly as if she were in the cab of the truck with him. The laughter in it, the late-night huskiness, the rough purr that came from having been recently and thoroughly satisfied.

He hadn't meant for her to fall in love with him, he told himself, trying to block out the sound of her voice. And it wasn't his fault if she had. He had done nothing to lead her to believe that they had any kind of future together. He was always careful that way, always, never fostering hope where there was no hope to be found.

*And why is there no hope?*

The question came out of nowhere, but he knew who had planted the seed for it. Alayna. Her and her psychological mumbo jumbo. Examine your feelings, she'd said. Listen to your heart.

Well, that would take about a negative two seconds, he thought wryly, because he didn't have a heart.

*You have a heart. You just haven't found it yet.*

"Damn!" he swore, slapping his palm against the steering wheel as Lacey's words came back to haunt him.

He'd warned her, hadn't he? He'd told her time and time again that he was a cold-blooded bastard. But had she listened? Had she heeded his warning? Hell, no! She'd fallen in love with him anyway.

And he'd fallen hopelessly in love with her.

Panic grabbed at his chest and he swerved his truck onto the shoulder and stomped on the brakes. Killing the engine, he collapsed against the seat and pressed a hand against the pain in his chest while he gulped in air.

Was he having a heart attack?

No, he couldn't be. He didn't have a heart.

Then why the hell was his chest filled with pain if he didn't have a heart?

*You have a heart. You just haven't found it yet.*

He stared at the road ahead, his breathing ragged, his fingers fisted in his shirt.

He had found his heart, he realized slowly. He'd discovered it the day he first met Lacey.

And he'd lost it again when she'd left.

Reaching for the key, he started the engine and whipped the gearshift into Drive.

He had to find her, he told himself, the panic returning as he pulled out onto the highway again. He didn't know what he would say to her when he found her, or whether or not she would even talk to him when he did.

But he *would* find her. He knew he would, because he wouldn't stop searching until he did.

# Ten

———

Lacey sat astride Buddy in the holding area, waiting for her turn to run. Out of habit, she reached down to check her cinch one last time, just to be sure it was still tight.

She stood in her stirrups, straining to see into the arena where the current contestant was making her run. Dust hung thick in the air, making it difficult for Lacey to see the rider and coating everything in the Astrodome a dull gray. Lacey sank back down in the saddle. Kind of like her mood, she thought morosely.

She gave herself a shake. Focus, she told herself sternly, and sat up straighter in the saddle. She couldn't afford to have her concentration broken. This rodeo was an important one, and even more so since she'd missed a few over the past week due to Buddy's injury. As a result, she'd slipped two positions in the rankings, and tonight she needed to make up for that loss.

She wouldn't allow herself to think about the other loss she'd suffered over the past week. The one to her heart. There'd be time enough to grieve over that later.

Travis dropped a twenty-dollar bill in the slot at the ticket window. "One adult," he said and glanced anxiously at his wristwatch.

"For this evening's performance?" the attendant asked in surprise.

"Yeah," he said. "And could you hurry it up? I don't want to miss anything."

"You've already missed quite a bit. The show started about thirty minutes ago. But I'm afraid you're going to have to miss it all," she added. "The tickets are sold out."

"Sold out!" he exclaimed, stooping to peer at the woman behind the glass.

"Yes, sir. Since yesterday morning. Would you like to purchase a ticket for tomorrow's performance?"

He dropped a hand on the twenty and drew it from the slot. "Tomorrow'll be too late," he murmured and turned away. He walked a few steps away and pulled out his wallet, stuffing the bill back inside.

"You wanting a ticket for the rodeo?"

Travis turned to find a man standing on the sidewalk, watching him.

"Yeah," he said, his eyes sharpening with interest. "You got one to sell?"

"Sure do."

"How much?"

"Fifty dollars."

"Fifty!" Travis cried. "That's highway robbery. They're only fifteen at the window."

"But they don't have any to sell, and I do."

Grumbling, Travis flipped open his wallet and pulled

out a fifty. He handed it to the ticket scalper and received
a ticket in return. He glanced at it quickly to make sure
it had the right date and time, then stuck out his hand.
"It's been a pleasure doing business with you, mister,"
he said and grinned.

Frowning, the scalper shook the offered hand then
stared after Travis when he turned and jogged away.
"Hey!" he called after him. "What are you so happy
about? You just paid me more than three times what the
ticket's worth."

Travis turned, jogging backward. "Yeah, but I
would've paid you a *hundred* times what's it worth. No,
a *thousand!*" he yelled, laughing as he turned to push his
way through the turnstile leading into the Astrodome.

Finding the entrance he needed, he loped up the ramp,
and stopped at the top, looking down into the arena while
he caught his breath. The enclosed area was three or four
times bigger than the arena at the Double-Cross. His heart
stopped when he saw that the barrels were already set up
in the cloverleaf pattern on the far side.

Praying he hadn't missed Lacey's run, he made his way
to his seat. "Can I have a look at your program?" he
asked the woman in the seat next to his as he dropped
down beside her.

She passed it to him without glancing his way. He
flipped quickly to the evening's lineup and scanned for
Lacey's name. Finding it, he passed the program back to
the woman. "Who just ran?" he asked, focusing his gaze
on the gate through which he knew the competitors entered.

"Wasn't paying any attention. I come for the bull riding. Five or six have run, though, I think."

And Lacey was running seventh. He scooted to the edge
of his seat, propped his elbows on his knees and dragged

a hand nervously across his mouth. The rodeo announcer's voice boomed from the speakers, cutting into
the country music that had been playing, to introduce the
next rider as Lacey Cline, a cowgirl from Missouri, who
was currently ranked number nine in the national stand-
ings.

Finding the anticipation unbearable, Travis fell back
against his seat, exhaling a nervous breath, but kept his
gaze fixed on the gate. He lunged forward again, his eyes
wide, when Buddy shot through the opening so fast it
looked as if he'd been launched from a hidden cannon.
Astride him, Lacey was nothing but a blur of green se-
quins and auburn hair flowing from beneath a matching
green cowboy hat. The horse streaked across the arena,
his legs stretched out, eating up the distance, and his muscles bunching for the first turn.

They rounded the first barrel and he watched Lacey's
legs fly out, then dig into the horse's sides, urging him
on to the second. He'd thought the run he'd watched Lacey make at the Double-Cross was fast, but she'd been
right. It didn't compare to this. *This* was speed.

Though her hat shadowed her face, he could see the
determined set of her jaw, the intensity of her expression
as she sat down deeply in the saddle and leaned back,
reining the horse tightly around the second barrel. He was
leaning right along with her as she stretched out over the
horse's neck, giving him his head as she pushed him for
the third.

He clamped his eyes shut, and pressed a hand over his
heart, wondering how Lacey stood the pressure, because
he was sure his own heart was going to pound a hole right
through his chest. A collective gasp from the audience
had his eyes flipping wide, and he watched, his stomach
dropping sickeningly to his toes, as Lacey's stirrup struck

the third barrel and it rocked precariously from side to side. He didn't know much about barrel racing, but he knew enough to know that if the barrel fell over, it would mean a penalty added to Lacey's time.

Fisting his hands against his knees, he focused all his energy on the barrel, willing it to stand, and sagged with relief when it slowly righted. Shifting his gaze quickly to the opposite end of the arena, he watched as Lacey raced Buddy past the finish line, breaking the laser beam, and on through the gate.

"Fifteen-point-twenty-six seconds!" the announcer's voice boomed. "What a run! Rodeo fans, we've got us a new time for our barrel racers to beat because Lacey Cline has just taken over the lead."

Travis's breath rushed out of him, leaving him feeling as weak if he'd just run the race himself. He sucked in two quick deep breaths, then bolted to his feet, pushing his way back out to the aisle.

Now, he had to find her.

The adrenaline high that usually followed a good run didn't stay with Lacey very long. By the time she had guided Buddy alongside her trailer, the blue mood she'd fought all day had slipped back over her.

Swinging a leg over the back of the saddle, she slid to the ground, then reached to unclip her reins. Her movements lethargic, she stripped off Buddy's bridle, replaced it with a halter, then tied him to a hitching bar on the trailer's side panel. Smoothing a hand down his neck and murmuring softly to him she moved to his side and flipped up the fender, hooking the stirrup over the saddle's horn.

"Nice run."

At the sound of the voice, her fingers froze on the cinch strap. She turned slowly, searching the shadows.

"Travis?" she whispered, sure that she'd imagined the sound. She watched, her eyes widening, as he stepped from the shadows and out into the illumination cast by the security lights.

"Yeah, it's me," he said and stuffed his hands deeply into his pockets as he crossed to her.

That he was there, standing not two feet away shocked her so much that she let down her guard enough to let hope slip in unaware. "What are you doing here?"

He lifted a shoulder. "I was in the area, so I thought I'd drop by and watch you compete. Nice run."

The hope that had filled her chest quickly dissipated, leaving her feeling foolish and more than a little angry with herself. She turned to tug on the cinch strap again, loosening it. "Thanks," she said tersely.

"You said Buddy was fast, but I had no idea he could run like that."

She squatted down to unwrap the shin guards from around the horse's forelegs. "It's the crowd. He gets all juiced up when he hears all the noise and sees all the lights." She shrugged indifferently as she stood. "I guess he just likes to show off."

"The announcer said you had the best time. Does that mean you won?"

"No." She dropped the equipment into her tack bag and stepped around Travis, refusing to look at him. "The results aren't final until the last night of the rodeo. I won't know until then if my time will hold."

"Well, it was a damn good run, anyway. How about we celebrate? I'll take you out to dinner."

Though tempted, Lacey knew that it would be foolish to accept his invitation, that it would only cause her more pain. He'd made it clear that he wanted only her friendship. And she wanted so much more. She reached for the horn to strip off the saddle. "No, I don't think so."

The weight of his hand on her shoulder stopped her.

"Ah, come on, Lace," he said and squeezed. "Have dinner with me."

She closed her eyes, willing back the yearning his touch drew. She knew she was weak, susceptible to whatever kindness or warmth he might show her, and, knowing that, she knew she had to get rid of him. Suspecting that the truth might be the fastest way to do just that, she rolled her shoulder, shaking free of his hand. Curling her fingers around the saddle horn, she stripped it from her horse's back.

"Listen, Travis," she said as she strode to the open door of the compartment where she kept her tack. "I know that you want to be friends, and all, but I can't do that, okay?" She heaved the saddle onto the rack. "So why don't you do both me and yourself a big favor and go find someone else who can handle the kind of relationship you want." She turned and dragged her hands across the seat of her pants as she brushed by him again, dodging his gaze. She reached for the saddle pad and blanket, stubbornly blinking back tears.

"I love you, Lacey."

She squeezed her eyes shut, her fingers convulsing on the pad and blanket. He didn't mean it, she told herself. He was just trying to sweet-talk her into his bed again. She jerked the pad and blanket down, then whirled for the tack bin again, blinded by tears. "I didn't think you'd stoop that low," she muttered furiously as she stomped past him.

"Low? What do you mean low? Hell, I said I love you!"

She flipped the gear over, damp side up, across the top

of her saddle, then slammed the door. She spun to face him, angry, hot tears streaming down her face. "What is it you want from me, Travis? Another tumble in bed?" Infuriated by the tears, she dragged the heels of her hands across her cheeks, wiping them away. "Well, I can't do that, okay? I made the huge mistake of falling in love with you, but that's my problem," she said and shoved past him. "And I'll get over it."

"Don't," he said, and caught her by the arm, stopping her.

"Don't what?" she cried, struggling to pull free.

"Don't get over me."

She froze, and turned her head slowly to meet his gaze.

"I love you, Lacey." He tugged her toward him, taking her other hand as well. "And I don't want you to get over me. I want you to love me forever, because that's how long I intend to love you."

She shook her head, not wanting to hear his lies. "No," she whispered, "don't do this."

"I can't help myself. You're kind of hard not to love."

Choking on the tears that crowded her throat, she jerked free of him and backed away. "I won't let you seduce me again," she warned him, swiping furiously at the tears that streamed down her face.

He closed the distance she'd put between them right back up. "You said that once before."

She stuck out an arm, bracing a hand against his chest to stop him. "But I mean it this time, Travis. I swear."

Making a tsking sound with his tongue, he slowly shook his head. "Lacey, Lacey, Lacey," he murmured sadly as he removed her hand from his chest. "You know better than to challenge me."

Frustrated when she realized that he had her hand in his, she cried, "That wasn't a challenge. It's the tru—"

His mouth closed over hers, stealing her claim before she could fully voice it.

Tears continued to stream down her face as she struggled against him. But he only tightened his hold on her, refusing to let her go.

She didn't want him to hold her or kiss her. She didn't want to need him or love him or want him so desperately, either. But as he swept his tongue across her lips, then took the kiss deeper, she was forced to admit that she was powerless against his greater strength, and even more powerless to fight her feelings for him.

And that knowledge upset her as much as had seeing him again.

Choking on a sob, she pushed hard against his chest, desperate to get away from him before he ripped her heart completely from her chest.

"Don't, Lace," he murmured, cupping a hand at the back of her neck and holding her. He dipped his head to meet her gaze. "Don't fight me anymore," he whispered. "Please."

Exhausted from fighting him, she dropped her head against his chest in defeat. "I don't want to love you," she sobbed helplessly, fisting her fingers in his shirt. "I don't want to hurt anymore."

He pressed his lips to the top of her head and rocked gently. "I didn't mean to hurt you, baby. I swear I didn't."

She snapped up her head. "But you *did* hurt me," she cried furiously. "You hurt me really badly."

Seeing in her tear-filled eyes the depth of the pain he'd caused her, Travis forced her cheek back to his chest and dropped his chin on top of her head. "I know, baby," he said, his voice heavy with regret. "But I was only trying to spare you more pain."

"Spare me!" she sputtered incredulously as she shoved from his arms. "From what?"

Dropping his hands to his hips, he braced them there and frowned. "Not from what, from who. Me," he added, jabbing a thumb at his chest. "I didn't think I deserved you. Hell," he said and turned away, tossing up his hands. "I'm still not sure I do. I was so eaten up with guilt over what I did to Jack, that I didn't think I deserved anyone's love, least of all yours." He stopped, dragged a hand through his hair, then turned to look at her as he dropped it to his side. "But you're the first woman who's ever mattered to me, Lacey. The only one I've ever let get close enough to need me." He snorted, then slowly shook his head as he rubbed a hand across the back of his neck. "The hell of it is, I think I need you a lot more than you ever needed me."

"But—"

He held up a hand to interrupt her. "No, let me finish. I may never find the guts to say this again." He braced his hands on his hips again and inhaled deeply, digging deep for the courage to say all that was in his heart. "I love you, Lacey. I've never told a woman that before, but then I've never felt for another woman what I feel for you.

"When you left, you took a part of me with you. The best part. I couldn't sleep. Couldn't eat. Hell, I couldn't even fish." He shook his head, smiling a little at the admission. "And no woman's ever had that effect on me before. I probably would've continued to fight my feelings for you, but then Alayna had a little talk with me, and she told me that if I wanted to find the answers to my problems, I was going to have to look here," he said and laid his hand over his heart. "When I did, I discovered that it was missing. You have it," he said, gesturing with his chin toward her. "And you've had it since that first night at the cabin." He ducked his head and blew out a long shaky breath before he lifted his face to meet her gaze again. "I guess what I need to know is this. What are you going to do with it?"

Lacey stared at him, her eyes dry, her own heart lodged so tightly in her throat she couldn't breathe, let alone form a reply. He loved her. He'd said he loved her. Really loved her. And he meant it. She was sure that he did.

Her mouth as dry as her eyes, she nervously wet her lips. "I—I guess I'd like to keep it," she stammered.

"Does that mean that you'll marry me?"

Her eyes went wide, her mouth dropping open. "Marry you?" she repeated, unable to believe what she'd heard.

"Well, yeah," he said uncertainly. "That is what people do when they are in love."

"Marry you," she said again, having a hard time absorbing the idea.

"We don't have to, if you have a problem with that, but I feel it's only fair to warn you that I plan on asking you again, every day if necessary, until you agree to be my wife."

Laughing, Lacey flew across the distance that separated them and flung herself into his arms.

The tension and the fear slowly melted from Travis as she pressed her mouth against his. She'd had him worried there for a minute, but he was beginning to believe that everything was going to turn out all right. He changed the angle of the kiss, taking possession of it as he slipped a hand across the seat of her jeans and pressed her against his groin. "I take it that's a yes?" he murmured, smiling against her lips.

She withdrew slightly and pressed a finger against his

mouth, avoiding his gaze by watching her finger's movement across his lips. "Maybe," she said vaguely.

"Maybe?" he echoed in surprise.

Laughing, she caught his hand and tugged him toward
the trailer. "Yeah, maybe." She stopped at the door to
her living quarters and turned, then looped her arms
loosely around his neck. "I may need some convincing."

Travis grinned and leaned into her, closing his mouth
over hers as he stretched a hand behind her to open the
door. "Baby, this won't take long at all."

Smiling smugly, she gave his cheek a playful pat.
"Wanna bet?"

Frowning, he stared after her as she stepped inside the
trailer. "And what's that supposed to mean?" he called
after her.

She stepped back into the doorway and smiled coyly
as she reached for the top button on her blouse. "Just a
warning. We McCloud women can be stubborn as mules
when the mood strikes us."

A grin quickly spread from ear-to-ear as he watched
her turn away. "Well, hell," he said as he hopped inside
the trailer. "I've got the time, if you do."

But it didn't take much time at all for Travis to get a
"yes" out of her. Even less time to help her out of her
blouse. With her stretched out beneath him on the narrow
bed, he looked down at her.

"Lacey Cordell," he said with a pleased smile. "I kind
of like the sound of that."

She sighed her contentment and shifted, creating a nest
for him between her legs. "Me, too," she murmured and
drew his face to hers. "Me, too."

\*   \*   \*   \*   \*

If you enjoyed what you just read,
then we've got an offer you can't resist!

# Take 2 bestselling love stories FREE!

# Plus get a FREE surprise gift!

---

**Clip this page and mail it to Silhouette Reader Service™**

| IN U.S.A. | IN CANADA |
|---|---|
| 3010 Walden Ave. | P.O. Box 609 |
| P.O. Box 1867 | Fort Erie, Ontario |
| Buffalo, N.Y. 14240-1867 | L2A 5X3 |

**YES!** Please send me 2 free Silhouette Desire® novels and my free surprise gift. Then send me 6 brand-new novels every month, which I will receive months before they're available in stores. In the U.S.A., bill me at the bargain price of $3.12 plus 25¢ delivery per book and applicable sales tax, if any*. In Canada, bill me at the bargain price of $3.49 plus 25¢ delivery per book and applicable taxes**. That's the complete price and a savings of over 10% off the cover prices—what a great deal! I understand that accepting the 2 free books and gift places me under no obligation ever to buy any books. I can always return a shipment and cancel at any time. Even if I never buy another book from Silhouette, the 2 free books and gift are mine to keep forever. So why not take us up on our invitation. You'll be glad you did!

225 SEN CNFA
326 SEN CNFC

| | | |
|---|---|---|
| Name | (PLEASE PRINT) | |
| Address | Apt.# | |
| City | State/Prov. | Zip/Postal Code |

\* Terms and prices subject to change without notice. Sales tax applicable in N.Y.
\*\* Canadian residents will be charged applicable provincial taxes and GST.
All orders subject to approval. Offer limited to one per household.
® are registered trademarks of Harlequin Enterprises Limited.

©1998 Harlequin Enterprises Limited

# MONTANA MAVERICKS

## *Big Sky Brides*

Legendary love comes to Whitehorn, Montana,
once more as beloved authors

Christine Rimmer, Jennifer Greene and Cheryl St.John

present three brand-new stories in this exciting anthology!

## Meet the Brennan women:
## SUZANNA, DIANA and ISABELLE

Strong-willed beauties who find unexpected
love in these irresistible marriage of
covnenience stories.

Don't miss
**MONTANA MAVERICKS: BIG SKY BRIDES**
On sale in February 2000,
only from Silhouette Books!

*Available at your favorite retail outlet.*

### V*Silhouette*®
™

Visit us at www.romance.net

PSMMBSB

# SILHOUETTE'S 20ᵀᴴ ANNIVERSARY CONTEST
## OFFICIAL RULES
### NO PURCHASE NECESSARY TO ENTER

1. To enter, follow directions published in the offer to which you are responding. Contest begins 1/1/00 and ends on 8/24/00 (the "Promotion Period"). Method of entry may vary. Mailed entries must be postmarked by 8/24/00, and received by 8/31/00.

2. During the Promotion Period, the Contest may be presented via the Internet. Entry via the Internet may be restricted to residents of certain geographic areas that are disclosed on the Web site. To enter via the Internet, if you are a resident of a geographic area in which Internet entry is permissible, follow the directions displayed on-line, including typing your essay of 100 words or fewer telling us "Where In The World Your Love Will Come Alive." On-line entries must be received by 11:59 p.m. Eastern Standard time on 8/24/00. Limit one e-mail entry per person, household and e-mail address per day, per presentation. If you are a resident of a geographic area in which entry via the Internet is permissible, you may, in lieu of submitting an entry on-line, enter by mail, by hand-printing your name, address, telephone number and contest number/name on an 8"x 11" plain piece of paper and telling us in 100 words or fewer "Where In The World Your Love Will Come Alive," and mailing via first-class mail to: Silhouette 20ᵗʰ Anniversary Contest, (in the U.S.) P.O. Box 9069, Buffalo, NY 14269-9069; (In Canada) P.O. Box 637, Fort Erie, Ontario, Canada L2A 5X3. Limit one 8"x 11" mailed entry per person, household and e-mail address per day. <u>On-line and/or 8"x 11" mailed entries received from persons residing in geographic areas in which Internet entry is not permissible will be disqualified.</u> No liability is assumed for lost, late, incomplete, inaccurate, nondelivered or misdirected mail, or misdirected e-mail, for technical, hardware or software failures of any kind, lost or unavailable network connection, or failed, incomplete, garbled or delayed computer transmission or any human error which may occur in the receipt or processing of the entries in the contest.

3. Essays will be judged by a panel of members of the Silhouette editorial and marketing staff based on the following criteria:

    Sincerity (believability, credibility)—50%
    Originality (freshness, creativity)—30%
    Aptness (appropriateness to contest ideas)—20%

    Purchase or acceptance of a product offer does not improve your chances of winning. In the event of a tie, duplicate prizes will be awarded.

4. All entries become the property of Harlequin Enterprises Ltd., and will not be returned. Winner will be determined no later than 10/31/00 and will be notified by mail. Grand Prize winner will be required to sign and return Affidavit of Eligibility within 15 days of receipt of notification. Noncompliance within the time period may result in disqualification and an alternative winner may be selected. All municipal, provincial, federal, state and local laws and regulations apply. Contest open only to residents of the U.S. and Canada who are 18 years of age or older, and is void wherever prohibited by law. Internet entry is restricted solely to residents of those geographical areas in which Internet entry is permissible. Employees of Torstar Corp., their affiliates, agents and members of their immediate families are not eligible. Taxes on the prizes are the sole responsibility of winners. Entry and acceptance of any prize offered constitutes permission to use winner's name, photograph or other likeness for the purposes of advertising, trade and promotion on behalf of Torstar Corp. without further compensation to the winner, unless prohibited by law. Torstar Corp and D.L. Blair, Inc., their parents, affiliates and subsidiaries, are not responsible for errors in printing or electronic presentation of contest or entries. In the event of printing or other errors which may result in unintended prize values or duplication of prizes, all affected contest materials or entries shall be null and void. If for any reason the Internet portion of the contest is not capable of running as planned, including infection by computer virus, bugs, tampering, unauthorized intervention, fraud, technical failures, or any other causes beyond the control of Torstar Corp. which corrupt or affect the administration, secrecy, fairness, integrity or proper conduct of the contest, Torstar Corp. reserves the right, at its sole discretion, to disqualify any individual who tampers with the entry process and to cancel, terminate, modify or suspend the contest or the Internet portion thereof. In the event of a dispute regarding an on-line entry, the entry will be deemed submitted by the authorized holder of the e-mail account submitted at the time of entry. Authorized account holder is defined as the natural person who is assigned to an e-mail address by an Internet access provider, on-line service provider or other organization that is responsible for arranging e-mail address for the domain associated with the submitted e-mail address.

5. Prizes: Grand Prize—a $10,000 vacation to anywhere in the world. Travelers (at least one must be 18 years of age or older) or parent or guardian if one traveler is a minor, must sign and return a Release of Liability prior to departure. Travel must be completed by December 31, 2001, and is subject to space and accommodations availability. Two hundred (200) Second Prizes—a two-book limited edition autographed collector set from one of the Silhouette Anniversary authors: Nora Roberts, Diana Palmer, Linda Howard or Annette Broadrick (value $10.00 each set). All prizes are valued in U.S. dollars.

6. For a list of winners (available after 10/31/00), send a self-addressed, stamped envelope to: Harlequin Silhouette 20ᵗʰ Anniversary Winners, P.O. Box 4200, Blair, NE 68009-4200.

Contest sponsored by Torstar Corp., P.O. Box 9042, Buffalo, NY 14269-9042.

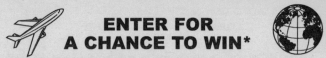

# ENTER FOR
# A CHANCE TO WIN*

## Silhouette's 20ᵗʰ Anniversary Contest

### Tell Us Where in the World
### You Would Like *Your* Love To Come Alive...
### And We'll Send the Lucky Winner There!

Silhouette wants to take you wherever
your happy ending can come true.

Here's how to enter: Tell us, in 100 words or less,
where you want to go to make your love come alive!

In addition to the grand prize, there will be 200
runner-up prizes, collector's-edition book sets
autographed by one of the Silhouette anniversary
authors: **Nora Roberts, Diana Palmer,
Linda Howard** or **Annette Broadrick**.

### DON'T MISS YOUR CHANCE TO WIN!
### ENTER NOW! No Purchase Necessary

*Silhouette*®

*Where love comes alive*™

---

Name: 

---

Address: 

---

City:                          State/Province: 

---

Zip/Postal Code:

Mail to Harlequin Books: **In the U.S.**: P.O. Box 9069, Buffalo, NY
14269-9069; **In Canada**: P.O. Box 637, Fort Erie, Ontario, L4A 5X3

*No purchase necessary—for contest details send a self-addressed stamped envelope to:
Silhouette's 20ᵗʰ Anniversary Contest, P.O. Box 9069, Buffalo, NY 14269-9069 (include
contest name on self-addressed envelope). Residents of Washington and Vermont may
omit postage. Open to Cdn. (excluding Quebec) and U.S. residents who are 18 or over.
Void where prohibited. Contest ends August 31, 2000.

PS20CON_R